Swans in the Dark

ROSEHEART BALLET ACADEMY
BOOK 2

MADELINE DYER

First published in October 2024 by Ineja Press.

Cover Design by Sarah Anderson Designs.
Interior eBook Formatting by Ineja Press.
Interior Print Design by Sarah Anderson Designs.
Editing by Ineja Press.
Proofreading by Madelaine Couch.

eBook ISBN: 978-1-912369-51-5
Paperback ISBN: 978-1-912369-39-3

The author can be contacted via email at
Madeline@MadelineDyer.co.uk

MADELINE DYER

INEJA PRESS

For Michael, my soul mate

Thank you for everything

ONE

Bella

Act normal. Act normal. Act normal.

I pace outside Madame Cachelle's office, a thousand thoughts thrumming through my head. Is this going to be it? What if she's heard the latest rumors? Why do all the ballet posters this year have a hot-pink border? Don't they realize it's too garish alongside the new neon-orange logo of the school, that it clashes? And who even thought that changing the school's logo to this abomination was a good idea?

My head pounds, and I turn so quickly I feel a twinge of pain in my ankle. Damn. Not again. But I don't slow down. If I can walk quicker than the thoughts in my head, I'll win. Win what, I don't know. But the feeling of winning is what I need, and just thinking of it makes the adrenaline in my system heighten.

Which of course is not what I want right now.

Come on, the calm box. The calm box.

I take several deep breaths, catch a glimpse of my reflection in the glass that covers the noticeboard; my face is only there for a split second, because of course I'm moving—Mum always says there are ants in my pants, which always *really* annoys me—but that split second is enough. My face is imprinted on my retinas, for me to study, scrutinize, dissect. Are my eyes too wide? Am I opening them too much? Can people normally see the whole of my irises, or should the top and bottom be cut off by my eyelids?

Cut off—like with a knife. A knife cutting my eyeballs. I hear the sound it makes, and my stomach does this squeezy thing that makes me feel sick.

No.

I narrow my eyes a little on my return journey past the noticeboard—'journey' as if it's a long way, not seven feet back and forth—and yes, I think it looks better. *I* look better. My eyes look better. More natural. I need them to look natural. But my head's still just as busy, and my hands—shit, they're shaking. I pull the sleeves of my oversized hoody down, as if it'll hide them, clench the fabric tightly in my fists. But I know Madame Cachelle is going to spot them trembling. Of course she is.

"The calm box," I mutter, because that's what I'm good at. Compartmentalizing. And now it's time to climb inside the calm box in my head, compress myself tightly so every part of me is in it. I have to be calm. Not worried or anxious or energetic or a mess. But oh, wouldn't it be good to run, right now? Run to my dorm, and back again. Or round the lakes at the bottom of campus.

No, can't do that now.

I wait exactly sixteen seconds, finally still, feeling fizziness in my legs and that twinge of pain in my ankle as I watch the second hand on the watch inside my brain—I've always been good at picturing what's not there—then I knock on the door.

"Miss Sotheby, come on in."

But it is not Madame Cachelle who calls me in—it's a man—and the shock of it, this new voice, makes my hands feel icy. The voice is as crisp as a dried leaf, and I'm thinking of dry leaves and damp leaves as I hurriedly realize I should be entering the room. So, I push open the door, my throat feeling too dry like I'm going to choke on the dried leaves, and enter the ballet mistress's office. Except does it even count as her office when she's not here?

"Please, take a seat."

It takes me a moment to see the speaker, because he's not sitting in Madame Cachelle's seat, at her desk, and—*damn*. It's Mr. Vikas, one of the company's ballet masters, in an office chair by the window, a chair that's not normally there. And… and there are other new chairs in here, by the desk, by the bookcase, and by the potted plants to the side of the room. And all three of these chairs are occupied. The physio, the nurse, the therapist.

Damn. Damn. Damn.

My hands immediately start sweating, profusely.

"Where's Madame Cachelle?" I ask, and my voice is a little too loud, a little too aggressive—that's what they'll say. I can hear it now. *Miss Sotheby exhibited aggression toward the staff.*

Panicked, I look around. There's one chair spare, the chair I always sit in, just next to the doorway I'm standing in. The seat's thinning, threadbare in places. Each month, I think it'll have been replaced, but each month it's here. Trusty, like clockwork, the cogs in my brain. I sink into it, dropping my duffel bag onto the tartan carpet. And—*oh, damn, my bag! What if they look inside it? No, they won't look inside it, because they never do. But this could be the first time!*

One eye stays on my exit, as always. Or at least it does until I forget, until I realize I'm nervously looking around, gaze jumping about nineteen to the dozen.

My heart thrums. Mr. Vikas's moustache is more refined than usual, sort of twisting up at each side. The physio has bags under her eyes. The nurse and the therapist look the same as the handful of times I've seen them—kind of bored out of their minds.

But they're all here—*no.* They know—they've heard about what he and I did…

Deep breaths, Bella. Calm box. Calm box.

Though wouldn't they have administration here too, or something? If they were going to kick me out? And why would they bring the physio and the nurse?

Quickly, I look around the room again, half expecting for more of Roseheart Academy's staff to emerge from the shadows.

"How've you been?" Mr. Vikas asks, but I don't really hear his words because all of a sudden I'm looking for the little container with the yellow lid. Sometimes the lid is white though, but I always think of it as yellow. When Madame Cachelle gives it to me, it's almost always on the desk or the bookcase, but where is it now? Or are they not going to bother? No point doing it if they're kicking me out, right?

"F-fine," I say, but my gums feel too heavy, like they're trying to weigh my face down. So, I look down at my bag, then wonder if I'm being too obvious about it. I force myself to look up again.

"I must say I'm impressed with your form these last couple of weeks," Mr. Vikas continues, then he rabbits on about how Madame Cachelle giving me my latest part was definitely the right decision, that my good behavior deserves a good reward.

Like I'm a bloody child. *Good behavior indeed.*

And I don't understand. Yes, I've got a very good part. Me and Ty. We're taking on the lead roles in the third-year diploma students' production of *Wild Swans*, following Harley and Fiona's withdrawal from the program—which in and of itself is a pretty big scandal, only topped of course by casting the resident junkies as the leads. Ha. Not that the others are supposed to know what me and Ty are going through. The school is pretty good at hiding it, being diplomatic and all that. Not that me and Ty are good at hiding it though. He even came to class earlier holding half a bottle of WKD and a pretty stoned expression.

I narrow my eyes a little as I focus on Mr. Vikas, careful not to show too much iris. The usual pleasantries follow. *There, I'm doing it right, right?* I nod, go through the usual script, but with Madame Cachelle replaced by Mr. Vikas. I know this script off by heart. Had enough practice. We're all just playing the game now. And speaking of games, where *is* the specimen cup?

Pee in it, pass 'go,' win the game!

Ah. *There.* On Madame Cachelle's desk. But it's behind a book. A hefty looking volume that I can't read the title of. A little time passes—and feels like it's not passing—and then Mr. Vikas hands me the specimen cup and tells me to go to the staff bathroom. And everything just seems…ordinary. Like just one of the usual monthly meetings, just with way more eyes present.

Nothing about what happened two nights ago.

Darkness, shadows, a bass that snaked through me, two shots of Tequila, a girl screaming bloody murder, and then brightness outside, tender voices, a company dancer joining me, a long look at his face, his jaw, under the moonlight even though it can't have been moonlight because we were outside the club with the bright lights and bouncers, thinking about how hot he is, this company dancer, and then leaning closer and closer to him…

My head pounds as I take the specimen cup outside into the hallway, momentarily feeling stupid for leaving my bag in there with them. Images of Mr. Vikas or maybe the nurse or physio or therapist going through my things fill my head, but I know I can't go back in to bring it with me. It'll look too suspicious. So, I go to the staff bathroom—empty at the moment, not like the academy bathrooms downstairs that always seem to be teeming with rats, the youngest of the ballet dancers-in-training—and I pee into the cup. A bit of my urine splashes onto my hand, and I curse—it's one thing that *really* annoys me. Almost more than anything. Still, at least this time it is *me* supplying my own urine. I haven't had to conduct a plan with Ava. Haven't had to in a while actually. Pride fills me. There's nothing worse than that happening then. Me finding the little container that I hid in the bathroom earlier, trying to decant it smoothly into the specimen cup without splashing onto me.

Just thinking about the time Ava's pee got all over me makes me shudder.

Time floats—*floats*, I like that word—and then I'm washing my hands, the cup on the counter staring at me, while I also stare at me. The mirror.

I like my new body—toned and strong, of course, from classes and practices. But the cocaine stops my appetite. Suppresses it. It doesn't really make me feel any different in my head—Ty says he gets more alert, sort of buzzing, seeing wonder everywhere, but then he also says his head is pretty *dull an' dreary* without it. My head's never *dull an' dreary*, but since I've been using the coke, I've found myself feeling, I don't know… different if I *don't* have it. Exhausted. Irritable. Sad. Not dull an' dreary.

Every day, I'm looking more and more like the dancers with eating disorders, and I understand *their* euphoria now. My body looks disciplined. I look like I'm in control. Stronger than the others. I look like a dancer—something I never managed to achieve before. But a few months on this stuff and wow. I'd been shocked. I'm still kind of shocked now.

I'm smiling—maybe a little too widely—as I waltz back into Mr. Vikas's office, still careful of my eyes and how wide I'm opening them. The nurse takes the urine sample from me. A little space has been cleared on Madame Cachelle's desk, as it usually is, for the drug testing to be done.

I stare at my duffel bag, trying to work out if the creases in its fabric were in that exact pattern when I left. Or if sticky fingers have been prying. *Sticky?*

"If you are struggling, you must inform one of us," Mr. Vikas says, just as the nurse begins the test.

"Of course," I say, all smiles, thinking of what I'll do when I get back to my room. And, anyway, why *would* I inform Mr. Vikas or any of the staff? As a ballet dancer, I'm trained to hide my problems, conceal them, pretend that I'm perfectly fine, that I'm naturally this thin and strong, that my body is natural, that I'm naturally great at dealing with stress. Everything's just *natural natural natural.*

"I'm fine," I say, feeling happier than ever. "I'm doing well. Really well."

I imagine my words as smiley faces floating around the office, and I smile wider, like I'm competing with them. A slight fizzy feeling fills my legs, and I resist the urge to jiggle them, then quickly remember about my shaking hands. But they're not shaking now. They're resting on my knees, so still.

I've got this. And—oh, damn!

There's a ladder in my tights. Right on my left knee. Dead center. I want to scream suddenly—feel the urge in me—because I hate trying to repair the tights. These are supposed to be non-laddering ones anyway. Spent enough money on them. *Jesus Christ. I'll be leaving them a bad review.*

But I force myself to be calm. Distract myself. "Uh, anyway, where is Madame Cachelle?" I ask.

"Called away on an urgent private matter," Mr. Vikas says, watching the nurse as she conducts the test. God, she's slow at it. Nothing like Madame Cachelle. "I'm stepping in for the foreseeable."

"Don't you have the company dancers to train?" I ask, trying very hard not to look at the nurse.

Mr. Vikas is the ballet master for the third-division of the Roseheart Romantic Dance Company, the division that the top graduating pair from the diploma course will join, before hopefully climbing the ranks to the second and then the first division. So, it's the third division that me and Ty actually have a chance of getting into now that our main competition is out. That'll be at the end of this year. We've got twelve weeks until the diploma finishes. And joining the company is all I've ever wanted. When we do, Ty and I will have the summer to learn some minor parts in the third-division's autumn production of *Roxana, the Beauty of Montenegro*.

"I do," Mr. Vikas says. "But desperate times call for desperate measures. Now, Sheila, have we got the results of Miss Sotheby's urine test?"

The nurse with her bumbling, round face and reputation for dispensing ice for any injury—which, to be fair, is pretty helpful at a ballet school—smiles widely.

The test is negative. Of course it is, because Mattie tells me when they're going to give me a 'random' test, and he usually gives me five days' notice. Four is all I need to make sure there's no trace of it in my urine. And sure, these four days aren't always easy—and yes, I get way more irritable and exhausted—but who wouldn't with the amount of thoughts I have in my head? Still, those four days drug-free are worth it. They allow me to stay here. Roseheart has a strict policy on drugs: *None! They're all bad!* But they've been surprisingly kind about my…problems. So long as I show them that I am making an effort. That I am winning.

The room is full of more smiles. So many of them, like we're all so happy, and I can't help but wonder why the extra people are present. Is that the way Mr. Vikas always does it? Does he not want to get his own hands dirty doing the test himself? Madame Cachelle is so much more down to earth.

I'm dismissed, and I head out, feeling again like I'm floating.

Floating.

A big, floating grin.

I can't wait to snort a line.

TWO

Alessia

"You are going to that school, whether you like it or not." Mother levels the full force of her gaze at me, as if daring me to challenge her again. "The afternoon session begins soon, and you have enough time to get there, so you are going." Her Annoushka earrings flash under the artificial light. Tanzanite and diamond, Mother's signature stones, wink at me. I still cannot believe she spent nearly twenty grand on a pair of earrings, for God's sake. But she always likes people to know who she is and that money is never a problem for her.

It is just a shame money cannot buy the type of family she wants.

I fold my arms, trying to muster as much courage as I can. "I do not want to go." I do not mean to sound like a petulant, whiny teenager, but I cannot help it. "Please, just see this from my point of view."

The Hermle Debden Mechanical Mantel Clock tick-tocks above the fireplace—not a real fireplace, just some huge marble construction Mother had put in when we moved here, along with an electric heater designed to look like an authentic woodburner. Any moment now, the clock is going to chime. It will make Father jump, because he does every time; his chair is right next to it. And, right now, he is doing his best to disappear into the deep-seated Howard armchair—the oldest thing we have in the apartment, dating to the nineteenth century, because bar that one piece of furniture, everything absolutely has to be new, for Mother. Father is currently hiding behind *The Financial Times*, the paper stretched between his hands like a shield, no doubt pretending not to hear Mother and me—ha, as if anyone can *not* hear us.

Angélique has stopped crawling about on the floor and now sits in the corner of room, on the plush baby-blue rug, holding her Jelly Cat teddy bear in a protective stance in front of her body. Her blue eyes are wide, watery. She never likes it when anyone shouts, and while neither of us is shouting right now, the air is thick, heavy with tension. We all know what is coming.

Mother's eyes darken, and she clutches a hand to her chest. She is wearing one of her smart-casual dresses, a teal fit-and-flare piece, and this one has got a large necktie. I always think they look ridiculous, but this is how Mother dresses every day. Oh and with heels, too. Of course. Even *in* the apartment. You never know when visitors will call, apparently—even though Mother is a stickler for booking guests in at specific times, having enough warning, and adequate amounts of tea, coffee, and biscuits on hand.

"This is what is best for you." Her voice is low, a warning. "*Mother* knows best."

It is not often I challenge her now—the last three years, we have pretty much existed in the same space as if we are roommates. Hellos, goodbyes, and that has been about it. I cook my own meals, clean up after myself, do my washing, all the while staying out of Mother's way. Because she finally relented, finally let me be my own person, even if she was pretty much ignoring me. But now, well, *now* she is back to her interfering ways.

She tricked me into going for an interview at Roseheart. Said we were going to a book signing that her friend had heard about. Some exclusive readers' club that was offering it. I do not know why I even believed her, trusted her, when she has always turned up her nose at my love for detective novels. But when she drove her brand-new 2025 Audi A6 in the direction of Roseheart, I became suspicious. When we drove through the wrought-iron gates of the academy, I knew. "Do not embarrass me," she said then, looking at me over the tops of her sunglasses—designer, of course. "I have pulled a lot of strings to get you an interview."

I assumed it was going to be an interview for the Ballet Diploma, but no, it was Dance Choreography. Apparently my being away from ballet for all these years worked against me, and Mother had to go to her plan B. Mother hates having to go to plan Bs, but even more than that, she hates having to use a plan C. There never even *is* a plan C.

Now I fix a steely glare on her. "I do not want to be at Roseheart." I take a deep breath. We have been through this conversation so many times in the last two weeks. "I am not interested in dance. I want *no part* of dance."

"Oh, even the neighbors know that." Mother's eyes narrow on me. She is standing by the Kelly floor lamp—an item I still cannot believe she spent over three thousand pounds on—her perfect white-blond hair a cascading waterfall over her shoulders. Her eyes are a rich brown, and her skin has a warm olive tone; if there is anything Mother is always concerned about, it is appearances, but I do not think the blond dye suits her, even though the hairdresser she goes to compliments it to no end—no wonder, the price Mother pays. It is not a secret why she has chosen that tone though; Allegra's hair is naturally that shade, as my oldest sister has albinism. And when Allegra went missing, Mother seemed to think that looking like her would bring her oldest daughter back.

Still, it has been ten years.

"This is a wonderful opportunity, Alessia," Mother continues, pointing a well-manicured finger at me. "You are going to make a great choreographer." She smiles at me, as if she has just proven that she does know me after all.

That bloody school. I take a deep breath, trying my best to remain calm. I fix my gaze on the paintings on the far wall—a collection of watercolors of the local harbors—but not looking at Mother makes me nervous. "I am not interested in choreography."

Dance has never been my thing, even when I was forced into it.

"You will do it," she says, and I glance at her just in time to see her eyes flicking invisible flames at me. "And you will do it *well*. You will uphold our family's reputation. And I expect you will have an advantage over the other students, what with your background in ballet; this is something that you would be well advised to use, not let it languish in the background."

She says 'background in ballet' like I used to be a professional or something. But I never was. I never even liked ballet. I just did it, being enrolled in classes at six years old, because Allegra was flourishing in ballet then. My sister had just joined Roseheart Academy's diploma program, and she was doing so, so well.

Then she disappeared, just a few months shy of her graduation—when she would have gained a place in Roseheart's prestigious company. I kept dancing for years after that, mainly under the instructions and insistence of my mother, but I am not a natural ballerina. I only did it because it was Allegra's thing, because Mother assumed that ballet must be embedded in our genes, and she apparently only wanted the best for me. Finally, at last, three years ago, I was able to step away from it.

Mother was not happy, but Nonna talked to her. Gave her a stern talking to—and Nonna was the only person who could make Mother back down. Mainly because Nonna is even scarier than Mother. And because Mother respects Nonna's opinion. Does not want to cause tension. Nonna said to me after that she had always assumed I must have liked ballet, because I did so much of it; she really was shocked when I revealed the truth.

Mother of course gave me the silent treatment, but I was able to be my own person. Be me. I found that I loved the piano, loved the way my fingers just swam over the keys, creating a harmony that seemed to speak to my soul. I discovered I really loved reading, liked being on my own, holed up with crime novels where I felt both scared and safe. When Mother had been in charge of my extra-curricular activities, there had been no time for playing the piano or reading. It was pointe class, barre class, stretches class, flexibility class—endless, nonstop. But it was a whole new world, learning about what *I* actually liked to do.

Until Mother woke up from a dream two weeks ago, where she had seen me performing on Roseheart's stage. It had reignited her dreams, her insistence. She went from barely speaking to me to being overly nice at first, trying to sweet-talk me at every opportunity, offering to buy me all sorts of novels if I just went along with her plan. When that did not work, her nice act dropped but her belief that I should be at Roseheart did not. She got me the interview four days after that dream, obviously pulled strings and paid a lot of money to get me in. Me being at that school is all she can talk about, and my suggestion last week that perhaps she should get some therapy to deal with Allegra's disappearance had not gone down well.

"Mother, please, I really do not want to do this," I say, but it is a mistake to think you can appeal to her emotions, her sense of heart, if it is conflicting her own vision. "I want to go to music college, I—"

The Hermle Debden Clock chimes, and it is not just Father who jumps.

"That is—that is what I want to do," I finish. "Music."

"Roseheart does not offer music courses," Mother says, tight-lipped. "And that is where you are going."

I look to Father for help, but all he does is noisily turn the page of his paper. On the floor, Angélique starts whining. Great. Approximately twenty seconds until we will have a full tantrum going and Mother will take my screaming baby sister out of the room, glaring at me, because of course it will be completely my fault that she is upset. Because I have upset the status quo of the household, yet again.

"You are going, and that is that," Mother says, tight-lipped. "There are to be no more arguments, Alessia."

"Nonna would never have made me do this." I glare at her, but Mother is an ice queen. She just glares back at me.

And I know that it is final. There really is no changing Mother's plans.

"You had better get going, else you will be late. We do not want people talking any more than necessary about our family."

Outside our apartment, I walk quickly. My rucksack digs into my shoulders, but I kind of welcome the pain. Mother thinks I am going to Roseheart—taking the tube across London right this second because I absolutely refuse to let her drive me or to use the private taxi company she loves— but there is no way I am doing that. I have got other plans, anyway.

"All right?" I nod at Mr. Burnton, our neighbor. He has just entered the foyer of the apartment block. He gives me a nod and a toothless smile, and then shuffles past me in his stained and torn clothing.

Melview Apartments are expensive. They are for the wealthy. It is definitely a pride thing, why my parents bought this place on the fourth floor. And so it always surprises me when I see Mr. Burnton's clothes. How poor he looks, even though he has got a pretty amazing home. Father reckons that he must own it out right and maybe all of his money goes on the bills. Mother reckons he has got the start of dementia, like Nonna, because his care for his appearance was the first to go.

They never speak to him though. Not like I do. Or rather, I did. Because now it is just the occasional 'all right', whereas before, when Allegra first went missing, it was his apartment I would be in a lot, when I was crying and upset, feeling left out and somewhat neglected, as selfish as it sounds. My parents would be out doing media interviews and appeals, and Mr. Burnton would be the one collecting me from school, making hot cocoa and getting in my favorite biscuits—biscuits that Mother never bought because *dancers must eat healthily and properly.* He feels like a member of the family, and my heart tugs as I think of how we have drifted away from him.

I am about to call after him—something more substantial than 'all right'—but he has already disappeared from the foyer when I look back. I make a mental note to go over to his apartment soon. I shall take *his* favorite biscuits. Custard creams.

My trainers squeak a bit as I leave the foyer. My toes still feel over-cushioned in them, and I am not quite used to wearing them all the time. But I have not worn any of my extensive heels collection out of the house now, since, well…

I swallow hard, trying to keep my breathing even.

I have been seeing a therapist—not that Mother or Father knows this, or why I have needed to see one—and she says I should *not* try and push away the thoughts, the memories. That avoiding them gives them power. Makes it worse. I still do not know how it can be worse, but she seems pretty convinced, and I suppose she is the expert when it comes to stuff like this.

Outside, the air is cool, refreshing, and it helps, being out here. Helps me cool down after the argument with Mother. Of course, she will think I am being the good little girl now, that my defiance was all words and no action.

I take my iPhone out of my pocket. It is on silent, but the WhatsApp group has been pretty busy all morning. We are meeting for the first time today, and several more messages arrive in the few seconds I am looking at it. Mainly the other girls giving reassurance, encouragement. *You can do this! We can do this! See you soon!*

Sometimes, I wonder what life would have been like if my parents had stayed in Italy after they got married. If they had not relocated to London, bringing both sets of their parents—my grandparents—with them. If maybe we would have ended up a whole different family. Different people. The three of us girls, maybe we would have been into science or something. Not ballet. Not dance. If maybe Allegra would have stayed with us. If we would have lived a life without pressure.

If maybe Mother and I would have had a better relationship.

I sigh, and I think about Angélique, the youngest of us. Two years old. Already, Mother is buying her tutus and leotards—*oh, you look so gorgeous, carissima!* Not even potty trained, yet already being pushed into a life where your body is valued over your mind, over your wellbeing. Where you are there for entertainment. To be looked upon, scrutinized. Where you have to be pretty and beautiful and skinny.

Allegra hated it, I remember that. A week before she went missing, she had a breakdown. Crying to me, on the phone. Telling me to get out of dance before it was too late. She told me that she wanted a different life. That she would do anything to get it.

And that is why I say she *disappeared*, when everyone else says she was *abducted*. Why I say she is *still out there*, when everyone else says she is *presumed dead*.

Because I think *Allegra Valenzi*, that name only, is dead.

I know my older sister, my beautiful, kind and intelligent sister, is out there, doing what she always wanted to do: being someone else. Away from the limelight. Away from judgment. Away from eyes.

Free.

THREE

Bella

The moment I reach the entrance to the dorms, Ava jumps up from the steps outside where several dancers are sitting. It's pretty much everyone from the final year of the diploma program out here. We've got into a habit of lounging about together before the afternoon classes begin. Makes me feel kind of cool, I must admit. *Cool like a cucumber.*

Okay, well I'm glad I didn't say that out loud. God, I can be so *cringe*.

This semester, the afternoon schedules are pretty light. Not like last term when we pretty much didn't finish until 8 o'clock most nights. Now, it's much better. One late-afternoon class on a Tuesday and Thursday. Character Expressions and either pointe class or leaps and jumps, depending on the student's gender. The rest of the time it's barre class and pointe class, romantic and classical classes, choreography and technique-refinement, fitness, flexibility, and Pilates. Oh, and rehearsals.

Still, we've got a good fifteen minutes or so before today's Character Expressions begins, so I wrap Ava in an excited whirling hug, and swing my bag from my shoulder. The other dancers barely pay me any attention as I dig out a small pouch.

"They're going to search my room again," I tell Ava. The drugs are hidden in my hand, and I press my fist against hers, until she takes them. "Some time tonight, Mattie reckons."

Mattie's a technical assistant for the company, often in charge of lights and smoke machines in performances, and he has the same loves that I do. He tells me when drug-testing is being scheduled for the company and academy dancers who apparently need it, as well as any extra intel about room searches, and I share half of my gear with him in return. It's a pretty sweet deal.

"Maybe even before the class," I add. There's often a room-check pretty soon after a pee-check. "Or tomorrow morning."

Ava's eyes widen, and she nails me with a piercing glare. "Hold on, you had that on you, while speaking to them?"

"They never search me then. Not when I'm doing the drugs test for them." I shrug. Still, she has got a point. Having the prohibited substance on me during my visit to Madame Cachelle's office probably wasn't wise. "Anyway, you take it."

She does, albeit scowling at me as she stuffs it into the gym bag that she carries everywhere. "I'd better take this to my room, uh, now."

I smile sweetly, thanking my dear friend, and promise her that I'll wait right here for her. She disappears. *Right here.* I plant my feet firmly on the concrete, looking down at my knock-off Ugg boots. And that ladder in my tights—dear God, it's even bigger than before. It reminds me of a snake. *Snakes and ladders.*

I start laughing—then I stop quickly when I realize a couple of the other diploma students are looking at me. Rhia and Candice, eyes narrowed. Felicity with one eyebrow quizzically raised. I give them all a big smile, and then look back toward the dorm doors for Ava.

They won't search her. They never search her. Never search anyone else. Always me. But at least they do it in secret. They don't broadcast to the other dancers that I've got…problems. Not like they do with the dancers who are anorexics or bulimics. Everyone's aware of who those are. But mine… mine's a secret—well, to those I want it to be.

I look at the dancers around me now, and I'm confident that the only one who knows is Ava, because unlike Ty, I never turn up to class with drink or drugs in my hands. And Ava's my best friend. I chose to confide in her. Have needed her help. Everyone needs a friend like Ava, anyway. She's cool. A massive fan of rock and metal music, knows some awesome bands like *Nightwish* and *Within Temptation*, and is always saying that one day she's going to put together a metal ballet. She also loves horror movies just as much as I do. Only last week we were watching *Suspiria*, eating popcorn, and then giggling all night as we texted each other lines from the film. I really wish she was my roommate—and I bet Stacia, my actual roommate really wishes that Ava was, because I'm pretty sure I kept Stacia awake all night that time, with my laughter.

Ava scowls as she returns, only a few minutes later, but then her scowl's lost among the others as everyone's moving about, ready to get to class.

We move like a flock toward the studio spaces where classes are held. We're still a little early, but we nearly always are. It started when Fiona and Harley were still here; they were proper obsessed with ballet and being the best, and they just kind of gee-ed us all up to put the extra minutes in, like how we see company dancers being early to their lessons. Even with Fiona and Harvey gone, the routine has stuck.

We file into the studio, and I feel a hundred times lighter now that Ava's looking after my gear. I bet she's got it under her mattress or something. She's a proper best friend, she is. And I never thought I'd find that here. Thought we'd all hate each other, be toxic rivals and all that, but no, our cohort is pretty sound. We gel together pretty good. *Pretty damn good.* For some reason, I think those words in a strong Texan accent and that just makes me want to laugh again.

"So, is it true?" Felicity asks me. She's one of those popular-type girls and she has the daintiest ankles I've ever seen. All glossy smiles and pretty eyes, the kind who tells you about how she had her own en suite in her room from the age of seven. Like that even matters. But the girls here lap that kind of shit up.

"Is what true?" I ask, feigning innocence. I like doing this with Felicity, seeing how long I can play with her for. Quite often, she'll over-explain, being all friendly too. All in all, she's pretty sound, even if she does love the goss.

"You and…" She widens her eyes at me.

Ah, *that* rumor. An ice-cold shudder runs down my spine. To be fair, I thought Mr. Vikas was going to bring it up. Maybe it hasn't reached faculty yet.

"Me and…" I widen my eyes back at her, a half-smile on my face.

She lets out a churlish laugh—it's a laugh that always and inexplicably makes me think of bubble-gum. "You know!"

"I don't know!" I mimic her tone.

Behind Felicity, Ava rolls her eyes. "Look, are we going to warm up or what before Miss Potts gets here?"

We all dissolve into excited little flurries—flurries, I like that word—and begin warming up. The warmup isn't as intense as it is for other classes, but we still do warmup because a lot of the time Miss Potts has us demonstrate various character expressions while performing different combinations, to get us used to doing them altogether. I always like Miss Potts's classes. All of us do. She began working at Roseheart the same year we did, so our cohort kind of feels protective of her. Apparently, for the cohorts before us Madame Cachelle took the majority of the classes, but now there are three who teach on the diploma.

A few moments later, just as I'm trying to remember whether I did twelve or thirteen stretches on my right thigh—because I did twelve on my left, and if it was thirteen for my right then I'll need to make it fourteen on *both* because thirteen is a bad number—Miss Potts enters the room with another woman. I recognize her immediately. Li Hua Zhao. She's one of the company dancers—recently promoted to second division with her ballet partner and boyfriend Trent Mason, whom I now know *very well*—and the room falls quiet immediately.

Don't look at Li Hua in case she can tell.

I point my nose in the opposite direction—and low and behold, there's another of those posters with the hot-pink borders. Whoever made those really needs to have a better color palette. It doesn't look good for a school that's all about artistic expression, right? Maybe I should tell them. But who would it be who made them? My mind races, but then I wonder if I'm being too weird, acting too suspicious, because what if I'm the only dancer not looking at Li Hua? So I force myself to stare right at her. She's looking around at us all, and when she makes eye contact with me, I give her a big, toothy grin. So wide that I swear I feel the corners of my lips stretching, straining.

What the hell, Bella?

Even I didn't know I was going to do that. And what if I've got food in my teeth? Oh, God. I didn't check my teeth earlier in the bathroom. I run my tongue over them as best as I can.

Miss Potts has been saying for a while that she should get one of the company dancers in to help us with character, because apparently we're just not quite 'getting it,' but I didn't think it would be Li Hua we'd get. Mainly because the second-division performers are known to have ridiculously busy schedules as it is. Thought we'd get someone from the third-division. Someone that the top-graduating pair this year might end up dancing alongside next year.

"Okay, people, are we ready?" Miss Potts yells, claps her hands, then begins giving us our instructions. She sets the scene, telling us the emotions that we're to convey on our faces, in the way we hold our bodies, and then rattles off a pretty complex combination of movements.

As we practice, holding onto the barre and facing the mirrored wall, Miss Potts and Li Hua walk behind us, observing, correcting where appropriate and complimenting various dancers on their expressive upper bodies.

"Li Hua is so beautiful," Ava whispers to me, about ten minutes later, just as we're told to pair up for the next exercise. Ava's half-Chinese and she told me once she wanted to be friends with Li Hua from the moment she started at the academy but thought it would be weird to just go up to her, even if—as she says—ballerinas of color have to stick together in an environment that favors their white competitors.

I wasn't too sure how to feel when she said that to me; I'd never really considered before that she might think I—and well, most of the other dancers on the diploma, and indeed those at the company and every other company—have an inherent advantage over her. A privilege to be born white. But it's important to be aware of it, I know. Awareness is the first step to correcting it.

Ava and I practice the exercise; in turn, each of us performs the same combination while channeling an emotion, and the other has to work out which emotion it is. I'm pretty sure that Ava's emotion is 'terror', but she keeps telling me it isn't.

"Uh, fear?" I shrug.

"No, I would've counted that as terror."

"I don't know, then. Maybe indifference?"

"Did my face look indifferent while I was doing all of that?" She looks shocked now—an emotion I have no trouble deciphering, because she does have a pretty expressive face. But the problem is when she dances—when anyone dances—I get more swept up in the beauty of it all, looking at her arms and legs, her lines, rather than her face.

I miss so much.

"No," I say. "Come on, you know I'm not great at this." It's always annoying, because Ava *always* gets what emotion I'm dancing with, during this exercise, on her first try. This time it was 'love.' All I had to do for that was plaster a dreamy, pretty witless-looking expression on my face. "I don't know what yours is then, I'm sorry," I say.

Ava looks crestfallen.

"But that's just me. I bet anyone else would know," I say. "Hey, Li Hua!" I spot her behind Ava's shoulder. "Come and watch Ava."

Ava glares at me for, like, half a second before she slips back into performer mode. She rattles through the combinations, ending with a sauté in arabesque and a jeté—a nice nod to George Balanchine, who Miss Potts seems to worship; rumor has it she's got a poster of him in her room. The whole time, I try and work out what expression is on Ava's face. *Concentrate, Bella, look back at her face… Oh those arms are so beautiful!* But Li Hua claps her hands together, apparently giddy with excitement.

"Oh, that is wonderful!" she says. "You've so perfectly captured the essence of heartbreak. And the way you held your arms in arabesque was beautiful."

Ava beams widely and gives me a *'see?'* look. So, it was heartbreak of all things. Heartbreak. God, this is like a badly scripted show.

I glance at Li Hua, very aware that there's heat flooding my face and I'm probably going tomato-red. Has she heard the rumors? I mean, she isn't looking directly at me now, is she?

It's then that I realize I'm smiling at her—like, when the hell did I start smiling at her again?—my cheek muscles aching, and I'm now probably looking a bit sinister or creepy. So I try to stop smiling, letting my expression slacken—only that weird thing happens where it's like my face glitches and I can't do anything.

"Are you okay?" Li Hua asks, her brows furrowed with concern.

I nod, turning away, still *smiling like a loony* as my brother says, *Bella the Loony*. Then bam! My face is my own again. Thank God for that. I breathe out what could seriously be the most ginormous sigh ever.

Li Hua moves on to work with the next set of dancers, and shortly after, Miss Potts sets us new exercises and expression work. The time passes quickly—it always does in this class—and soon we're all grabbing our water bottles and bags from the back of the room.

"Wait, who's this?" Felicity asks, her voice loud, and I turn to see she's pointing at a framed photo of a dancer at the back of the studio. The portrait's pretty large and has been hung above the door. It definitely wasn't there last class.

"That is Allegra Valenzi," Miss Potts says.

"Who?"

Several people ask that same question, and I move forward to get a closer look. The dancer's slim with near-white hair, super pale skin—maybe she's albino?—and a leotard that looks a tad too small. It's straining over her breasts.

"A dancer who was once at this academy," Miss Potts says, with a glance at Li Hua—and I see that the company dancer is about to say something, but Miss Potts's glance has silenced her. "Her sister is joining the academy—uh, today, actually, I believe—and the administration department thought it would be a nice touch to have Allegra's portrait up."

"Why? Allegra's not in the company, is she?" Felicity asks.

A shadow falls across Miss Potts's face. "No, uh, she isn't."

"Allegra was abducted many years ago," Li Hua says.

Abducted? My eyes widen.

Miss Potts shoots another look at Li Hua, but the company dancer doesn't appear to see this time—mainly because she's now facing toward us. Her eyes are sparkling—it's the same spark that I see in my brother's eyes when he talks about the latest true crime podcast he's obsessed with.

"It's almost ten years to the day, since the abduction," Li Hua continues. "Two other dancers were taken at the same time, too, but they were returned when the ransom was paid. Allegra never was."

Well, of course this has everyone's attention, and *of course*, Miss Potts being Miss Potts refuses to let Li Hua say anymore. She scolds us all for being gossips and reminds us it's true life and we shouldn't be finding excitement in any of this. It's a disservice to the family. "And don't say a word of this, should you bump into the younger Valenzi girl," are her final words to us, before class is dismissed.

I'd kind of expected everyone to be talking about Allegra Valenzi all evening, and although we do—and we Google her but don't really find a lot—it's not long before attention turns back to me. And the rumor.

"So, it is true then?" Stacia asks me slyly, once we're all in the common room. She's my roommate, though she and I have never really become closer than what I consider a normal friend. Like, we look out for each other, we're kind and that to one another, and we'll hang out in a group, but not really on our own outside of our room. I've always wished I could room with Ava. "You and one of the company dancers?" But Stacia says it like it's a question, like she's still fishing. I mean, she doesn't even offer a name—so that's a dead giveaway that she knows nothing.

But still, I smirk. "Yeah, we got it on under the gazebo last night."

See, *that's* the way to stop the rumors. Own them. If people think it's not a secret, they'll stop talking about it.

Even if they're not technically rumors.

Even if they're the truth.

Because me and Trent Mason? Well, it totally *did* happen. Just not last night; it was two days ago. At a random club. He didn't recognize me—or at least he didn't let on that he did. I knew who he was. Wanted to see how far I could get. My dark purple lipstick, my cat eyeliner. Ava's dress. I looked hot, and he looked troubled, and we met outside after a girl had a panic attack on the dance floor. When he asked how old I was, it was easy to lie and say I was eighteen.

And this is where it gets tricky. Because yesterday, he found out—summoned me to the gazebo and barked at me, unfortunately witnessed by some of the academy's younger students. No kissing or anything there though. But, apparently, there was a photo of us on his phone—he'd already deleted it by the time he told me, but some of his friends saw it. Recognized me as a diploma student at the academy. Him, a man in his early twenties, with a student. *Naughty naughty.*

"Don't worry," I told him last night. "We'll both deny it."

"That's not the fucking point," he snapped. He looked way less hot than he had in the club. Those brooding eyes weren't so brooding now. Just full of anger. "You lied to me about your age."

"It's not like I'm fifteen," I said. "I'm seventeen. That's a year *over* the age of consent, you know." I hadn't meant my voice to sound patronizing, but it had.

He just shook his head, breathing hard. "Anyone asks you about us, you deny it."

I promised I would, but as soon as I got back to the dorms, I found the diploma students were talking about it. I managed to evade the questions then—until now.

But it doesn't really matter what I say about me and Trent. It's not like either of us is going to get into trouble. Right?

Then why were you so worried about Mr. Vikas finding out?

I laugh at Stacia's other questions, and one of the other girls tells her that I'm obviously lying, that there's no truth in any of this. *Good.*

But I can't shake my feelings of unease, and as Ava and I get dinner, as I try and relax, back in the common room again afterward, the huge tide of dark fatigue, as I call it, is beckoning me. It's swirling round and round, and then Trent's and Li Hua's faces are there too, circling me. Everywhere I look, they're there. Watching me. And maybe it's the stress of today—the meeting with Mr. Vikas and the drug test and having to go four whole days without any—but I know what I need now. And now that it's close, now that it's doable, I can't think about anything but the cocaine.

I need it.

My hands shake even more, and fifteen minutes later, in the shared dorm bathroom—which is almost always quiet because each room has an en suite and so people rarely use this one—I meet Ava, having summoned her by text to bring my baggie from her room.

I tip the powder out on the countertop and glance quickly back at her. She's standing by the door, on guard, a disapproving look on her face.

"I have to," I tell her. I know she doesn't get it. But right now, I'm positive the coke's the only thing that can keep me from falling into the swirling abyss.

FOUR

Alessia

I do not feel like a survivor. Sitting here, ignoring the vibrations of my phone in my pocket as my afternoon meds alarm goes off, my legs crossed, body slouched a little even though I know it is bad for my posture, right foot twitching as I stare at the minute hand on the clock, beg it to go just a bit faster, faster, faster.

But it does not, so I look at the other girls and the other girls look at me, and then of course I look back at the poster—the only one on the notice board in this back room of the community center. *We are all Survivors*, it says. They must hold a lot of meetings like our one in here. Either that or whoever booked this room told the person what our meeting was for and they thought they could help by pasting this up here. One lone poster trying to make people feel better.

"Well, who's going to speak first?" one of the girls asks.

You would think that we would all know what to do. That we would want to talk, feel connected or something. But we just stare around at each other. I recognize three of the girls from their online profiles. Annmarie, Tiger, and Amaryllis. They are seated together on the other side of the circle, opposite me. They all live in the same part of London, and they were traveling here together. Tiger gives me a tentative smile, but she does not speak.

Chair legs squeak next to me as a girl moves. "I don't want to be here," she says, and then she is standing, pushing her chair right back, grabbing her bag and running from the room. Her feet slap slap slap. My brain starts doing the calculations, automatically: she is about seventy-two kilos, I would say, and that is ten steps. 0.04 calories burnt per step, so barely half a calorie used there. Huh. Does not even seem worth it.

My feet twitch, and I tuck them under my chair. I am not supposed to do this—the calculations—anymore, but that is not the only thing I have not been able to stop.

"Okay, well, I'll talk then," the same girl who spoke earlier says. She pushes a curtain of blonde, slightly wavy hair behind her shoulders, then tucks strands behind her ears. She has big ears. "I'm Emma."

As she talks—telling us she lives near Elephant and Castle, works in Starbucks, and what all her dogs and cats are called—I try and match her with one of the profiles. Not everyone used their real name though, of course. I did not. I was ShadowGirl07. Only Tiger, Annmarie, and Amaryllis used versions of their names. I had thought Tiger was a nickname at first, but on WhatsApp she assured me it was her real name. Her brother is called Bison.

"And that's it, that's me," Emma concludes, flashing a shy smile at us all.

"Really?" Tiger says. "Because you've talked about everything apart from what we're here for. What we're all here for."

I slump a little more, try to ignore the pain around my ribs, how my spine is aching. Just twenty more minutes here, and then I can go.

The *We are all Survivors* poster winks at me, and I wonder what a survivor is supposed to feel like. Strong? Confident? Reassured?

I do not feel any of those things.

Most of the time, I barely feel like I am living. Like I am caught between the real world and some shadowy dark place. And not just because of what happened to Allegra. Or to me at that party…

I take in several sharp breaths, feel a speck of saliva going down the wrong way—Oh, God, I am going to start choking. My eyes will sting, and all the girls will look at me. It will look like I am crying, panicking, suffocating. Dying.

Dying.

"We're not going to make her talk about *that*," another girl speaks up. "This is a safe space."

I swallow frantically, somehow managing to stop my body exploding. But I feel heat rise to my face, soft dampness collecting under my arms and between my shoulder blades.

"Of course," Tiger says.

"Really? Because you just said—"

"It doesn't matter," Annmarie says.

Amaryllis has not said anything yet, but I see she is holding a pen now—a pen that seems to have appeared out of thin air—and she is writing something in neat capitals on the back of her brown hand. I want to see what she is writing—but of course I cannot from here.

I sit up straighter, my left hand gripping my right wrist so that my thumb and pointer finger make a loop around it. Then I slide the loop up, as far as it will go, toward my elbow.

It doesn't go as far as it used to.

"No, it's fine," Emma says, looking flustered. "I was—"

"You don't have to," interrupts a voice from my right. Strong Manchester accent.

"But we're all here because of the forum," Tiger says. "It makes sense. How else are we going to connect, heal? My therapist said there's comfort in finding others like you, others who've experienced what you have."

Emma nods. I grip my arm tighter, until the fingers of my right hand start to tingle. The wonderful numb sensation follows.

"I was raped," Emma says. "Six months ago. He… I knew him. My neighbor."

There are several gasps, all around the room—even though it should not be a surprise. That is why we're all here. Victims of rape and sexual assault. But it *is* a surprise, for me, hearing the word. The power of the word still gets me. The word I cannot say. Even to my therapist, I struggled.

I just push it down inside me, fold the word neatly into a box, padlock the box, bury the box under old roots and too much earth so that it can never be found accidentally. That box is too dangerous.

But the boxes of the other girls are opening. All around the room, there are padlocks unlocking, boxes lifting up, throwing earth and dirt and mud everywhere. Keys and chains are flying.

He was my step-brother… my teacher… a taxi driver… a man I met at a bar… I thought he was my boyfriend…. my friend… I didn't realize there was anything wrong at first… He seemed nice… He bought me presents… He bought me a drink… It was at school… at the cinema… at the beach… at a party… a party… a party…

He got angry.

He loved me.

He hurt me.

I grip my arm tighter. Realize my fingers have slipped, my nails digging into the new flesh that's there, drawing the same blood that all these other girls are spilling inside themselves. We are all just sacks of blood. Sacks of hurt.

"But hey," Emma says, her voice weak, her face flushed. "We're all survivors, right?"

"This train is being held at a red signal."

I lean back, trying to calm my nerves. It is not so bad when the tube is moving, when I can focus on the rattling and the movement in the carriage. When everyone is doing their own thing, looking at phones and books, chatting, listening to music, whatever it is. But now they are not doing that. Everyone is looking around, at each other.

I try to shrink back into my seat, pulling the gray hood of my oversized hoodie up. I feel safer with it up, covering as much of me as possible. Two men near me—not together— begin talking. One of them is trying to catch my eye, so I pull out my phone.

There's a message from Tiger in our smaller WhatsApp group, as well as several from the main group where all of us chat. Although we met on a forum for teenage girls who had experienced sexual abuse, we did not feel comfortable staying on a platform that someone else owns, where someone could read all our 'private' messages.

The main WhatsApp group is mainly filled with messages from the other girls saying they have got home safely after our meeting.

I look at the latest message—which I am tagged in. Tiger asking if I have got home yet. Her concern touches me. Mother is not like that.

Still on the train, I type back, then I switch to our smaller group. Tiger has asked again there too, but she has added something more: *You're so brave going on trains alone. I still can't go anywhere by myself.*

I do not feel brave as I hunker down in my seat, trying to avoid the gaze of the two men, my face half swallowed by my hood.

I do not know if I will ever feel brave again.

But that is okay. That is what I tell myself. Annmarie messaged that to our group—that it is okay not to feel brave—when Tiger and Amaryllis were talking about how they do not think they can be brave now. Because it hurts too much. Because getting away and telling someone about what had been going on used up their capacity of bravery. No more lurks in the well.

I did not say anything in that discussion, just read their messages. Knew that they would know I was there, reading. But it felt better for me that way, and now I often tell myself it is okay—even if it is hard to believe.

The train jolts suddenly, then lurches into a smooth momentum. I breathe a sigh of relief. The two men stop talking, each going back to what they were doing before.

Good. I breathe deeply.

I shall be home in twenty minutes, I am about to tell the main WhatsApp group, when I pause. Think of what Mother will be like. And Mother, well, she is hurting—of course she is. The anniversary is coming up.

Of course, we do not talk about the anniversary at home. But there is one person I spoke about it to, someone who is not my therapist. Darius. He was one of my friends, back when I was in ballet training. He was set to go far, but then a knee injury when we were seven changed everything. It happened just before Allegra disappeared, and his grief for his body—and his abrupt departure from ballet—and my anguish for my missing sister meant we fell out of touch. I learned through others that he got in with a bad crowd. I tried to reach out to him when I was nine, up until when I was thirteen. Just the odd message, every now and again. But when he did reply, he just wanted money from me.

But recently, he messaged me—four-and-a-half years on. He seemed friendly, like he really *did* want to reconnect. Properly. He remembered the anniversary of Allegra disappearing was coming up. He seemed interested. I also told him about Mother's plans. He said at least she cared. And at least she was still letting me live at home, rent-free. When he fell in with the wrong people, his parents made him move out.

I soon discovered, however, why he had got back in touch with me. He was still in with the wrong crowd. It did not take him long to ask me for money, just as he had when we were thirteen.

That was a few months ago, and I stopped replying.

I breathe out hard, leaning back into the train's seat. The choreography course lasts two years, but I have only got two months until I am eighteen. At that age, it will be easier for me to move out. Easier to rent my own place. Maybe I just do this course for two months? Keep Mother happy until I do not have to be under the same roof?

I click my knuckles, twice, then I delete my message for the WhatsApp group, retype it: *I will be at Roseheart in twenty minutes.* I wince at my use of the school's name, but the girls already think I am a dancer there. One of them had heard about my sister, just assumed it meant I would be a ballet prodigy too. It was easier just to go along with it, even if it meant I could not share with them my annoyance about starting a course that I do not even want to be enrolled on.

Anything to please Mother.

I shall message once I am there.

I shall message once the next stage of hell starts.

But when the tube finally gets to the stop where I would change, if I was going to Roseheart, I stay seated. I cannot bring myself to *actually* go there—even though I have apparently made up my mind, told the girls.

Tomorrow, I tell myself. Promise myself. *I shall start tomorrow.*

FIVE

Trent

Three. Two. One. This is it. Let's get this over and done with.

I take a deep breath and force myself to move forward, up the path, ignoring the voice in my head that's screaming at me, telling me that I am going to fall over. Or be sick. Or both.

Maybe faint too? Huh. How manly would that be?

I hold my breath and straighten my jacket, my feet coming to a halt on the white gravel. The suit's too big for me, but my parents said it would be best to look professional, when I go to see Mr. Appleby. Last night, on Skype, my parents were pretty shocked when I told them I wanted to leave ballet. Leave it for good.

"But this is all you've ever wanted to do!" my mum exclaimed.

I almost wished that there was a dodgy Internet connection at Roseheart. That there would be a lag or something to give me an extra few seconds to process what I was going to say, even though I'd spent the last few months rehearsing my decision.

Still, after the initial shock, my parents took it pretty well. Even if they were apprehensive. Mainly because it was about the money.

"What if he wants repaying?" My dad looked worried. Very worried.

The only way I've even been able to train at Roseheart and join the company was because of Mr. Appleby. He's sponsored me since I was little, first at my other ballet school, and then moving to Roseheart with me, and now he's one of Roseheart's biggest financial investors—if not *the* biggest. There's no way my parents can afford to pay him back for all he's done for me. For us. He even sends extravagant gifts to my parents—presents that they really need: a working oven, a gorgeous three-piece suite, a brand new bathroom after theirs flooded when the flat above had a leak.

And now I'm here, outside Mr. Appleby's place. Ready to turn my back on everything I've ever known.

My breaths shudder.

Mr. Appleby's house is, well, a mansion. I've been here before, and no matter how many times I visit, I still get this moment of complete and utter jaw-dropping *awe*. Oh, how I would love to live in a place like this. Extravagant steps and marble pillars, gorgeous rose beds leading to the front entrance, seven floors of perfection and exquisiteness. The life of luxury.

Feeling sick, I continue to the door and ring the bell. I hear the maid's heels as she approaches, tap-tap-tapping away.

"Ah, Mr. Mason!" It's Bessie, and she looks genuinely happy to see me upon opening the door. "Come in! Come in at once! Mr. Appleby's just upstairs playing the violin. I can see if he will be available."

She leads me to the visitors' lounge, where another of Mr. Appleby's maids offers me a biscuit from a selection artfully arranged on a plate and places a pot of hot tea on the table—that's the thing about coming here. Even announced, I'm always given hot tea that just seems to be at the ready.

I pick a Viennese whirl, and then when I take a bite, it crumbles all down the front of my suit. Hastily, I try to wipe the crumbs away, then realize that I'm brushing them onto the pristine red carpet under Mr. Appleby's very eyes. Because he's right here—standing tall, proud, smiling. When the hell did he get here?

"So, Trent, to what do I owe this pleasure of seeing you again?" He sits opposite me, at the small table, but I swear I feel his touch on my shoulder. That big, bear hand. I shiver.

"Sir, I thought it best to let you know as soon as possible. At the earliest opportunity. Thought it a curtesy, to let you know, given all you have done for me." There's a lone crumb on my trouser leg, balanced precariously on my left knee, and

I stare at it. "And I've thought long and hard about this, for a long time, so I don't want you to think this is a rash decision or anything." I take several deep breaths, then feel the scratchiness in my throat that sure as hell means there are crumbs stuck there. Oh no. I'm going to choke.

I grab my cup of tea and take a couple of gulps. For a moment, I think I'm going to choke on the tea too, but thankfully, that doesn't happen.

"Yes?" Mr. Appleby asks.

"I… I no longer wish to… and it's not that I'm not grateful. Because I am—for everything you've done for the past few years. Well, more than a few. Ten, now, isn't it?"

"Trent." Mr. Appleby gets up and then he's coming over. Kneeling by my side.

Shit. Exactly what I didn't want.

"I'm leaving the company," I blurt out—and it works.

He freezes, a few inches from me. But he's not touching me, and he doesn't look inclined to. Because Mr. Appleby can be very touchy-feely. *Over* touchy-feely. When I mentioned it to the other danseurs he sponsors, seeking solace or something similar, I don't know, they just shrugged. Said it was his style. Said that he's just passionate about the arts. That that's why he's sponsoring several of us anyway.

Now, Mr. Appleby looks down his nose at me. For a long, long second, his expression doesn't change. Then he laughs.

Actually laughs.

"Oh, my darling boy, this couldn't have come at a better time, for I am planning on buying a new villa out in the south of Spain and I've heard that two of my dear theatre friends are looking at setting up a new dance venture over there. We can transfer you over there, no problem, and of course we can still work together."

And here it comes—his hand on my knee. Heavy, warm, right where that crumb is. Was. I'm already sweating so much, and I swear I can feel his sweat imprinting through the fabric of my trousers, mixing with my own. "No… no, sorry, I should have been clearer. I'm leaving… Well, I intend to leave the whole industry." I take a deep breath. "I no longer wish to dance."

Silence. The whole room is filled with it. A fragile kind of silence.

My breaths are shuddery, like hummingbirds are fluttering in my airpipe. They want to get out.

So do I.

I daren't look at Mr. Appleby so I look down at my hands.

"Well, this isn't going to work." His voice is all choked-sounding. "Not at all. You are one of my danseurs."

I'm not your danseur.

"There's no reason for you to leave. Is it money? Do you want more?"

I shake my head. "You've been more than generous." Not only has this man paid my tuition fees since I was eleven years old, but even now that I've got a salaried position at the

Roseheart Romantic Dance Company, he's still there, not only being the biggest annual funder for Roseheart but also depositing a monthly shoes-and-food allowance into my bank account and setting me up with private medical insurance. I'd questioned this, upon joining the company, but he said it was standard for him to give this to all of his danseurs. To make sure they're well cared for. And he added, when he throws his private parties, he'd love to have some of his danseurs perform.

That's not happened much—only twice have I been asked to this very mansion where a stage had been set up in the Greeting Room, where I was asked to dance, alongside two other danseurs. I'd been nervous, immediately thinking something untoward would happen afterward, because you hear about all these kinds of things—and well, there was no denying it, Mr. Appleby is touchy-feely.

But nothing did happen.

We did a private performance, me and Manuel and Luca.

We were invited to mingle with the guests afterward.

We ate canapés and extraordinarily delicate-looking pastries that had been made by a French-trained patisserie chef especially for Mr. Appleby's party.

And then we left, the three of us danseurs in one of Mr. Appleby's private cars, complete with driver and chauffeur. And that was it.

"Then for what reason could you possibly want to leave ballet?" Mr. Appleby asks. "You're not injured, are you? I've had no medical expenses come through on my policy."

"I'm not injured." I look down. "Not physically."

"Not physically?"

I don't want to say it. It was hard enough talking about it with my mum and dad yesterday. Hard enough saying the words. I'd really been hoping that Mr. Appleby wouldn't press too hard for a reason. But of course, I'd known deep down that he would.

He'd never just let me walk away without a good reason.

"It's the environment," I begin with. "The pressure."

"So, you *do* want a change of scenery?" He squeezes my knee, and I look up and see a muscle in his jaw twitch. He's got a thinning beard—patchy in places—and the bristles twitch in turn. "I can of course arrange this at a drop of a hat. You only need ask, my darling boy."

"No, it's all of it. It's too much."

I don't know what else to say. How to say it. How the pressure is just always there. So much of it, all the time. The back-to-back company classes, the pressure the ballet masters and mistresses put on you, the pressure you put on yourself, wanting to advance up the hierarchy, the sheer disappointment that comes with another year stuck in the same division, and then when you are promoted, the sheer pressure of showing everyone that you were right to be promoted. The wear and tear on your body, the injuries you've never allowed to heal because pain is supposed to be pushed through. Pain is nothing. The objectification of your bodies, how you are constantly scrutinized—not just by the ballet masters but the public too. How you scrutinize your own body. How you come to hate it. Hate having to fuel it with food that you can't stand the taste of.

How you end up pushing yourself harder and harder because there's always something you think you can do better, something you think you've let everyone down on, how you think you just have to try harder. How you sacrifice sleep for extra training. How sick and tired you feel all the time, because you just want to be the best but you never can be. And even if you could, there would always be something more.

And so you do something stupid, in the moment. You're under so much pressure that you decide to go out clubbing.

You see a girl. A girl that you've seen at the academy, in the diploma program. Bella Sotheby. The loud one. The one you always hear rumors about. The one whose eyes sparkle when she laughs. The one who manages to look so confident all the time.

And you know she's a student, but you've been drinking and you don't really care. You ask her how old she is, and she says eighteen and you choose to trust her, knowing it could be a mistake. Knowing she could be lying. Knowing that you shouldn't even be kissing someone else—let alone doing more—because you've already got a girl. Li Hua.

One fucking moment of weakness.

A moment that's been following you, tormenting you.

Mr. Appleby clears his throat. "Did you not always want to be a Roseheart dancer?"

I nod. I always wanted to train at Roseheart Academy, and when I got accepted there, at age thirteen, after two years of being sponsored by Mr. Appleby, we made acceptance onto Roseheart's diploma the next goal. Then I achieved that, and the next step was the company. When I got there, it became rising up through the ranks. When I got to the second division with Li Hua, we still wanted more. Needed more. And Roseheart, being so exclusively focused on romantic dance and pas de deux doesn't offer the other promotions that other companies do. No soloist positions I could aim for.

Just be the best, or nothing.

I've got anxiety—anxiety I went to an NHS doctor about because I couldn't bear for Mr. Appleby to learn about it. Even though the private medical appointments are said to be confidential, I didn't feel comfortable having it on those records. I know that money buys things. Access.

"I want a *complete* change of career," I say, and I try to project as much confidence and determination into my voice as possible. "This is something I've been thinking about for a long while, and I've applied to go to Exeter University to study English Literature and—"

"University?" Mr. Appleby stares at me, then makes a spluttering sound that he hastily turns into a laugh.

"I've made up my mind," I say, firmly. "And I've told Li Hua too, and she's fully supportive of me." It's a lie—another one, when it comes to my girlfriend.

She asked me if the rumors about me and Bella were true. I said no.

I didn't tell her that I wanted to leave the company. Leave ballet forever.

"Supportive of you, even though it means the end of her career, too?" Mr. Appleby asks the question in such a way that is obvious he believes he's got the upper hand here. The advantage. The power.

The end of Li Hua's career? "No, she'll be staying. It's only me who'll be leaving."

"She cannot stay at Roseheart without her romantic dance partner." There's a slight hint of amusement in Mr. Appleby's voice. "It is against the rules."

"No—it'll work," I say. "Marion and Victoria and Peter were all asked to leave two years ago, but Marion's partner stayed on. Although he's not been in company performances, he's still training with us—and Li Hua has trained with him a few times." I try to present it confidently, like I've got it all worked out—like it's so obvious, that there's nothing *to* work out. "They can dance together once I'm gone."

"You think it's that simple?" Mr. Appleby leans back, finally removing his hand from my knee. His action is enough to make me breathe a sigh of relief, even if his words suggest the opposite.

I watch as he busies himself pouring more tea into his cup. He then settles back in his own chair. He even sticks his little finger out as he raises the teacup to his thin lips.

"Do you know why I picked you, Trent, all those years ago?"

I know he's not actually waiting for a response from me, so I just look at him. His eyes seem to bulge. There's a small droplet of tea clinging to one of the wiry hairs just below his mouth.

"Because I saw a little boy with passion for art," he says, giving an extravagant flourishing gesture with his free hand. "For movement. For storytelling. I saw your determination, and it reminded me of my own at that age. Did you know I wanted to dance?"

I shake my head.

"I was never given the chance. The opportunity. But you, my darling boy, you've had it all. And, Trent, my dearest, you are one of my finest danseurs, and you will stay as a danseur at Roseheart."

"I can't."

He stands up, drawing himself to his full height. He's at least six-and-a-half feet, but he holds himself with the presence of someone even bigger. Taller. Stronger. I don't like looking up at him like this, so I force myself to stand as well, even though my knees feel too weak.

Oh God. I'm actually going to fall over.

"Well." Mr. Appleby rubs his hands together. "I cannot continue to invest in Roseheart if my favorite danseur is no longer there."

I stare at him. "You'd really pull your investments?" I swallow hard, thinking of all the dancers this will affect if the Roseheart directors can't get a replacement investor. Because Mr. Appleby, well, he has to be responsible for at least eighty percent of the annual investments in the last couple of years, especially.

The company, and quite possibly the academy, wouldn't survive without him.

But I can't be emotionally blackmailed. I won't let myself be.

This is him bluffing, anyway, it has to be.

"I would have no choice." Mr. Appleby's thin lips arrange themselves into a smile that makes my stomach churn. "It would be such a shame. All those dancers without a job. The collapse of the Roseheart Romantic Dance Company. All because of your…selfishness."

"I have made up my mind," I say. I breathe deeply. I had a feeling he'd do something like this. My parents and I talked about it, what I'd say and do if he said this. We came up with whole scripts for different scenarios, varying reactions—scripts that I cannot even remember now, in the moment.

"You know, it will be very hard for some of the Roseheart dancers to gain positions with other companies," Mr. Appleby says. "Scandal has tainted more than one of these dancers and although Roseheart overlooks things—to a degree—other companies simply will not want the press. It doesn't matter how strong a port de bras is, not if it's *unfortunate* media attention."

I don't say anything, because I know he's trying to goad me, wind me up.

"And even if the other dancers manage to find themselves new work, your girlfriend definitely won't."

For a moment, I can't believe he's actually said those words. Threatening Li Hua? Because of course that's going to get to me. He knows it.

My fists tremble.

"You know, a lot of traditionalists within the ballet world are still quite backward," Mr. Appleby says. "Not at all *woke*, as you might say. I've shown fairness by sponsoring Black danseurs, Asian danseurs, even that Deaf danseur, across the years. But most people in my position, they like to see… Well, I'm sure you know."

Rage boils inside me.

"Such a pretty girl isn't she, your girlfriend?" Mr. Appleby smiles suddenly. "Would be a shame if something were to happen to her."

"What?" The word bolts from my mouth.

"I think you'll find it's in everyone's best interest for you to stay at Roseheart."

SIX

Trent

By the time I make it back to Roseheart's grounds, I cannot contain my anger. It's bubbling out of me into the ink-black sky, and I feel so sick and just so fucking angry with it that I don't know what to do. I don't want to go straight into my apartment, because there's a good chance Li Hua will be back from her Pilates class now, doing stretches in our living room, and every time I see her at the moment, my emotions are all over the place.

It's only a matter of time, I know, before she finds out about what happened between me and Bella. And it's also only a matter of time before she finds out about my conversation with Mr. Appleby. How I was apparently willing to sacrifice her career too. Because Mr. Appleby's got power, influence around here, and I knew before I even set foot in his house that if I didn't get my way, really insist that I leave and make him understand and agree that it is in my best interest to, that he'd hold it over me. Now, he'll make sure everyone at the company finds out what a flake I am. He'll frame it as a betrayal. And if there's anything company dancers don't like, it's when someone's not *dedicated.*

When performing a ballet, everyone has to put their utmost effort in. One hundred-and-ten percent. Nothing less. Word will get out about me wanting to leave, and they'll feel betrayed by me.

Li Hua will feel betrayed by me. Like she so rightly should feel.

My face crumples. I don't want to cry—not out here in the rose gardens—but I am. I curse, wiping my face so aggressively that the button on my sleeve catches my cheek, makes my skin sting sharply.

I take several deep breaths. I feel sick, and I want to scream and scream, never stop screaming.

Trapped, that's what I am.

That's what dancers are, when they're here. You don't leave unless you age out or you're kicked out.

And you don't get kicked out unless you've done something really bad.

I take a deep breath, and stare down at the nearest rosebush—dormant, a collection of sticks, poking up through semi-frozen soil. No blooms or leaves in January. There's one little lamp out here, for the whole of the garden—a lantern, right in the middle—and it casts a soft glow over the rose twigs, makes them look otherworldly, ghostly talons rising from the soil. There's going to be a frost tonight again. I love looking at the frosty lawns in the morning from my window.

I take a deep breath.

I wonder just how bad it would be if the administration department found out about me and Bella. Me, with a student. If it's even worth confessing to. It's not like she's underage. Just not an adult. But is that as bad?

I groan. Roseheart would probably sweep it under the carpet anyway. It's not like I've got her pregnant—I wasn't drunk enough not to be careful. And after the last few tumultuous years, the company and academy are not going to want another scandal.

No, I'd still have to be a danseur here, even if the truth about me and Bella was out there. Li Hua would know, and I'd still be expected to dance with her. At Roseheart, you're lifelong dance partners. Even if we break up romantically, we'd still be forced to spend so many hours of every day together.

It's why they advise that you don't get involved with your dance partner unless you're really serious.

But since when did Li Hua and I ever listen to anyone? We just fell in love hard, fast.

And then I started doing stupid things, messing it up.

Just as my fingers and toes are about to freeze, I finally head inside the block of company flats. A couple of first-division ballerinas are in the communal kitchen, and they watch me with wide eyes as I gulp back two glasses of ice-cold water from the dispenser on the countertop, having to drink them quickly because I don't know how much longer my numb hands can hold the glass for. The coldness of the water gets right inside my teeth, makes me shiver.

"She's still not here," one of the women is saying as I rinse my glass.

She? I nearly drop the glass. Li Hua—she's not got back okay? Because she was popping into town for the evening, wasn't she? One of her usual Pilates classes. My eyes widen. Mr. Appleby—is he sending a message to me?

I spin around to look at the ballerinas. "Who?" The glass is still in my hands, and I'm holding onto it so tightly that the tendons in my wrists start to ache from the strain.

"Alessia Valenzi," one of them says. "Didn't you hear she was starting at the academy today?"

Alessia Valenzi. I stare at them blankly, but then a moment later, something that Li Hua said to me rings through my brain. I think she's the younger sister of that dancer who went missing ten years ago. Li Hua's been obsessed with that case, reading everything she can find. She's been watching too many police dramas, because I've seen all the notes she's been making on the case. There'll be a corkboard up in our flat soon, faces of suspects and people of interest pinned up on it, with string connecting different papers and notes and whatnot.

"Though it's probably going to be tomorrow now," the other says. "It's, like, way too late now."

"Yeah, and she doesn't even want to be here—that's the rumor," the first dancer says.

That makes two of us.

The two women continue chatting, gossiping, and I say goodnight to them.

Finally, I know, I have to face Li Hua. She should have got back from Pilates an hour ago.

Roseheart provides full lodgings for its company dancers: a range of dorm-style rooms and a number of flats. Li Hua and I roomed separately for the first two years we were in the company—two years in which we had a lot of 'sleepovers' just like we had in our diploma days—and then last year, when a flat became available, we applied for it. Got it.

We're not the only couple who shares a flat. The two principal dancers within the first division do as well, and then several others are shared by pairs and trios of friends.

I get to our flat all too soon. The door creaks as I open it.

"You okay?" Li Hua calls out as I drop my keys on the small table by the doorway.

I nod, and then she's suddenly by my side, reaching for me. Dressed in baggy jogging bottoms and a tank top, she looks good. She always looks good, even when she's not trying. A set of headphones hang around her neck—no doubt she's been listening to one of her true crime podcasts—and the headphones twist and dig into my chest a little as she hugs me. I'm a head taller than her, and her soft hair brushes against my chin. She's got the red ribbon in her hair, still, and I smile a bit, despite myself. Ever since I told her red is her color, she's always made sure to wear something red. *For you*, she always says.

She pulls back a little and looks up at me. "You look tired." She cups my face, and I want to just lean into her again, let her hold me, tell me that everything is going to be okay. Even though I know it's not.

I stare into her heart-shaped face, into her eyes—always so beautiful, so pure, so full of love for me. And trust. That's the thing about Li Hua. I've never met someone who trusts me with all their heart. Because she does.

This morning, when I told her there was no truth to the rumor about me and Bella—a rumor that one of the company dancers had 'helpfully' messaged her about—she believed me. I know that she'll never ask me again. My word was enough for her.

My word should be enough.

But there's a ragged wound inside me, something rotten, something contaminating.

I hold her close to me, tightly, and I promise that I will never do anything that could hurt her again. No, I'll ignore Bella. And I'll keep dancing.

I'll do it for you, Li Hua.

SEVEN

Bella

Freezing fog hangs in the air as I battle my way down Old Freeman's Street, my teeth chattering. My feet are blocks of ice, and twice I've nearly slipped and fallen flat on my behind. *It's too early for this. Way too early.*

I turn right at the junction, stepping over a pile of what I believe to be semi-frozen vomit on the ground. *Gross.*

Pigeons coo at me, and the cash in my pocket weighs heavily. Though it's almost five in the morning, there are a lot of people out. Of course there are. It's London. But these aren't the posh morning commuters and keen gym-goers. This isn't *their* part of London. This is the homeless men and women stirring, shaking out blankets that have tried to freeze as they slept—or tried to sleep as winter raged on. This is cyclists speeding through the cold back roads, avoiding the odd fox who runs suddenly away from the tipped dustbins. This is broken glass littering pavements, and a woman walking quickly along the narrow pavement with a large suitcase whose wheels twist and turn the wrong way.

When I first moved to Roseheart, at the start of the diploma, Mum wasn't happy that I'd be in London. All she knew of London really was its seedy underbelly—the part portrayed in gritty crime dramas and psychological thrillers, where everyone's addicted to something, where crime is rampant, and where there's a good chance someone you know is going to be murdered—if not you, yourself. I had to work hard to reassure her, and my brother Bobby helped a lot. We talked her around, and she came to open days with me. We transformed her view of London, taking her to the posh shops, the food markets, the tourist attractions, and I promised her that when I lived here, I'd stick to the nice areas on the *rare occasions* I left Roseheart.

If Mum knew where I was right now, she'd have a heart attack, I'm sure.

The streetlights here work only intermittently, casting a little light, but mainly it's just what I call the London grogginess here. There's always light pollution, and it never really gets completely dark in most places in the city. So even though it's not daylight, I can still make out shadows and shapes. Everything's mostly covered in a gray-brown hue.

I turn left, down the next alleyway. A road no wider than the corridors at Roseheart. Nearby, I hear vehicles, cars accelerating and then braking sharply. Someone hoots their horn.

A couple of scrawny-looking women in their late twenties step out of the doorway to my right. They're skinny, their twig-arms unclothed, tank tops stretching over braless bosoms, both with their thin hair pulled up into buns that emphasizes the gauntness of their faces. I nod at them, and in the gray light, I just about see their nods back at me.

"He in?" I keep my voice low, quiet.

The taller of the two nods then smiles. She's close enough that I can see she's missing her two top front teeth. The teeth either side look darker, like they're rotting.

"Thanks," I say, and I duck behind them, into the doorway.

It's dark inside—as always. But it's a different kind of dark. Heavier, muggier. Dense. The smell of weed hangs thick in the air, and something scratches my throat with every breath I take. Movement down by my feet catches my eyes. I pause for a moment. *That better just be his cat.*

"All right, Bella?"

From the depths of the room to my right, Mac emerges, backlit by one weak lamp in the corner of the room. He moves like how I imagine a sloth might if it was turned into a human—arms always reaching out, baggy clothes draping from every limb. I can never quite tell how old he is. I've never seen him in daylight, for he always prefers pickups are done at this time. I was surprised the pickups were even at his place—these couple of rooms that he rents—but he told me I'm one of the lucky ones. Not everyone he trusts with his address. I've only ever seen women, just like those two, outside. Never any men making pickups here.

"Just the usual amount," I say, trying not to breathe too deeply. There's something else in the air too. Not just the weed. Something that's really getting to my head.

I sent Mac a message last night, before I went to sleep, asking if he had some available. It's sooner than I usually pick up, but I've gone through it quicker this time.

"You still giving some to that tech guy, right?" Mac asks. For a drug dealer, he's pretty talkative, always seems interested in what I'm doing, what's going on. Or maybe many dealers are. Maybe I'm just running on stereotypes here. But Mac knows I'm a dancer, and he also knows that I'm not just collecting for me.

"Yeah," I say.

"I'll give you a little extra then." He gives me a wink.

"Cheers," I say, and I feel myself blushing and I don't even know why. Not like I'm attracted to him or anything.

Nah. But Mac's a pretty decent guy—for a drug dealer. I've been getting my gear from him all the time. Well, all the time that I've needed it. It started when I first joined Roseheart. The pressure, the stress, the anxiety—all of it had me in a crying heap in the rose garden one Friday afternoon. I was considering quitting, but then Mattie came along. He introduced himself, said he had something that could help. Gave me a bit of his stash—not the cocaine then, just some weed—but it got the two of us talking, meeting up. And I found it did help, and it continued helping, until I found I wanted the harder stuff.

Mattie was apprehensive at first. Said that cocaine wasn't a good idea. But I persuaded him, and then he gave me Mac's number. Asked if I could get the gear for him too because he'd heard that Mac gave better deals to girls. And sure enough, that seemed to be true. And even when I accidentally told Mac that Mattie was taking a cut of my gear, Mac still continued giving me a good amount. He said he had to look out for people like me.

Now, Mac turns away to where I think the table with the lamp is, and I hear rustling. Then he's back, pressing two small baggies into my hand. There's a sliver of light leaking through a window behind him, and it lands across his hand as he gives me the gear, illuminating a small tattoo of a crescent moon on the inside of his wrist.

Pretty cool.

I love tattoos. Have wanted one forever. *Shame you chose to be a dancer*, Bobby said to me on his last visit when he showed me his latest pieces on his upper arms. I'm not the only one in the family who loves inking art onto their skin. I've got big plans for when I'm no longer a dancer.

I hand over the cash, and Mac takes it in his big bear hand, pockets it without counting. He never counts mine. Just gives me a warm smile, tells me to take care.

I leave, and the moment I step outside, a breeze that seems even colder than before wraps around me. I can breathe better now, away from the smog and the weed and whatever else that was in Mac's house.

It doesn't take me long to walk back to Roseheart—twenty-five minutes really—and the gear's safely tucked in my jacket pocket. When I'm a few minutes from the academy gates, I text Mattie, letting him know I've got more and asking if he wants to meet now.

Sure. His replies are always instant. The guy never seems to sleep. *Usual place.*

It's coming up to six o'clock now, and I've got just enough time to whizz over to the company-side of campus. Mattie's in one of the older buildings mainly used by the technical staff, his place being a flat at the top, but we always meet by the back door, next to the block's boiler room. It's a fire exit that's rarely used. I get there first, but he arrives maybe thirty seconds later.

"Any word on new tests?" I ask him.

Mattie shakes his head. "Nada. Yesterday's go okay?"

"Yep. No problems there."

He smiles. He's only about four years older than me, got a strong jawline, white skin that tans easily, and a full head of golden curls. I've heard many of the girls in the school fawning over him. Not only does he have a nice face, but he's six feet four—which apparently is hugely important. I've never really felt sexually attracted to Mattie, but there's something intimidating about his looks all the same. He knows he's hot and he's aware of the effect he has on people.

He expects that effect, and half the time, I think he's waiting for me to make a move on him.

Still, I wouldn't. Not worth the risk of it going badly. Not when we've got our arrangement, and I need to know when the random tests will be.

Conversation with Mattie is always focused on our arrangement—never any small talk—so we nod goodbye and head our separate ways. I tuck my remaining baggie of cocaine into the bottom of my jacket's pocket, making sure it's secure, then drop by my room to grab my canvas flats and pointe shoes. I keep my jacket with me, because I don't entirely trust Stacia not to go through my things, looking. She'll do anything for a juicy bit of goss, and though she likely doesn't know about my 'drug problem,' she'll probably be looking for a scrap of paper where I've supposedly penned Trent's number with love hearts alongside it. She's such a romantic.

Ballet time, I tell myself as I head down to the studios.

I've always wanted to be a dancer, a dancer at the Roseheart Romantic Dance Company, wanted it more than anything in my life. When I'm dancing, it's the only time my brain really feels truly quiet, relaxed. Ava thought I was crazy when I told her, insisting that when she's dancing her head is busy with remembering all the combinations and to hold her arms just right and thinking about her character expression. But when I dance, I feel free. I feel myself. I don't worry about the size of my irises or if I should've really spent nearly

£50 on that expensive kind of toothpaste that promises to whiten your teeth.

I can lose myself in the music, the dance, and I need it. I need ballet. Being a professional dancer has always been my goal.

Since being cast as the leads, Ty and I have got so much more work to do, and Madame Cachelle previously suggested we book in our own rehearsal times. I took her suggestion seriously, booking the 6am slot in Studio 23—my favorite one—every day for the next four weeks. Ty was delighted when I told him. His eyebrows did that little scrunchy thing and he shook his head, a bemused look on his face as he waited for me to tell him it was a joke. His face fell when he realized it wasn't. He'd stuck two fingers up at me, told me there was no way he was getting up that early, but so far for every practice he's actually been here on time. Even if he looked bemused every morning he stepped into the studio.

He often looks bemused when he dances with me though—wait, is he *humoring* me? I feel my eyes widen, and then I'm thinking about my irises again and the whites of my eyes and… and those posters with the hot-pink borders are down this corridor too. My fingers itch to tear them down, and I see myself doing it, collecting their shreds, bunching them in my hands.

Just concentrate.

I push open the door to Studio 23, and step inside the darkness, feeling for the light switch. *There.* My hand catches it, and I flood the room with light and—

"Oh my God! Ty?"

He's lying in a heap in the center of the studio. At my exclamation, he lifts one leg into the air and waves his foot at me.

"Uh, what's going on?" I rush to him, my heart pounding. Is he hurt? Has be been attacked? Has he—

My gaze falls on the two empty beer bottles next to him. "Seriously? At this time."

"Big night," he mumbles, and his voice sounds all thick, like his tongue is too big for his words. He rolls his head toward me, and I see his pupils. "And I wanted to make sure I was here on time."

"You are so high right now," I whisper, annoyed. "Why can't you just take this seriously?"

Ty giggles softly, something he always does when he is indeed under the influence of drugs. Myself? Well, I'm feeling pretty good this morning. Clear headed. I've got another month or so before I get called in for another 'random' drugs test and talk, and while Mr. Vikas is taking over from Madame Cachelle, I'm pretty sure I've got an easy ride through it all. That man may have looked a little scary, but I can tell he's pretty soft. But the point is now that I just want to train. I want to dance. Want to rehearse.

And Ty is letting me down.

This isn't the first time, either.

While I may use coke, I don't let it affect my performance. I am *dedicated*. I never turn up wasted or high to rehearsals or classes. I'm always on time, always putting my best in. And the annoying thing is that Ty can dance well when he is in such a state, so I know that if he really tried, if he turned up sober and clean to class and rehearsals, he'd be even better. With Harley gone, Ty's already the best guy in the diploma. But doesn't he want to be *his* best?

"I'll get you some water," I say.

He dissolves into more laughter, and I'm cursing him as soon as I'm outside the studio, where the little water dispenser is. I grab a paper cup, irritability lacing my movements. There's another one of those awful posters above the water dispenser, and I rip it down in one clean movement, then screw it up, spilling the cup of water in the process. I let out a small scream, then chuck the ball of paper behind the water dispenser and grab another cup.

When I enter the studio again, Ty's at least standing up now. Even if he is singing to himself, swaying slightly, and turning to tell me how beautiful I look.

"Drink this, now," I snap.

I spend more time than I'd like getting Ty to drink water. In fact, a lot of us diploma students do. Usually right before class. I'm well aware that the others have expressed annoyance over his behavior at varying times. "Madame Cachelle is just too soft on him," Felicity always says.

Someone who isn't soft, however, is Madame Yelland. Alongside Miss Potts and Madame Cachelle, she's the third ballet teacher who works regularly with the diploma students. I'm pretty sure it's Madame Yelland on the rota later. And so while I practice now, running through choreography and doing my best on my own—while Ty tries to sober up in the corner—I'm thinking about Madame Yelland and the horn-rimmed glasses she wears. The way she snaps her fingers so enthusiastically but kind of aggressively too. I can't get fully into the beauty of dance today, can't use it to calm my racing head, because it doesn't even feel like a proper rehearsal when it's just me dancing half the pas de deux.

Seven o'clock slips around, and Ty and I have a quick break—for water, a piece of fruit, and a toilet trip—before heading to barre and center class. Madame Yelland greets us as she always does, with a prim nod.

"Howdy," Ty says.

Once everyone has arrived, we all warm up and then line up along the back of the room, each of us resting our left fingers on top of the barre, our feet in first position. Every time I do this, I always think of my very first ballet teacher— Mrs. Peters in the Community Center, and how she'd say *"Your legs are barbershop poles, and so energy spirals which way? Upward and outward!"* One time she even drew on her own tights to show us this, a line from her third toe, up the center of her shin, and through the center of her thigh, on each leg. *"See how the lines are facing away from each other, like they're lovers not talking after a passionate argument?"*

Not entirely sure that was an appropriate simile for seven-year-olds, but it made me have possibly the best first position in Essex. But it means that as we're beginning barre class, I'm thinking of Mrs. Peters and her strong Scottish accent—which has me screaming inside, *No! I just want to be calm and in ballet mode*—but it's not long before I get that serenity of dance in my head again. The class goes through the usual order of pliés, tendus, and dégagéz, before moving onto frappés, ronds de jambe, and fondus. All the while Madame Yelland plays soft notes on the piano.

We're given a quick water break before moving onto grand battements and adagio, and then we move into the center of the room, for jumps and leaping steps. I always like the parts of class where we do jumps and leaping steps. While the guys have dedicated classes just for this, these are the only times us girls really get to practice them. Our individual classes are for pointe work instead.

"We'll start with entrechat quatre," Madame Yelland says. "Then entrechat six and dix. Feet in fifth, please."

I hold my head strong and center, and jump, rapidly crossing my feet for the required number of times, making sure for six and dix that I end with my foot that was in front in the back, in unison with everyone else in the class.

"Good," Madame Yelland says. "Felicity, watch your arms. Ava, remember to land in a tighter fifth. And you group of guys, you're all arching a little too much in the six. We want to engage the abdominals."

Ty, who was included in the group of guys, then demonstrates the movement again, but this time overcompensates, tightening his abdominals way too much, then laughs loudly. Madame Yelland doesn't laugh. Neither does anyone else. We just move on to the next steps: jeté, pirouettes, and the tour en l'air, before finishing class with the révérence.

Felicity sidles over to me after class. "So, Stacia heard that the company dancer you got with was Trent Mason. And I also heard that he has a girlfriend. Does she know?"

"Know what?" I'm breathing hard, and I just want to swat her away like the annoying little fly that she is currently being.

"Uh, you literally admitted it, last night?" She gives a laugh, but it sounds as natural as her blond hair is. Felicity just likes creating drama that she can sit back, watch, and enjoy. My mother says there are always girls like her at every job, in every profession.

I don't give Felicity the satisfaction of a reply. I just ignore her and go about my day. It's a busy one. So many classes, rehearsals, fitness sessions. And I'm not going to let another person ruin my calm.

No, today is going to be a *perfect* day.

EIGHT

Alessia

"Ah, Miss Valenzi, how good of you to join us this fine morning!"

I take a seat at the back of the classroom and murmur a quick apology to Madame Jurgensen, feeling my face flush. Thanks to a delay on the tube, I am a couple of minutes late. I was hoping I could slip in unnoticed, but Madame Jurgensen, it seems, has eyes like a hawk.

"I assume you are indeed Miss Valenzi?" Madame Jurgensen asks, raising a quizzical eyebrow. "For Miss Valenzi is the only name I didn't tick off my list when this class started."

Ah, so it is going to be like this.

I maintain eye contact with her. She knows full well who I am, but she does not like me. That was made clear right from the start, when I was reluctantly sitting at the interview table with two other choreography teachers. Whereas they had smiled and been encouraging, Madame Jurgensen had looked me up and down. *Another failed dancer*, she said, like she knew me. Like she knew anything about me.

But I am not my sister. And I am not a failed dancer. I am not a dancer at all.

And I am definitely not going to be a choreographer. But maybe, just maybe, being here can be a good thing—that is what I decided upon last night, when I was trying to talk myself into this even more. Maybe I shall feel closer to Allegra by being here. Maybe I shall find a clue as to where she is now. Which country she chose to start her secret life in. Maybe I can even fly out, visit her. All in secret, of course.

"Try to be on time next time," Madame Jurgensen says.

There is a blackboard behind her; this has to be the only classroom in this day and age in London that actually has a blackboard, like we are in the 90s or something—and she writes uneven, scrawly letters on it in chalk.

"We're just looking at the abbreviations," says the girl across the aisle from me. She's got a strong accent, but I can't place it. Irish or Scottish—I always get them mixed up. On her desk is a folded piece of paper with 'Francesca' written on it; a quick look around the room shows me everyone has made these name tags.

While the choreography course has intake options in January, I assumed everyone else would have enrolled last September, but maybe not. Or maybe Madame Jurgensen has just not taught most of the students in this class before.

Francesca smiles at me, warm and friendly. It is a stark difference to what I am used to—at school, I never really had friends. I did my GCSEs, and then did AS-levels and left. I have just been at home since last summer, on my own, mostly. Reading crime novels. Listening to classical music. Teaching myself the piano from YouTube videos, even though I could have easily afforded lessons—but it was more fun that way. But the point is that I never needed friends.

"But you'll be fine with these," Francesca adds, smiling wider. It really does light up her whole face. Her close-cropped hair would not be tolerated in a ballerina, but it really makes her cheekbones stand out. She's got a thin face. "I expect you'll know them all already."

I give her a thankful smile, even if it means that she obviously knows who I am.

There are three aisles in the classroom, and about ten rows, so we are all separated somewhat from each other, and Madame Jurgensen turns and sweeps her way down the aisle between me and Francesca. "Girls, I hope my class—my class that you are paying to attend, might I remind you—is not interrupting your conversation?" She titters and any respect I had for her evaporates.

But, still, I cannot mess this up, so again I apologize. Francesca apologizes, too, and Madame Jurgensen gives an approving sort of nod to her. Not to me though—instead, she just snaps at me to make my name card and drops a folded piece of paper in front of me.

I write 'Alessia' in big, capital letters and then struggle to get the folded piece of paper to stand. Several of the other students watch me, and I cautiously meet their eyes, hoping for sympathetic looks, but I get none from them.

I focus on the board. Abbreviations I am already familiar with from my time in ballet fill one side. SR for stage right, SL for stage left, US for upstage, and DS for downstage. Some more complex ones such as SRL and DSR follow next—upstage left and downstage right—but then we have got ones I am not too sure of: b/w, tog, and C2, C4, C6, and C8.

I pull my notebook out of my rucksack.

"We can use others too." Madame Jurgensen taps the board as she speaks. "EDH can be en des hours, and FL and BL are front leg and back leg respectively. The number 2 is often used for 'to' as in the dancer goes from stage left to stage right in line 12. Shorthand, we would write *L12 go SL2SR*. Of course, everyone's abbreviations will be a little different," Madame Jurgensen says, back at the front of the room. Her long skirt swishes in the most annoying way. "But I am a firm believer that making these more universal to all can only benefit everyone. Once you all have built up your repertoire of the abbreviations, I would like you to use, then we can quickly and precisely make notes on directives that you give to your dancers—and of course, this applies whether we're talking about ballroom, jazz, contemporary, or ballet." She does not attempt to hide the way disdain drips from her voice as she says the last dance type, like it does not deserve to be there. "Now, what do you do if, say, you have four dancers on stage, and you want two of them going from stage left to stage right during line 12 while the other two go from right to left? Well, this is where naming your dancers comes in."

She launches into a spiel about how important it is to label each of your dancers—alphabetical letters randomly assigned or the first letters of their names. "It really is vital to remember and record where exactly all your dancers are at any given beat in the music. Now, say I put each of you in a room now with eight dancers and a piece of music, what would your first actions be?"

One of the boys at the front raises his hand. "Naming each of the dancers."

"Yes, and then?"

"Deciding what kind of dance it's going to be."

"The genre?" Madame Jurgensen raises an eyebrow. "I would hope you would already know the type of dance you're choreographing before this stage. Anything else?" She looks around the room.

I raise my hand, trying to be the good student, ready to say, *Listen to the music.* But her gaze skims right over me and settles on a boy a few rows in front of me.

"Dylan, yes?"

"Finding out any strengths and weaknesses of the dancers."

"Knowing your cast, yes, and their abilities." Madame Jurgensen nods. "And Avery?"

"Medical history of the dancers?"

She makes a considering noise deep at the back of her throat. "Anything else?"

Listen to the music and count the beats. My arm begins to ache—which kind of shocks me. I should be able to hold positions for ages. I am weaker than I thought. But I wave it a little, and I know the teacher sees me but chooses to ignore me.

"There is one thing that you're missing though," Madame Jurgensen says. She scans the room, clearly seeing me again but then looks away, pointing her nose out the window for a second. So, it is going to be like this. Great. "We must listen to the music and count—else how do we identify a particular part? How do we know how many sections we can evenly divide the piece into if we do not know the count?"

I withdraw my hand, and I do not even try to get involved in the rest of the class as Madame Jurgensen drones on and on about the history of dance notation. She spends a good half an hour lamenting how dance moves often are not named, and I want to tell her that that is not the case in ballet, but there is no point. She just encourages us to be creative and name every move ourselves—and share our names among each other, so we are all using the same terminology.

I suppress a yawn and look down at my notepad. I have been doodling without realizing. Drawing a stage, marking the ballet dancers' positions for the opening act of some performance. I have used a dot for each dancer, but now I go over each one, replacing the dots with the letters A through to L.

"Miss Valenzi!"

I jump and find Madame Jurgensen standing over my desk. There is a rather long hair protruding out of her left nostril that I failed to notice earlier.

"If you think you'd be better suited to teach this class, then be my guest."

My mouth dries as I look up at her, and there are a thousand things in my head that I want to say, but I just end up bowing my head. Meek. I hate it, but I do not want to get kicked out of this class. I cannot deal with Mother if that happens.

Madame Jurgensen makes a *hmmf* noise deep in her throat and then after an excruciatingly long time, her shadow over me moves backward. She resumes teaching, and I resume breathing.

I keep a low profile until the end of class and then practically run out of it. I swear I feel her burning gaze on my back.

"Hey!"

But it is Francesca.

"Wait up!"

I slow and nod at her. "She really hates me."

"It's because you're a Valenzi," she says, rolling her eyes a little as if it's obvious.

I frown. "But what difference does that make?"

"Because she's jealous. Rumor has it, she, uh, didn't like your sister," Francesca says. "They trained together, in the diploma. Jurgensen's just a jealous bitch."

I laugh softly, but my eyebrows are raised so high that the skin on my face seems tauter. Madame Jurgensen wanted to be a ballet dancer? Ex-professional dancers end up teaching dance. Terrible dancers teach choreography. That is what Allegra said to me once. I cannot remember why. But Madame Jurgensen is the same age as my sister? Twenty-seven? Wow. I thought she was at least forty. That woman has not aged well.

"Anyway, I'm getting the tube back to Stratford now," Francesca says. "Wondered if you wanted to come too, to my house? I know it's totally short notice, but I thought we could work on the choreo homework together? We haven't got any other classes today. Or we could totally go to a café or something nearby? Sorry, I forgot it's weird to invite someone over who you've only just met. But I'm not an axe-murderer. Promise!"

"I would love to," I say, "but I have got an appointment." And plans to go to the music shop, to play their grand piano. "Sorry. Maybe another time?"

"Sure." She smiles, and I am relieved to see that I have not offended her. "See you tomorrow?"

"Tomorrow." I nod. "And I will not be late to Jurgensen's class!"

Francesca surprises me by hugging me goodbye, and I hope she cannot tell how much I stiffen. I am just not used to people hugging me.

Most of the students on the choreography courses do not live at the Roseheart campus, unlike the ballet dancers. Even the dancers in the lower school have dorms, Mother told me, but there are a number of courses for 16+ that take day students, so there is a lot of movement in and out of the academy.

I sit for a little bit in the canteen at Roseheart, just people-watching really, even though I have got C.L. Taylor's latest paperback in my bag. I have got about an hour before it will be time for me to get the tube across London for my therapy appointment, and what I really want to be doing is looking for signs of Allegra here. Because there must be signs around here. Clues she left. If ten years is not enough time for all traces of her to be eradicated.

But I cannot bring myself to move. To get up.

"That's her! Yeah, sitting there!"

I turn wearily at the sound of gossip and see two girls who look about twelve years old pointing at me. Their eyes are wide as they see me looking at them, but then they begin stage-whispering. About my sister. Of course.

I get my phone out, mainly for a distraction, thinking of playing some music so I cannot hear them—but damn, I have not got my earphones. Instead, I look at my messages. Emma and Tiger have both messaged in the WhatsApp group, trying to sort out when our next meeting will be, but they have not had many responses.

The rest of my new messages are from Mother.

I trust you have told them you are a Valenzi?

Take a photo of the portrait they have apparently put up for your sister, would you? I had an email about it. It is in Studio 12.

Have you made sure everyone knows you are a Valenzi?

Do not let people walk all over you.

Send me photos. I want to see what it is all like.

Is it making you want to be a ballerina again?

I sigh and turn my phone off. My breaths seem to rattle through my body. Mother never even asked how I am, how my course was. I did not even see her this morning—or last night, when I got back after spending the day just walking around town, really. The house was so quiet. This morning, as I ate breakfast, Father said that Mother had taken Angélique out. Something about checking out a new nursery. The last one they went to said that they could not offer my sister a place. Of course, they only said that after Mother disclosed that Angélique is being assessed for autism.

I look around the room, my ears tuning back into the conversations all around me as students drink bottles of water and fruit juice, peel bananas, and eat flapjacks.

"I'd never want to set foot in this place if that was my sister," the annoying twelve-year-old continues. "What?" she says to her friend, her eyes all big and expressive. "This school killed her—that's what Claira was saying."

I feel forced to look at them, to set my heavy eyes on the pair of gossipers. "Allegra is not dead." My voice is loud, and now a lot of people in the canteen are looking at me. I did not even think there would be many in here, not at this time of day, but I guess it is breaktime or something for the lower school.

"Then where *is* she?" the girl asks. "Because the ransom was paid, and the other two girls were released. But Allegra Valenzi wasn't."

"She is out there," is all I say as I gather my things. *Of course* my sister is out there.

She is waiting for me.

NINE

Trent

"Hold that arabesque for just a moment longer once you come out of the grand jeté en tournant," Madame Petrov says. "We need to make sure you're fully in the shot."

I nod, already feeling sweat dampening my costume, and look back at the videographer. He's nervous, and I think this is the first time the freelance agency have sent him to us. Twice he's got in my way on stage, trying to circle me as I leap because Madame Petrov requested 360-degree visuals, as if this is a performance in the round. But of course, as soon as Tilly starts up again on the piano, I do the leap again, and again, as Madame Petrov requests, making sure to hold my arabesque until she gives a curt nod.

Li Hua's on the other side of the stage, just visible in the wings, standing elegantly as she waits for her turn, but Madame Petrov gives me more variations to perform for the filming, before she brings Li Hua on stage and says we will perform the adagio pas de deux where our characters, the prince and Odette, dance together before she must return to her swan form.

Li Hua gives me a warm smile—just for me—as she stands at the stage's edge, before she slips fully into character. It's like a mask sliding over her face. It's the first time we've danced in full costume in our new roles—we were cast as the leads for *Swan Lake* only a week ago—and she looks magnificent as Odette: a full-feathered pure white tutu stems from a fitted magnolia bodice bejeweled with hand-stitched sequins, highlighting her curves—curves that I keep finding myself even more drawn to now. Even though I wish I wasn't. Her face is flushed, and her forehead is shining a little through her makeup. Her dark hair has been interwoven with the extravagant white feather headpiece.

Madame Petrov gives the signal to Tilly, the pianist, who nods. Normally, the company's pianist sits to the left of the stage, toward the back, but the ballet mistress has had Tilly move to below the front of the stage, to mimic The Royal Opera House's setup in their ballets. Not that we have a live orchestra. Yet, anyway. The other week, Jaidev and Taryn said they heard the board discussing it. Probably something that the first-division company productions would get. Not us.

Tilly begins, clear notes swimming toward us, and I look across the stage at Li Hua. I nod to her, then we glide forward, as if compelled to one another, and stop when the two of us are exactly seven feet from each other. We bow deeply. Tilly's piano strokes speed up, a Tchaikovsky piece, of course, and our steps are light, bouncing. Li Hua pirouettes toward me as I near her. I keep my breathing just as light, and join her, supporting her, my hands firm as I lift her once, twice, three times. The videographer whizzes around behind us—something that threatens to make me dizzy—and the soft-pink spotlights overhead change to white.

"And slow down," Madame Petrov says, just as I anticipated her saying it in my head. As ballet mistresses go, Madame Petrov is pretty predictable. Not like Mr. Vikas, the ballet master for the third division—though I've heard he's now teaching on the diploma, standing in for Madame Cachelle. I always found him a bit fiery, scary, but Madame Petrov always seems down-to-earth. Dependable. Predictable.

Li Hua and I slow, maintaining perfect eye contact and tension with each other, as we move across the stage, the videographer circling us. We continue with the adagio pas de deux until Madame Petrov calls for a halt and says that that's enough of this dance for the film. Onto the stage, she summons Anna, Momoko, Rin, and Kara to enter for a shortened version of the Dance of the Cygnets. Their costumes are similar to Li Hua's, though less grand. *Swan Lake* was the first performance I ever danced in at the amateur ballet club I joined at six years old, and watching the other scenes being performed still makes me stop in wonder.

Typically, Madame Petrov said she'd have picked the four smallest dancers to be the Cygnets, but there are two dancers in the second-division who are much shorter than anyone else, and pairing those two with the third and fourth shortest would still have created a height difference. Instead, Anna, Momoko, Rin, and Kara are all roughly the same height; they've really gelled together too, capturing the magic and beauty of the dance as they move sideways, holding hands with arms interlaced, performing sixteen pas de chat.

A stagehand beckons Li Hua over for her costume change, and she disappears into the wings. More dancers troop past me onto stage—the Dance of the Cygnets complete for the videographer's footage, it's now time for the courtiers' dance, according to Madame Petrov's schedule.

I stay just out of sight of the stage; a moment when I can pause and watch the ballerinas and danseurs on stage. Then Alexander, as Von Rothbart, is beside me with the most magnificent headpiece on, and his sudden presence makes me jump. The pace is always faster when we perform for the videographer to get footage for the trailer, as quite often we're not performing complete scenes and most of it is out of order.

"Li Hua ready yet?" Alexander asks. "We've got the ballroom scene next."

Before I can answer, Li Hua reappears, her ivory tutu, bodice, and hairpiece swapped for the ebony ones. As Odile, she somehow looks even *more* striking. The black costume seems to bring out the definition of her face more, really makes her eyes sparkle. But I notice she's breathing hard, rubbing her neck.

"You okay?" Immediately, concern floods me. Was it our lift in the adagio pas de deux? Did I hurt her?

"Fine," she says. A couple of tendrils of her dark hair have escaped her bun and now they float wispily around her head. I think they make her look beautiful, but I smooth them back along the sides of her head, so they reach the perfect bun, knowing what Madame Petrov is like.

A moment later, we're all given our cues. I join the courtiers on stage, ready for the start of the ballroom scene. Rin—now playing my mother, the queen—stares haughtily across at me, one arm extended, ready. She's breathing hard, and I can just about see that the queen's extravagant gown has been pulled on over the top of her swan costume. While the tutu flattens somewhat, it's making her gown bulkier. She'd pointed out that this would happen earlier, when Madame Petrov had told us which scenes she wanted filming and the time that we had for the transitions, but she just told her to make it work. Now, Rin's breathing heavy, and her face is rather red. It's hot in here, especially when the majority of our dancing is performed under the bright lights.

Off stage, trumpets sound—a recording, alas not the real thing—and Tilly takes her cue on the piano. I plaster my dance smile on my face as the lights turn up, and I flit across stage, from one group of courtiers to another, assessing prospective lovers for my character, Prince Siegfried.

Show despair at these potential fiancées, I remind myself as I dance with each bridal prospect, only to shake my head in an exaggerated 'no' at the end of each pas de deux, for Prince Siegfried can only think of the beautiful Odette. Rin provides a convincing performance as the angry queen when I tell her I cannot marry any of these women. But just as the queen shakes her head in disapproval and annoyance, the lights dim and another trumpet announces the arrival of two unexpected guests: Von Rothbart and his daughter, Odile, now charmed to look like Odette.

The videographer manages to get in the way as Alexander and Li Hua dance onto stage, causing Li Hua to come down from pointe suddenly, but she recovers fairly well and elegance and grace fill her movements.

I act out my surprise at seeing her—a woman so lovely and alike to my beloved Odette. Li Hua's only been dancing this choreography with Alexander for about a week, but their movements are precise and fluid, graceful and measured as they act the evil father and daughter. It's not just my *character* who's swept away by the beauty of Odile, but me too, as I am also held under the illusion, for I can't help but be mesmerized by the beauty and command in my girlfriend's performance.

Li Hua's gaze is completely focused on her art and the circling videographer among us all, and so when I move forward as the prince selects her, she looks up and makes sudden eye contact with me, eye contact that appears to make her flush, like she hadn't expected me to be so close. Of course, I know it's part of the performance—because Li Hua is an amazing dancer, so wonderful with her character expressions—but there's something in the way our eyes connect, our souls connect, that makes me really feel it. Her dark lashes flutter as she curtseys toward me, before making her movements light and fluttery, mimicking combinations that Odette, the White Swan, performs in both the prologue and act two.

With Alexander as Von Rothbart watching us, Li Hua and I begin the Black Swan pas de deux. As our duet heads toward the climax, a projection of Li Hua as Odette, the White Swan, appears on the wall behind us; in it, she's desperately trying to get the prince's attention, but of course, my character is not to see her, and Von Rothbart casts a spell over the courtiers and the audience to trance them to forget. Dancing with Li Hua as Odile rather than Odette shouldn't feel any different—yet it does. More enticing, dangerous, exciting.

As the Black Swan pas de deux ends in its dramatic climax, Madame Petrov calls out "Cut," just before the prince is due to inform the queen that it is Odile he wishes to marry. It's silly to feel annoyed that we're not dancing this scene to completion, but I do.

"Excellent," Madame Petrov says. "Let's go back and redo the Dance of the Cygnets again. Laurence, I want a different angle used on them this time—and can we have the smaller spotlights on too?"

A minute or two passes as Li Hua and I watch the action on stage. Madame Petrov has Momoko, Anna, Rin, and Kara redoing their scene, and she instructs Anna to maintain better unity with the other three dancers.

One of the backstage crew lurks near us, while another stands in the opposite wing—just visible from where we are—making notes on her notepad.

"It's the best we'll get," Madame Petrov says. The lights come up and I see she's looking at her watch, then the videographer. "You really have to go now?"

The videographer nods. Behind him, the rest of the dancers move onto the stage too. "We can make this work, especially if we supplement it with footage from previous *Swan Lake* performances."

"Those don't have the current dancers," she says, "but okay." She thanks the videographer, then turns to us all. "Evangeline will be here soon—I've got to meet the governors now, but let her know that I want her revisiting the choreography of the Dance of the Cygnets. It's not quite working with Anna on the end still. But I'll see you all later for the evening rehearsal." She retrieves a folder from under the edge of the stage, then steps closer to me, and lowers her voice. "Can I have a word with you outside, Trent?" Her tone, normally so light, is now anything but.

I feel sick, so suddenly, but I nod and follow her outside of the studio. The air suddenly seems much colder, stiller, tenser.

"Silas Appleby is a great friend of mine," Madame Petrov says. "And he has been in touch about the future of Roseheart's funding."

My heart sinks. She knows? Oh God. The ballet mistress knowing I'm not committed—when I have no way of actually leaving and getting out—is the last thing I want. Nervously, I wait for Madame Petrov to say more.

"I have already spoken to Luca and Manuel about this, and I am asking if you'd mind buttering up Silas, so to speak? I know he really values the three of you and it really is imperative that we get this funding."

I let out a shaky breath. "Uh, of course." So, she doesn't know about my previous plans?

"We will also invite him for a special tour day here, so he can really see further how his funding benefits the company and academy. In fact, I've got the invitation here." She produces a thick white envelope from inside the folder. "Would you mind hand-delivering it to him?"

The voice inside my head is screaming as I take the envelope. "Uh. Sure." Even the paper the envelope is made from feels expensive. Not the ordinary invitations Roseheart sends out. "Though there's a stamp on this?" I frown. And Mr. Appleby's address has been written on, in an exquisitely neat hand.

"I was going to post it," Madame Petrov says. "But the directors suggested one of his beloved protégées take it to him. Which of course is much better."

"Yes, much better," I parrot.

Just holding the envelope makes me feel sick. Is it not enough that I've got to be in a profession I desperately want out of, but now I also have to go back to that man's house? Hear him talk down to me, manipulate me, blackmail me, threaten my girlfriend? Because he's never going to let me forget what I said.

I bid farewell to Madame Petrov and leave, the invitation burning a hole in the inside pocket of my jacket. I've got two hours before my next class and that is just about enough time to go and deliver this damn card to Mr. Appleby—yet I just can't bring myself to do it.

Instead, I head to Roseheart's gardens. The rose gardens, with their geometric designs.

I sit on my favorite bench, and I just stare. After a few moments, my eyes no longer focus on the winter-bitten stubs of plants in front of me, and everything's just this blurry haze. Brown and gray and white, colorless. Formed, yet formless.

"I can't do this anymore," I whisper into the still air. Above, heavy clouds linger. Looks like snow's coming. "I really can't."

I take a deep breath. This is what breaking point feels like. It has to be breaking point, this. And I can't even begin to describe the churning well of turmoil inside me.

And then it's all just too much—all this pent-up energy inside me. I'm crying, again. Fucking crying. I turn, and I punch the arm of the bench before I even realize I'm going to. Punch it so hard my knuckles split open. A delicious redness oozes out, and the pain—well, the pain feels real. It feels like *something*.

"Trent?"

I jolt, look up. Someone is leaning against the tree. A girl. *Bella*.

My heart sinks.

TEN

Bella

When Trent made his way into the garden, I didn't know whether to say anything. Didn't know whether to just sneak away or wait for him to leave. But when he started crying—when he punched the bench—that's when I just spoke up. Spoke up without thinking, totally giving myself away.

So now he thinks I'm a creep, a stalker. But whatever. I push that thought away, only it doesn't want to go so I shove it harder—picture throwing it off a mountain or something dramatic, while I'm screaming a war-cry, and where that last bit comes from I don't know. I don't know where a lot of the things in my head come from.

I make my way toward him, for some reason just taking really little steps. Tiny steps. Mouse steps. "Are you okay?"

Now, standing up, shaking, he looks anything but okay. His eyes are so dark and full of pain; they're brimming with it, going to overflow. *Stupid question to ask. Why the hell did I ask that?*

"She's going to find out, isn't she?" Trent breathes out hard, and then drags a hand aggressively through his hair before pulling the skin down under his eyes so the fleshy pink bit under his lower lids is visible. "Everything's just going to crash down."

He looks tired. Well, he looks awful really.

"I'm not going to say anything." I keep my voice low, as if it—as if *I*—can be a comfort.

He lets out a bitter laugh. "It doesn't matter if you say anything or not! The whole company's talking about it, which definitely means the academy is."

I feel my eyes narrow a bit—then realize I've not been being careful about my eyes and my irises and all that. But maybe it doesn't matter? No one's said anything. *Or they just think you're too weird to say anything to.*

But, wait! I focus back on Trent. Li Hua already knows about me and him? "I don't get what you're saying."

My brows furrow as I look up at him. He's only about two or three inches taller than me but looking up at him now reminds me so suddenly of what it was like, that night in the club. How I looked at him, how I knew he was conventionally attractive, and so I felt like I *should* be attracted to him sexually. How I was trying to force myself to feel something—because everyone's talking about sex all the time, and though I do it, I never really feel that urge. That need. And so I went to that club to prove that I could do it, still, again. Have a one-night stand because I wanted to. Because it's what normal teenagers do.

But even as we had sex, outside the club, in the alleyway, I still didn't feel anything, other than cold and awkward. I was just listening to the bass of the nightclub's music, the buzz of some flies nearby, the whole time thinking about my newest pointe shoes I had to break in, and wondering what color leotard to order online next. A dusky pink, maybe. Or a blush. But then Stacia ordered a blush before, and it was so close to her skin tone that it made her look like she was dancing in the nude.

"She trusts me, okay?" Trent says. "I already told her that there was nothing there. Nothing happened between us. And I have to keep that trust. Which means you and me, it's not going to happen again." He sounds angry, suddenly, accusatory.

"Whoa!" I hold my hands up, stepping back. Gravel crunches under my feet. "I never said anything to indicate otherwise."

"But you're here, aren't you?" he snaps. "What did you do, follow me? Spying on me? Ready to jump on me again the moment I show vulnerability?"

"That is not what I'm doing—and not what I did."

"But you're *here*," he yells, and spit flies from his teeth.

I take a deep breath and lift my head higher. "I am here because I like the garden."

"You like the garden?"

"I like the flowers."

"The flowers?" He snorts. "It's the middle of fucking winter. The roses are just stumpy twigs. Come on, Bella, you're going to have to try a bit harder than that."

"Fine," I say, and I grab his arm, pulling him toward me. "I'll show you."

Just as I'm leading him back to where I was stationed, between the plants that in the spring and summer will give the deepest pink roses, I realize that grabbing his arm probably wasn't the wisest idea, so I drop it quickly. He looks at me, his face all flushed, when I stop by the bench on the other side of the gardens. I point at the sketchpad and pencils that are on the wooden slats. I've left them all in a mess, and several ants are now walking over my drawings. *Brilliant.*

"I draw the roses, okay?" I say.

He doesn't answer me, just bends to slowly pick up my sketchbook. A pencil rolls off the page and drops onto the ground. I wince. Great. That's probably broken the lead.

But Trent isn't paying attention to my expensive Faber-Castell pencil that he's broken—a pencil that I absolutely cherish and protect at all times. Hell, I love the whole set of them. It's the most expensive things I own that isn't related to ballet. A whole set that Bobby bought me for my birthday last year.

Trent stares at my drawings. I feel my face begin to heat up. I'm not exactly an amateur—I've been drawing flowers all my life, drawing rose designs that I want to have tattooed on my body the moment I can no longer dance due to injury or ill health or whatever. Most dancers lose a part of themselves when they retire—through plans or circumstances forcing it—and I'm sure it's because they've not thought about themselves as anything other than a dancer. They've not thought about who they are, who they can be. They have no backup plans, nothing.

But I've got this. And just looking at my drawings now, comparing them to the bleak winter remnants of the garden, fills me with hope, because there's always hope for beauty and life in the future, even when things might look barren.

I draw the hope that is currently lost, but I know it will be back.

I've started uploading little cards of some of my rose drawings to a top-secret Etsy account—making a surprising amount of money, which is mainly how I've been funding my coke—and the moment I retire, I'm booking myself in for tattoos. They'll be everywhere. All over my body. My body will still be my art, always, and the things I look to for hope will always be with me.

"Shit, these are really good," Trent says, finally. He looks up at me, and there's so much emotion in his eyes that I'm caught off balance for a moment. "You should show people these."

"Whatever." I laugh, and I know how false my laughter sounds. So instead I busy myself with collecting up the remaining Faber-Castell pencils and fitting them neatly back into their box. "Anyway, I have to get to class now—are you… going to be okay?"

He nods, breathes deeply.

"No more fighting a bench that can't fight back?" I say. "Because that really isn't a fair fight, you know." Then I flinch. *What the hell, Bella? That sounds like flirting.*

But he just nods, once, so I nod too.

"I'd better go then," I say. "Got class." And before I can say anything more or really look at his eyes again and feel the hurt and the pain in them, I scamper away.

After a long day of classes, just as I'm walking back to the dorms from Roseheart's lakes—a place I go to run sometimes when my head's too busy for me to be inside the gym, with all the buzz of noise and voices and machinery clanking—I realize someone is following me.

I'm sure of it.

Follow. Follow. Follow.

My heart pounds fast as I cut through the rose gardens— the same gardens Trent and I were in earlier. I step against the stone wall in the courtyard, by the trellis that's home to so much beauty in the spring. I narrow my eyes, as if that will help me look around, see more, somehow let more light in and reveal who it is. Because it's *someone*.

I clutch my water bottle tightly, feel two of my knuckles click. "Hello?" My voice is wavery, shaky, and I could kick myself.

No one answers.

You're just imagining it, I tell myself, even though I know I'm not. My skin prickles with it. Someone is there.

And now the air is different. Heavier, and brighter too. Someone is after me, I can feel it.

Just my gut feeling.

I take a deep breath.

Time to move, Bella.

I picture myself in my room, drinking hot ginger tea and relaxing with the autobiography of Vadim Muntagirov's memoir *From Small Steps to Big Leaps,* because he's one of my favorite dancers, while I maybe trace over some more rose designs in my notebook, and I will myself forward, across the courtyard, down the avenue on the left, around the corner and—

Footsteps, behind me.

I whirl around, quickly, eyes scanning the dark tones and the shadows. Leaves rustle near me—just the wind. I swallow hard. Those were footsteps I heard. I'm sure of it. Yet there's no one here.

"I'm going crazy, just like they said I would," I mutter, and I don't even know why I say that because no one has actually said I'm going crazy or that I will. *So what the hell, Bella?*

I turn and I walk as briskly and swiftly as I can to the academy dorms. Relief fills me when the building's at last in sight.

Last year, Roseheart installed an ID card system—not just for the company but the school too. In the day, there's a receptionist at the front of the dorms who monitors everyone going in and out, but in the evenings, security relies on technology. I swipe my card, breathe an even bigger sigh of relief when I'm fully inside. The glass doors slide shut behind me. Safe.

I take the stairs up to the second floor, then let myself into my room.

I walk around Stacia's bed, to get to mine. She's not here—in fact, I didn't really hear anyone in the dorms. They could all be at the gym still. Pretty much the whole of our year does everything as a flock.

Then I frown. My bed. It's… it doesn't look right. Not as I left it. I frown, tilting my head to one side. So, someone's been in and searched my room—that happens pretty regularly. And I did say to Ava yesterday that Mr. Vikas or whoever is probably going to search my room very soon.

But… but I can't shake the feeling that this is different.

I double check the door's locked, then look under my bed, in my wardrobe, behind the full-length curtains either side of the window, in the en suite—all potential places where someone could be hiding. But each time, there's nothing.

You're just paranoid, Bella, I tell myself, but my words sound like a lie.

ELEVEN

Bella

By the next morning, I've smoked myself out of my worries, drunk a bottle of gin with Ty—the two of us hanging out at the back of the bike shed, like we're back in school—which means we totally skipped our 6 o'clock rehearsal, and yet I somehow arrive fresh-faced at pointe class. The gin and everything have helped. I'm no longer a jumpy mess. And I know it's not like me, to really go overboard with this sort of stuff—to actually conform to the image that I'm pretty sure some of the staff have of me—but I couldn't help it. I just needed to calm down.

Of course, last night, I tried to dance in my room. Tried to use ballet as my drug to calm down, to get that serenity. But every time I took a step, I heard another step behind me. Someone else. Someone who'd disappear every time I looked over my shoulder.

When Stacia returned, she watched me dance, helped correct my form a bit, and let me use the portable ballet barre that she has by her wardrobe. When I heard the mysterious steps, I asked her if she did too. Now, she thinks I'm a weirdo—*weirdo, weirdo, weirdo*—and she's in this class too, with Mr. Vikas—*because he's taking it, Mr. Vikas of all people*!—and I'm sure she's talking about me every time she speaks in a low voice to the other girls.

I think Mr. Vikas is talking about me too, to them. Because they're all looking at me. And when I look at them, directly, they look away. Even Ava. Ava, who's supposed to be my best friend.

I try to concentrate on the class, on Mr. Vikas's instructions, but I just can't. My head feels too…weird. Sort of spacey, empty. But not empty in a good way. I'm twitchy, jumpy, startling even when Mr. Vikas claps his hands or every time the speakers emit any sounds.

My head spins, and I can't quite see properly either. My hands shake, and I know I need to do a line, so when Mr. Vikas announces a five-minute break, I rush out, to the dorms. My steps are fast, urgent. There's a clock ticking in my head, and I know I'm likely going to be late back, but I just need to do a line. Need it. Then I'll be calm. So calm. Perfectly calm.

I grit my teeth, weaving in and out of other students milling around, and then at last I'm in the dorms. I don't even go to the shared bathroom this time, just use the en suite. Messily cut a line of cocaine using my debit card. Snort it quickly. Wait to feel something.

Wait and wait and wait.

And why's there nothing?

Maybe it wasn't enough. Or maybe the quality isn't here with this baggie.

I do another line, then curse as the alarm in my head goes off—time's up. The clock's ticking even louder now. Time to get back. So I run. Run as fast as I can, nearly careen into several people, but that doesn't matter. I get back to Mr. Vikas's class, breathing hard, feeling a little bit sick, but otherwise a bit like myself. And the best part is that no one followed me. There or back.

I smile, feeling triumphant. A success. Yes!

I throw myself into the swing of things, volunteering whenever Mr. Vikas needs someone to demonstrate. I put everything into it, push my body harder and farther than ever. My muscles are burning and my big toe on my left foot is bleeding profusely by the time pointe class finishes. The platform and part of the box of my Gaynor Minden shoe has turned a murky brown.

Someone touches my arm, lightly, and I whirl around.

"Ava!" I smile, and I'm doing that smile again—that smile I keep doing, the one that seems too big for my face—but I can't stop doing it.

She pulls me to the side. "Are you…" Disappointment flashes onto her face. "Really, Bells?"

"Really, *what*? I'm fine—perfectly fine. More than fine!" I feel something crawling on my arm, so I slap it away with my other hand—but whatever it is doesn't go, so I slap it again.

"Was it in the break?" Ava asks. "Is that when you did it?"

"Did what?" I laugh, but I'm still trying to get these things off my arm. I stare at it, trying to see the tiny insects there that are irritating my skin. But they're so small. Tiny. Too small to see. Panic rises in me, suddenly. Have I got fleas? *Actual* fleas. "Oh my God, Ava! I've got fleas. I've really got fleas."

Calm box, Bella—the calm box.

But the calm box isn't working now. This is too much.

"What?" Ava stares at me. "No, you're just... you're just being you." Her voice is low, and I'm vaguely aware of others around us now—diploma second years, filing into the studio ready for their class.

Ava takes my arm—my arm with the fleas which I don't know how she can bear touching—and pulls me out into the corridor, then out one of the fire exits. "You need to sober up before flexibility class," she says, her voice firm. More firm than I've ever heard it. "And have you been drinking as well?"

She stares at me in disgust, and then... then things get strange because suddenly she's not here anymore. And I'm not outside the fire exit. I'm back in the rose garden. I'm sitting on the bench—the bench that Trent punched yesterday.

"It's okay," I tell the bench's arm that he punched. I pat the wood, gently. "You'll be okay."

There's a bottle of water next to me. It's not mine—or at least, I don't think it is—but I drink some of it, gulping it back.

My head starts to spin, and the reality of what I've done sets in. I'm just like Ty, drinking, smoking, getting high before class. And I don't do that. I don't.

I shiver, then look up as I see someone approaching. Li Hua. She makes her way over to me and I try to smile, but my facial muscles don't seem quite right anymore. So I wave instead. But she doesn't wave back.

She just walks right up to me, sits next to me. There are bags under her eyes and her makeup is smudged. "Hi Bella. Uh, h-h-how well do you know Mattie Levenson?" Her hands are shaking, and she places them on her lap, then smooths out her skirt.

"Mattie?" I blink. This was not what I expected, because for a moment there, I was pretty sure she was going to confront me about me and Trent, and I wasn't entirely sure that I'd be able to give a convincing answer, given my brain feels like it's currently doing Twister. "He's, uh, a nice guy."

"I know he's a dealer." Her voice is flat, and she stares at me expectantly.

Is she trying to score some gear? My eyebrows shoot up. "Oh, Mattie's not," I say. *I'm* the one that gets the stash from Mac, and I give Mattie a share of mine, in exchange for warning on the random drugs tests. But it's not like I can tell Li Hua this.

"I'm pretty sure he is," she says.

I frown. Well, maybe he deals the small amounts I give him? Shares them among company dancers.

"I just don't think you should trust him," Li Hua says. "A lot of men cannot be trusted, can they?" And there's something in her eyes now that lets me know she *does* know—I'm not imagining it. She bows her head a little. "Is it true? You and Trent? At the club."

To be honest, I thought this would've happened. Yesterday or the day before. Sooner. Not now. Not sitting here with my head feeling strange and my arm crawling with fleas and this bottle of water, which really is quite nice water.

But Li Hua's asking me calmly. She's so calm. Even though she's sad.

"I am sorry," I say, and it's strange, because there's a moment where I've said the three words, when they're out in the open, in the real world, yet I still feel them inside me. Squishy shapes on my tongue, that I roll over, press behind my front teeth. *I am sorry.*

Li Hua nods once, then leaves.

I drink some more water from the mysterious bottle. I flex my fingers. I look at the time on my phone, vaguely aware that I should be in class. But my head… my head is quiet. It's actually quiet now.

I lean back against the bench, close my eyes.

I listen, but there's no one else out here. No one following me.

I'm not being stalked.

I'm safe.

"Safe," I whisper. The weak sun tries to warm my face, and I smile. "Safe."

Then my phone buzzes. I'm not sure how much later it is when it buzzes, but I jolt—feeling like I've just woken up— and stare at my phone. I'm clenching it tightly in both hands.

A message flashes up on my phone. A number I haven't got saved. But there are no prizes for guessing who's sent it.

How could you have told her?

I don't reply.

TWELVE

Bella

Of course, it's just my luck when I run smack into Trent later that evening. He's carrying a cream envelope and looks greatly annoyed at me. Probably rightly so.

"How could you have told her?" He spits the words at me.

We're just outside the administration building—me, because I was taking a walk to try and clear my head. I'm feeling better now, more myself again, but I know I've got making up to do. Ava is furious with me. So are most of the diploma students; apparently, my state earlier was obvious. And when I checked my email, I found I've been called in for a meeting with Faculty and Administration tomorrow morning. That's enough to get anyone down from the buzz.

"Why did you tell her?" Trent yells at me now, and I realize I've just been staring at him for probably a good ten seconds.

"I don't like lying," I say slowly, even though that in itself is a lie. I know I lie a lot. To be honest, I'm not really sure why

I *didn't* lie when Li Hua asked me. Why I just told her. Because Li Hua is so kind. So lovely. I didn't want to upset her. And yet I did.

Maybe it was because I wasn't thinking right. The drugs, the alcohol.

"She's taken off and I can't find her now—and this is all your fault," Trent yells. "And here—you can do this." He shoves the cream envelope in my hands. "The address is on that. You take it there. Deliver it yourself. Don't go chucking it in a post box."

"What?" I stare at him, confused.

"Given what *you've* done, I've got to sort things out with my girlfriend, so the least you can do is take this for me. And see that it gets delivered ASAP. It's already late getting there."

Without waiting for my response, he turns away. And I'm left staring at the envelope. It's addressed to a 'Mr. Appleby' and it's got what is presumably his address on in an elegant cursive, along with a first-class stamp.

Don't go chucking it in a post box.

The address is the most posh and expensive part of London, and I find myself wandering down to the main entrance of Roseheart thinking about what it would be like to live there. To be rich enough to order a car to pick me up and drop me off whenever I wanted.

There's a girl dallying there now, by the gates, like she's waiting for someone. She looks about my age, and she's got long medium-brown hair and a rather upturned nose that makes her seem a little pompous, like she's filled with airs and graces. Her clothes are expensive—I can tell that by the fit of them, the cut of the fabric—yet she's carrying the scrappiest rucksack that's practically falling apart. And her shoes: trainers that look like they're from Primark. Maybe she's from the poshest part of London and she's trying to blend in. Trying to be undercover.

"What are you staring at?" she shouts suddenly—at me. She has the most annoying whiny voice. "Come to gawp at me as well?"

I start to hold my hands up, complete with the envelope. I'm right in front of her—did I walk right up to her, while I was lost in my imagination? Have I been staring at her? I'm, like, two feet from her. So close I can see dark circles under her eyes that she's tried to cover with concealer. "What?" My voice sounds small.

"Yes, my sister went missing, but no you cannot talk about her like she is dead," she snaps.

My frown deepens. "Are you Alessia?"

"'Are you Alessia?'" she mocks.

This girl doesn't really look much like the girl in the portrait, Allegra. Allegra was so pale, albino maybe, whereas this girl has olive skin and dark, glossy hair. I look at her nose—how small and delicate it is, even if it is upturned—and I try to remember what Allegra's nose is like. But I can't.

I glare at her. "There's no need to be rude. I've literally said nothing about your sister." Haven't even given Allegra a second thought after Miss Potts and Li Hua were talking about her. And does that make me odd? Shouldn't I have wanted to know more?

"Whatever," this girl, who I'm pretty sure *is* Alessia Valenzi, says. "I did not even want to be here."

And with that, she flounces off—apparently she wasn't waiting for a car. She just walks off down the road, tossing her dark hair over her shoulders. I shift my weight from foot to foot, feeling bewildered.

A car pulls in next, to the gates. An expensive-looking taxi firm, and for a moment I'm living in this parallel world where I've got enough money to just order a car to take me places. To take me to this Mr. Appleby's house, where maybe the Valenzis are his neighbors. They'll each have one of those super big houses, where they have, like, a butler, who answers the door. Like they're in Agatha Christie novels.

I'm smiling away, imagining it all, scenario after scenario running freely in my head, when a voice calls my name.

I turn to see Li Hua waving at me.

Immediately, the hairs on the back of my neck rise as I stare at her.

"You going into town, too?" she asks. Her voice is careful. "This is my taxi. Want to hop in with me? I saw it's going to rain awfully in about twenty minutes."

I stare at her, a slight smile taking over the bottom half of my face even though I haven't a clue why there's this half grin on me. Get in a car with her, seriously? She's going to hate me.

"You coming, love?" the driver calls through his open window.

Li Hua turns to me, holding her arm out. "Are you coming?"

"Um, I thought you hate me?"

"You're just a kid." She shakes her head. "*He* should know better. It's not your fault."

A *kid*. "I'm eighteen in April." Just three more months until adulthood.

Li Hua makes an *uh-huh* noise at the back of her throat, but then waves for me to get in her car. "I can drop you off wherever you're going."

It doesn't feel right, getting into the car, but I almost feel like I don't know what else to do. And refusing would be rude, right? She's being so nice. Once we're inside, both sitting in silence, my worries spiral. Where exactly is this car going anyway? How do I know I'm going to be dropped off? What if she knows, like, gangsters or something?

But, no, this is Li Hua. I sort of know her. Don't I?

"Uh, I can get out here," I say about five minutes later—five minutes that were filled with an awkward silence between us—vaguely waving around at the streets around us, even though I don't know where we are.

"Nonsense," Li Hua says. "Where are you going again?"

I show her the envelope.

"You just need a post box?" She looks confused.

"No, uh, it's to be hand delivered." Just in time I remember not to mention Trent's name.

"Okay." Li Hua leans forward and talks to the driver for several moments, arranging a detour. Then she looks back at me. "You can do it once I've been dropped off."

My throat starts to feel too thick, blocked, as I realize what Li Hua means. I don't know that this is a *genuine* taxi. And soon I'm going to be alone in here, with the driver. And Li Hua hates me—she *has* to hate me.

I lean forward, trying to get a glimpse of the driver. A man, mid-forties. Bald head. Wide shoulders. He spoke with quite a typical London accent earlier, didn't he? My head spins.

"Or we can take the detour after," Li Hua says quickly. "If you'd rather? I mean, I'm going to my Pilates studio. But you can come with me. You can wait there—there's a café. It's quite nice. Or you can join me for the class."

My mind is a flurry of questions and scenarios and possible situations. Which is the better option? A Pilates class—if it's genuinely an actual class. "I can't afford it," I say, then kind of wish I hadn't said that because that just makes me sound weak and like I'm asking her to pay for me.

"What's it going to be?" the driver asks. The way he speaks reminds me of Phil Mitchell in *EastEnders*, like we're wasting his time.

"We'll go after," Li Hua says. She looks across at me and smiles what I think is supposed to be a reassuring smile. Then she bows her head a little, and her face drops. Her voice is quieter when she speaks: "He's done it before, you know?"

He. Trent. My chest feels too tight.

"I, uh, I didn't know."

"You're not the first." She shakes her head. "Look, come to Pilates with me. They always do your first class as a free taster session anyway. Look, we have to stick together. It'll be fun."

"Why are you being nice to me though?" I ask her.

"Because, well, I'm fed up with him. Everyone thinks I'm just quiet and soft. That I don't retaliate. Don't stand up for myself. But I do. I am." She breathes hard. "Did you know I've been meeting with two other women he's slept with?" She laughs a little. "We've sort of become friends. As odd as it sounds."

"What, and you're all going to get revenge on him?"

Outside, it begins to rain: huge, fat, heavy raindrops splatter spectacularly on the windows.

She laughs. "Something like that."

"And are you all at this Pilates class? Am I about to walk into a big criminal organization or something, plotting his demise?" I laugh, but her eyes widen a bit, and I realize I've probably taken it too far. "How can you even stand to be near me?" I ask. "To be near any of these women?"

Li Hua shrugs. "Sometimes I tell myself that it's only fair he seeks… intimacy elsewhere." Her voice is quiet, too quiet for the driver to hear.

I frown. "What?"

Li Hua's phone buzzes. I see a message flash up on the screen, but she clicks off it and looks straight at me. "We used to, uh, do it all the time. But then… well, a new dancer joined the company."

"And you've got a thing for them?" I frown.

"No. No, nothing like that. No, it's Taryn Foster. She's, you know, out as being asexual."

I nod. I've heard of Taryn, but I don't really know her at all. Haven't spoken to her. Only seen her across the campus a couple of times, I think.

"It made me realize that I'm ace too. I… I always knew there was something different about me. But as soon as Taryn joined us, and everyone found out she was ace, I just… well. I didn't want to be hiding anymore. I'm not publicly out or anything—but I stopped living a lie. I told Trent. He, uh, said he'd still be faithful to me, even if we didn't sleep together. But I was silly to think that would be true… It's not that he's slept with other people that really hurts me," she says. "It's that he just keeps lying about it. Hiding it."

"So you want an open relationship?" I ask.

Tears fill her eyes. "I don't know. I just want him to respect me. I just want the truth."

I don't know what to say. I tell her I'm sorry and she just nods.

A strange, but somewhat uncomfortable, silence settles over both of us.

We seem to get to the drop-off point for Pilates very quickly, and then Li Hua's ushering me into what is indeed a very posh exercise class. A woman wearing very expensive jewelry welcomes us inside, hugging both of us and engulfing us in a cloud of what I assume to be very expensive perfume.

"How wonderful to have you joining us!" she says to me, clasping her hands together in a display of exaggerated glee.

"Just a taster class," I mumble, weakly.

For the next forty-five minutes, I feel awkward. The whole Pilates class Li Hua acts like we're best friends, even throwing her arm around me in a friendly way, pairing up with me when we're asked to do work in twos, not once making a snide remark. She's friendly and I'm just not sure what's going on.

I don't really know what else to say as we walk out of the class, so I don't say anything.

"I think the driver's going to pick us up two blocks away," Li Hua says. She indicates for me to start walking, and I do. "Normally, he can't even drop me off right outside, so earlier was unusual. But he often waits to pick me up where the roads are wider, right by the Pret. You know it?"

I shake my head. "Well, I know the chain. But not the specific one you're meaning." Again, I'm wracking my brain for something else to say. Something meaningful. But I can't think of anything, still. I just… think. *Asexuality.*

I have heard of it. I mean, I did *wonder* about it. Once. Whether I was asexual. If that word was right for me, if it explained why I just don't feel anything sexual for anyone, even when I really want to. When I seek out a man to sleep with, every now and again, to try and make myself feel it. Prove to myself I'm not broken.

My head is a tangled web of thoughts and feelings I don't understand, and instinctively, I want to do a line—the need is just there, sharp, sudden, strong.

No.

I take a deep breath and—

Footsteps, right behind us.

I turn, panic immediately rising in me, but there's no one there.

"What was that?" Li Hua's voice is low, and I look at her, see her eyes are wide too.

"You heard it too?" I ask. I push my hair from my face, and light raindrops land on my skin.

"Hello?" Li Hua calls out.

We both listen, but I don't know if we'd hear anything— not with the traffic that's constantly going past us—and then we both jump as nearby a car backfires.

"Um, I don't think there's anyone here," I say.

"But you heard it as well as me," she says. "There were footsteps—someone on foot. Here." Then she takes a deep breath. "Are we being watched right now?"

I look around. There has to be someone here. There has to be. But all I can see are the narrow streets, the closed shop fronts. There isn't anyone about on foot, but there is plenty of traffic. A constant stream of cars.

Li Hua's also looking. "Probably. I've been being followed for the last two weeks."

I stare at her, my throat drying. "Me, too." Because those footsteps that I heard yesterday? When I was so certain I was being followed? What if I *was* right?

Her eyes flicker for a moment, then Li Hua nods and indicates for us to cross the road when we can. A moment later, a woman in a red Ford Fiesta waves us across and we move quickly. We get to the place where Li Hua says the driver will meet us, but she frowns when the car isn't here.

"I'll call the driver now," Li Hua says.

This road is wider. There's still a lot of traffic though that I keep an eye on as she taps on her phone.

"Three-minute wait," she says. "He's just been delayed, that's all."

I nod. There's a van speeding up along the road, behind Li Hua, and I see her turn slightly toward it, frowning. She steps back onto the pavement farther and looks at me. "One more thing," she says. "I—"

The white van screeches to a halt beside Li Hua, brakes and tires squeaking, and then the side door opens. Two men appear—all dressed in black—and they grab Li Hua.

She doesn't have time to scream. One puts his hand over her mouth, his arm snaking around her chest, pinning her arms to her sides. The other man grabs her legs, and then the two lift her up.

Oh my God. What is... Is this a...

I surge forward, stumbling, my legs suddenly feeling too heavy. "Li—" is all I manage to say, as she disappears into the van, as the vehicle speeds off.

And Li Hua has been… abducted?

THIRTEEN

Bella

I'm walking.

No, I'm *in* a car.

The driver's talking.

Li Hua's screaming—except she's not. She's not here.

Her feet… her feet kicked out as they lifted her up. Didn't they?

I can't remember.

My head hurts.

There's a rip in the back of the driver's headrest. Like a cat's claw has dragged some of the stuffing out. The stuffing is red.

Why can't I remember?

"What do you mean Li Hua's been abducted?" Trent stares at me.

He's the only one in here. The company lounge. I headed straight for it, even though I've never been in here before—but I felt compelled to come straight here, my head pounding nineteen to the dozen. I needed to find Li Hua's friends. Needed to tell them. But instead it's only Trent. The cheating boyfriend.

I feel sick just looking at him. I grab at the back of a chair, can hardly breathe. My chest is too tight, and it's too hot in here. The smell of the cleaning products is too strong, and the contents of my stomach churns.

"She's… she was…" I shake my head, clapping a hand to my chest. "A van. It… It took her."

"Li Hua?" Trent raises his eyebrows. At first, when I burst in here and told him, he laughed, said I was such an attention-seeker—but he's not laughing now. The lines on his face seem deeper, darker, etched more permanently. He takes a step backward, crashing into one of the sofas. "Fuck! I'm going to kill him."

"What?" I stare at him, but he's grabbing his phone, tapping at the screen furiously.

He turns away from me, and I can see he's breathing hard because his whole body is shaking. "Is this you?" he demands, the moment someone answers the phone.

I can't hear the reply—only that I think it's a man. I hear a low, gruff-toned voice.

"Li Hua's just been taken—are you trying to make a point? I already said I was staying!" He swears loudly, and then he punches the wall.

The movement is so quick that I nearly miss it, yet I flinch at the same time, my heart pounding. The wall is all… dented. Trent hit it with that much power.

"Fine!" he yells into the phone, and then he chucks it to the far side of the room, where it hits the wall and drops down behind seating. His eyes burn as he turns to me. "Have you called the police?"

"The police? No." I flash hot, then cold. Should I have called the police straight away?

"Uh, why not?" He frowns at me, and his voice rises. "So, it wasn't an actual abduction? It was staged?"

"Staged? I don't know." I shake my head.

I… I suppose it could be. I touch a hand to my chest, feeling lightheaded and sick. It could've been staged, I tell myself, and I want to believe that because it's better than the alternative. Maybe… maybe she'll walk right through that door now. And I look toward it, hopeful.

Li Hua didn't fight them, did she, her abductors? I replay it all in my head. She didn't kick or thrash. Or did she? But it's like I blink, and I see both scenarios. Her kicking and her not. And I don't know which is… which is true.

Trent rushes over to the window and pushes it open, leans out. "Hey!" he shouts, waving his arms. "Get in here now— it's urgent."

I move to try and get a glimpse of who's out there, in the little garden. It's dark but I spot several figures, and then people are stepping into the room. More and more dancers. I should know their names. But I don't. All are wearing jackets and the faint whisp of smoke hangs around them. What, were they smoking? My heart beats faster, and I'm trying to taste it, feel it.

I need it.

Then I tune back into what's happening now: Trent, telling them that Li Hua's been abducted.

Abducted.

It doesn't feel real.

Can't feel real.

I mean, she's a grown woman. She's strong. She can't have just been taken off the street like this. No, this has to be some prank. A wind-up to frighten me or something.

"I'll call the police," a ballerina finally says, her face paling.

"We need a full head count of ourselves and the school students too," another guy says. He's Asian and I think I recognize him. He might be Jaidev Ngo.

"And I'm letting the board know," a woman with the shiniest, sleekest bun says. "It's, uh, January 14th."

I stare at them. "The board?" I turn to look at her, taking in her flustered appearance, then taking in everyone's worried faces. "Wait what's going on? What has the date got to do with this?"

"The Valenzi girl," one of the guys says, his eyes widening. He turns to look at the woman behind him. "This is like that, isn't it?"

"It could be," she says. "That was the 14th January too."

"The Valenzi girl," I echo. "Allegra…"

But the woman just shakes her head at me. "Was Allegra stalked too in the weeks before?"

"Stalked?" Trent and another man both exclaim.

The woman runs her hands through her hair. Tension rattles through her body and she spins around in a full circle. "They're not going to get away with it this time though—because we've got you, Bella." She spins toward me, grabs my shoulders. "You're a witness."

"What good is a witness," Trent whispers, "if they copy what they did to Allegra and kill Li Hua? Because Li Hua told me all about that—she was researching it. It only makes sense that Allegra was killed—that's why they didn't release her with the other two they took. They disposed of her body instead. Oh my God. The kidnappers, they've found out—they knew Li Hua was looking into them and… what if she worked out who they were?" He shakes his head so violently I swear I hear something click. "This cannot be happening. This really cannot be. Oh my—" He lunges suddenly to the side of the room, grabs the waste-paper basket, and heaves the contents of his stomach into it.

I start shaking even more. My feet feel too big.

I stare at Trent, and suddenly I get the most slimy feeling filling my stomach. Because I've seen his… *thing*. And I don't know why I'm thinking about this now. About that. About us. When I shouldn't be. I shouldn't be at all. Not with Li Hua being abducted.

But I had sex with him.

I…

Oh *God*.

"It's okay," a woman with a kind face says to me. She puts her arm around me, starts leading me to the side. "We'll get this sorted."

FOURTEEN

Alessia

I used to love walking in the dark, alone. Used to feel free. Strong.

Not anymore though.

It is not even that late. Only just gone half-past nine. I breathe in the cool, fresh air. Crisp. Has a bite to it. And I think. Think about how I loved the dark before.

We are all Survivors. The poster's words flash through me, and I snort. Then it is here again—sudden rage that makes me want to run back to the community center and grab that poster, rip it up into a thousand shreds and watch the scraps float down to the ground. I want to scream and scream and scream—the urge is just suddenly here.

That has been happening more, recently. I take several deep breaths. Part of me wonders if it is because my parents do not know what happened. Because there is only enough trauma their hearts can hold, and of course

Allegra took it all. That and their disinterest in me after I left ballet.

"Just a few more minutes," I tell myself, pulling my hood up, as if that alone can protect me. Stop all the monsters lurking in the badness from jumping out and getting me. I clench my hands into fists, repeatedly, feel my fingers *click click click*. A slight slickness over the knuckle of my left pointer finger. I do not need to look to know that it is bleeding again.

"Just a few more minutes, and then I can go back to my room."

It should not feel like a test. Walking out here. Scuffed trainers. Rain in the air, misty.

It has been months since it happened, and for a long time after, I thought I would never be able to walk alone at night again, not without being scared. Without feeling like my skin is not right, like it is crawling with someone else's touch. Remembering…

It did not even happen here. Yet in my mind, it did. It happened *everywhere*. By the trees, and in the tube station, and at the back of a café, and behind the Co-op, and next to the bins, and on the top floor of the shopping center—all of these places, as soon as it is dark.

"I cannot be scared of the dark," I mutter. And so that is why I am here. Reclaiming the night.

I am not even that far from Roseheart, perhaps the only place that, oddly, feels truly safe to me right now, despite all the gossiping students and all the annoying ballerinas running around everywhere in leotards with their hair in buns—all looking so much like my sister—yet my heart is pounding. I lift my hands up to the inky night, breathing in the coolness. I used to run at night, too. Not here—over at the tracks, a seven-minute walk from my old school. I would sprint until my lungs burned, until my head pounded, and I was weightless, floating, my breath feeling like the heaviest thing in my body. But it was okay, because I was expelling them. Exactly forty-four laps around the track, starting at 2 am. Then back to my room, giddy, doing pullups next to my bed, the carpet burning my spine. A few hours of sleep before the new day started.

An owl screeches somewhere behind me, and I flinch, whirling around. My stomach twists, and my bottom lip wobbles as my gaze darts from branch to branch, searching shadows anywhere at all where someone could be hiding.

"Come here, babe." His voice runs like velvet over me.

I take a deep breath, wrap my left hand around my right wrist, squeeze it as tightly as I possibly can until my fingers feel numb.

I want to be numb. I want to… not exist. No—that is not… I groan.

A twig cracks behind me, and I whirl around, eyes wide, chest rising and falling so quickly that I cannot breathe, feel like I am not getting any oxygen as I stare into the darkness.

"Hello?"

I do not know what I expect to happen. If I think someone will answer, step out of the darkness, wave a greeting. Or maybe they will just come at me, a hand over my mouth as they wrestle me to the ground.

But there is nothing.

No one here.

Or no one who wants to make themselves known.

In my pocket, my phone buzzes, startling me. I do not want to pull it out of my pocket, look at the bright screen because then it will make the darkness seem darker, harder to see if anyone is still here. And so I turn quickly and walk.

Just a few bloody more minutes, and then I can go back. I will have proven I can walk in the dark. And then it has to get easier than this, doesn't it?

Life has to get easier—and it will. It cannot get worse.

Nothing can get worse. Nothing can—

"Hello, Miss Valenzi," says a silky voice behind me, and I scream.

FIFTEEN

Bella

The company dancers practically pull me through the grounds, toward the academy's part of campus where the administration buildings are located. We weave through a crowd of petit rats—the younger dancers in the lower school—and I swear the company dancers' heads are swiveling like they're trying to count them all, check no one's missing.

One of the oldest receptionists is on the desk, and her face pales when she sees me and what seems like half the company, and the speed at which we enter.

"Put the school in lockdown and start the alarms," the woman in front says. As we came over here, they all told me their names. She's Netty Florence Stone. The *principal*. I don't know why I didn't recognize her before, because of course she's Netty Florence. She's sweating hard. "Li Hua Zhao, one of the company dancers, has just been abducted on the street."

The woman's face pales even more. "What?"

"It's Allegra Valenzi all over again," Netty Florence says. "It's the same pattern as Allegra because Li Hua has been being stalked for the last two weeks as well."

Li Hua was stalked for two weeks? My eyes widen.

"Someone's been following me, too. I think." The words are out before I even realized I was going to say them.

"There we go then," Netty Florence says, shaking her hands in front of her in a sudden motion. "It's possible they were going to take both of you then. Maybe a third person too, if they're keeping things the same. And Li Hua was also sent a threatening note this morning."

What? She was? My heart pounds.

"Look, we've called the police already—but you must have protocols in place for this again—because it's not just going to be one dancer who's been taken or is in danger, is it?" Netty Florence breathes hard. "So raise the alarm, whatever you have to do. We need to see if anyone else is missing."

Anyone else? My head spins.

The receptionist nods and picks up the telephone next to her. She speaks into it, but my adrenaline is suddenly peaking, sending rushing sounds all through my ears and I can't hear her words.

Then fire alarms go off, blaring, and I jump.

"Come on," Netty Florence says, pulling me along suddenly.

"Couldn't *we* have set the fire alarm off ourselves?" Trent says. I forgot he was with us, in this group. In fact, I forgot it was anyone but me and Netty Florence. His voice—just the sound of it, the tone—makes me feel sick.

"Not until administration knew what was going on. That it wasn't a prank," Netty Florence replies. "We need to get to the company grounds now. Join the line-up."

Some of the company dancers stay at the reception of the administration building, but Netty Florence and Trent lead me back to the company blocks.

"Are you expecting anyone else to be missing?" someone asks Netty Florence.

"If it's a repeat of the Allegra Valenzi situation again, yes," she says, tight-lipped, glancing at me.

"How many?" the other girl asks.

"Three were taken in total last time," she says. "The two that escaped, they weren't killed. But they were… tortured. I don't know." She's breathing quickly and my stomach drops. "I don't know the exact details—I just read up on it before, when I joined the company because I like true crime." She suddenly claps a hand to her mouth and bursts into tears. "Just like Li Hua."

"Look, it doesn't mean it's the same," Trent says, patting her shoulder. A muscle in his jaw twitches, and his words sound forced—like he's trying to say them just as much to reassure himself as he is trying to help Netty Florence. "The Valenzi girl was ten years ago."

"Ten years doesn't mean it's not a copycat, that it's *not* going to be the same," Netty Florence snaps. "And that all started with stalking and a note, too."

As the company dancers line up at the fire meeting point for the company, I still can't believe it. Li Hua has been abducted. None of this feels real. I concentrate on my breathing, trying to keep it even, trying not to panic as I stare across the darkness. So many moving figures. The school is assembling nearby, under flood lights, and while we haven't got our own lights here, some of it is transferred across in fractions and glimpses, making us look like ghosts.

Ghosts that are asking me so many questions, swarming me. Not just the company dancers but staff too. Every time I try and move toward the diploma students, hands pull me back. Ghosts wanting to talk to me, keep me away from my friends.

"What did the man look like?"

"Did you see him?"

"Did you get the registration number of the van?"

"Why didn't you help her?"

"Did they hurt you too?"

"Did they try and take you?"

"Why did they take Li Hua?"

Tingling sensations run down my arms, and I cross them over my chest, look toward those to my right for a friendly face. But Netty Florence is frowning.

"I just don't get it," she says slowly. "Why *didn't* you call the cops as soon as she was taken?"

"Yeah." Accusing eyes turn on me. More company dancers whom I don't know. "Instead you got into *her* taxi and came here."

I stare at them, feeling something strange and numb flitting around my body. The journey back in Li Hua's taxi feels like it was days ago, not hours. It was strangely silent, even though I was making small talk with the driver, answering his questions like how the Pilates class was and what being a professional dancer was like and even more, whether ballet is a lot harder than other types of dance. Just the usual questions really and I was glad to answer them. Gave me something to concentrate on, though I was shivering and sweating at the same time. There was a rip in the back of the driver's headrest, and I stared at it for so long as I spoke, until my vision blurred and the rip seemed to gape open.

Like a skull. I shiver, suddenly seeing the rip again, but it's superimposed onto Netty Florence's face now, only her face is changing, the nose smaller, the jaw narrower, the hair darker, until it's Li Hua. Li Hua with her head cleaved in two. One eye is drooling, dripping blood. Blood that lands on me.

I jolt, and a tear runs down my face. It shocks me, almost more than Li Hua in front of me. Only of course it isn't Li Hua. I blink and it's Netty Florence. No blood.

I take several deep breaths, my head full of rushing sounds. *Get a grip.*

"Hey, Bella's in shock," Ava says, suddenly appearing here—my friend. My best friend. "Anyway, you shouldn't be questioning her."

"What?"

"Bella shouldn't say anything until the police get here." Ava fidgets a bit on the spot, then she's trying to tug me toward her—back to where I see the diploma students are. All their eyes are on me.

Then Ava's words sink in.

"You think I'm guilty of something?"

"No!" Ava says. Her eyes narrow, and I shrink back. My legs feel wobbly, like I'm going to fall over. "But I know about eyewitness testimony and how unreliable it is in any circumstance. We need to wait for the police to be here before we do anything."

"What time are they getting here?" Jaidev asks.

"Miss Tavi has phoned them too," Trent says. "Shouldn't be long."

Shouldn't be long. I mouth the words to myself.

"This is *just like* the Valenzi girl," one of the second-division dancers says. She has a wide face and a nose stud, a nose stud that glints and makes me think of glitter. I focus on her. She has a petite frame, olive skin, shiny black hair, and dark eyes, and then I do a little bit of a double take as I realize who she is. Rosella Ramírez-Alfaro has been in the company for quite a few years. She's one of the most breathtaking performers I've seen. Last year, when the diploma students were invited to watch the first-division's production of Sylvia, Rosella had the title role and her solo dances were so captivating, elegant, mesmerizing. Madame Cachelle was teary-eyed, praising her for weeks after.

"What exactly did happen, with Allegra Valenzi?" I ask Rosella. I've never spoken directly to her before. Whereas Netty Florence, the principal of the company and lead of the first-division dancers, has always been friendly and encouraging, and other dancers like Li Hua have visited our classes, Rosella's usually at the back of rooms, in the shadows. Not very sociable, I heard someone say about her.

"The Valenzi girl, well," Rosella says in a low voice. Her words are hushed but fast, and she's looking around, scanning the area as she speaks. "Ten years ago—I was in the lower school here at Roseheart then—she was abducted when she was walking back here. She'd been to some sort of posh gym. Private classes and all that. She was with three friends. Two of them were taken with her. The other raised the alarm. Of the three abducted dancers, two of them were either let go or they escaped—most likely they were released, because three different ransoms were put out. Of course, Roseheart paid all of them, no questions. But Allegra didn't show up with the other two dancers. I don't know all the ins and outs, or why she didn't reappear once the money was paid up, but the cops found her blood. In the back of a car. Enough of it to pronounce her dead."

I feel like I've been punched. I try to picture Li Hua now. Is she tied up in some trunk of a car somewhere, or some basement, screaming? Is she already lying dead in a ditch? I shiver. Has her head been ripped apart like the leather headrest?

"Who... who did it?" My voice trembles.

"It was never solved," Rosella says.

"Then why haven't we heard much about it?" I stare at her. A major crime has taken place at the academy that I've been at for years, and the first I heard of it was a few days ago when the administration team decided to put up a portrait of Allegra, all because her sister was joining.

"The governors," Netty Florence says. "That's my guess. Or the investors. They'd pay a lot to stop the media doing anything that might tarnish Roseheart's great reputation. Money and greed always come before us."

I gulp in the cool air. Roseheart's investors paid off anyone who wanted to investigate an unsolved murder? Is that even allowed? Surely the police wouldn't obey that?

Netty Florence, Trent, and Rosella are talking more, but the coming night air carries their words over my head. I shiver as I look around.

Staff are now walking about, talking in low voices. Several of them have earnest and worried and scared looks etched on their faces. I see my ballet mistress from the diploma, Madame Cachelle, striding over from the school's assembly point. She's back on campus? She's got a radio in her hand, and though I can't hear what she is saying, she looks fierce.

A little way away, a car backfires, and I jump, then hear vehicles hooting. Someone shouts—someone in the lower school. Trent says something loudly, and all the company dancers are talking quickly.

Everyone is doing something.

Except for me.

I turn again, a slow ache creeping through my body.

Madame Cachelle is right by me, her eyes scanning over the company dancers. "Yes," she says, into the radio. "Mr. Vikas is on his way. But Sara and I have done the counts and we've got the same answer. Two unaccounted for, in total."

Two?

My heart drops. I look around, my heart pounding as I try to see all the diploma students. There's Ty, and Felicity and Bobby, Aaron and Haley, and—and are those diploma students, there, too? Everyone is starting to mix together.

"Yes," Madame Cachelle says, and she makes eye contact with me but only very briefly. A fraction of a second or so. Then she looks away, and her skirt swishes as she takes several steps. But somehow I still hear her words. "One of the day students. She should still be on campus, for the evening classes, but we cannot find her. Yes, it's Alessia Valenzi. It's… it's proof, isn't it? Them taking her, too. It really is happening again."

SIXTEEN

Alessia

I feel sick as I stare at the man. He is all shadows and sharp angles, but when I try to look at his face, it just blurs a bit. Like he does not want me to see him, commit his face to memory.

The roof of my mouth dries. "Wh-what do you want?" My heart pounds. Is it him? The man who... I thought I would recognize him, but... but there is nothing. It was dark, at that party. More than anything, I remember his hands. How cold they were. But how strong, sturdy.

But this man knows me. My name. And he is here. It has to be him. I look around, but there's no one else. Unless there are more of them, in the shadows.

"I just want to talk." His voice does not sound like how it does in my memories. It is softer.

"I do not want to talk," I whisper.

He steps closer, but he holds his hands up. A surrender gesture that is supposed to make me feel better, but it does not.

"Just remember," he says, and I see he has a scar on his face: two parallel lines that glow white below his right eye. He inclines his head slightly. "You're the only hope now," he says. "Darius wants you to remember."

"*Darius?*" My eyes widen, and the name bursts from me.

Suddenly, I'm six years old again, back at the start: nervous, trying to find the shoe cupboard. The teacher told me to get a pair that matched my skin tone better, and I had been wondering around for a few minutes, completely lost, when this boy had appeared. Deathly-pale skin, short dark hair spiked with hair gel, and glistening blue eyes. He had dimples when he smiled.

And that is… that is how I try to remember him. Not him as he was when I last saw him: *I really need this cash, Alessia. You don't understand.*

Have you got it?

Are you coming round with it or what?

Fuck you, Alessia. You're never there when people need you.

"Darius needs you to remember," the man says, and then he just… disappears. Slips back into the darkness, and he has gone. His footsteps make no sound at all.

Darius. I breathe deeply, looking around, and of course it comes back. The little things about him that just *made* my best friend. His shuffling walk. The sunglasses he often wore, even when it was cloudy.

If… Darius needs me to remember something, why not just message me? We are connected again now, even if I have not replied to the latest.

I swallow hard. I need to get back home—I am too late for the evening class anyway, now. Will have missed most of it by the time I get there.

I need to just ignore this.

It will all go away.

It has to.

Two police cars are parked outside Melview Apartments, and lights are on in almost every window. People are milling about—other residents, but also policemen and women—and when I walk up to the door, everyone is staring at me.

"That's her," Mrs. Townsend, a neighbor two floors down, says, pointing to me, and two policewomen look over at me. Then they are approaching and my mouth is drying.

"Alessia Valenzi?" The shorter of the women asks. She's Asian and has what I think is a Singaporean accent.

I nod.

She and her colleague—a white woman with a scar on her chin—exchange a look, before asking if I am okay, where I have been, and if anyone has hurt me.

I stare at them, panic unfurling in my chest. "What is going on?"

They share another look and then ask if they can come up to my apartment with me. You cannot really say no to police officers, so I just nod, head up numbly. There is more commotion inside the apartment block, and several people are staring at me.

"Alessia! Oh my god, thank goodness!"

Suddenly, Mother is here, in the fourth-floor foyer, wrapping me in a tight hug. I freeze, every muscle in my body unsure what to do. It has been years since Mother's hugged me.

"We thought… we thought…" She is crying, her expensive makeup smeared. She turns back. "Marco! Marco, she's here!" Then she switches into Italian, shouting and crying, and not letting me go. I can feel her shaking.

The officers try to calm her down, but then Father appears, and he is shaking and crying too. Angélique is in his arms, looking very red-faced. "My daughter, my daughter," he whispers against my face as he joins the hug.

At last, the officers separate us, lead us into our apartment. I find it is quite busy inside. Mother's best friend Deborah Levenson and her husband are both here, along with a couple of the neighbors. Deborah's eyes widen when she sees me, and she claps a hand to her chest.

"Thank goodness," she says. "Thank goodness. See, Guilia, it isn't happening again—it really isn't!"

"What is going on?" I ask.

Mother is still hysterical—and so is Father too, now with Deborah and her husband fussing around them—so I look at the policewomen. They introduce themselves, but I cannot hold onto any of the names they give me. I just stare at them, waiting.

"We need you to answer some more questions first," the white officer says. Perhaps we could go somewhere quieter?

I nod, lead them through to the kitchen. Mother is still crying noisily behind us.

The police officer takes a notepad out of a pocket, and a pencil. "Has anyone been in contact with you this evening, or earlier today, or tried to harm you in any way?"

My heart pounds, and I think of the man. The man who mentioned Darius. "What is this about?"

"It appears we have a copycat," the white officer says. "Today is ten years since your sister went missing, alongside two other Roseheart dancers, correct?"

I nod.

"An abduction of one of the company dancers was witnessed earlier this evening," the Asian officer says. "Roseheart staff also reported that you were missing from your evening classes."

Mother appears in the doorway of the kitchen. I can feel her glare burning on me now. So much for the hugs.

"So we need to get an account of your whereabouts in the last three hours."

I open my mouth, about to tell them about the man at the park. The man who knows Darius. But then I stop. That has got nothing to do with this—this new abduction, is it?

"Which dancer's been taken?" I ask.

"Li Hua Zhao."

The name is not familiar to me, but then why would it be? I have not been keeping up with who is at the company.

"Now, we need to know where you've been."

I tell them that I was walking alone in the park. That it is something I like doing. There is a war inside my head about whether to mention the man who knows Darius or not. I mean, he did not hurt me. And he cannot be part of the abduction. And I do not want to get the police looking into Darius. The cops are not always kind when it comes to drug users and the addicted, and I feel this strange sense of loyalty to protect Darius. Because he is obviously still finding things hard. Still needing money to support his addiction. His lifestyle. He needs support, not judgement. And it cannot just be a coincidence that he, through that man, reached out to me today. At *this* time.

I take a deep breath. I do not mention the man or Darius. It is not relevant.

"Thank you," the officers both say as they leave. The Asian officer gives me her card and says that if there is anything else I want to share, I can contact her at any time. DI Sofia Chan, the card reads.

A strange silence falls over us once the officers have left. Mother is still standing by the doorway, and I cautiously make my way toward her, but she backs away, as if she cannot be close to me. A moment later, and she's sitting in the window seat of the lounge, next to Father in his armchair. Angélique is on his lap. Mother's posture is as tense as a pencil, and I wait for them to say something. But neither does. They stare at me. There is no trace of the warmth and relief in Mother's face now, and another hug seems like the last thing she will ever do.

"Do you… do you think it is someone copying… what happened before?" I ask. Because I have never truly been able to work out whether the abduction ten years ago was real. My sister wanted to disappear, and if it was not for the taking of the other two dancers—and their very real injuries from torture—I would have been so sure that the whole kidnap was fake. Just a story, to allow my sister to leave the country.

I swallow hard. Allegra was kind and compassionate. There is no way she would have set up her abduction if it meant two innocent dancers got hurt.

But her abduction also cannot be *real*, I know that. Because she *is* out there. No matter what conclusion the police came to, how much of her blood they supposedly found in the trunk of a car, and the verdict of 'assumed death' that they came to, Allegra is out there. She is finally free, living her own life. In Greece, maybe. Or Albania or Bulgaria.

She has not been dead all this time.

She is alive.

But now another dancer has been taken.

"It does not mean it is the same people behind it," Father says at last. "Anyone can copy what happened."

Mother is just staring at me, her eyes cool, her facial expression slack—a strange contrast to the tension in her shoulders, her back, how carefully she's holding her legs. "I should phone the academy. Let them know for sure that she is okay." She's still staring at me, yet speaking like I am not here. "Marco, you had better drive her to and from Roseheart from now on. We cannot be too careful."

SEVENTEEN

They round us back up, into the buildings. Everyone is here, apart from Li Hua. Word arrived not long ago that Alessia Valenzi is safe after all. *It's just one abduction.* Like that's a good thing.

"Like that's a good thing." I'm whispering the words before I even realize I'm going to.

Some company dancers look at me. I look at them.

We are all packed into a lounge in their accommodation block. Somehow, I'm still with them, separated from Ava and Felicity and the diploma students, squashed on a soft chair with Rosella and a second-division dancer called Momoko. Rosella has her arm around me. Netty Florence kneels in front of me, along with Allie, who I think was introduced to me earlier as the third-division's costume designer and seamstress. So many of the company's non-dancing staff are here too: stagehands, electric and lighting specialists, artistic directors. I think I saw some of their faces outside, earlier, but I can't quite remember.

It's hot in here. The lights are buzzing and I'm sure I can hear the annoying whine of mosquitoes, too. Where are they? I turn, trying to find them, look directly at one of the light strips. It leaves murky red shapes in my vision, and I blink frantically, trying to blink twenty times because suddenly that seems important.

Sixteen, seventeen, eighteen…

Someone hands me a cup of tea. It's too hot, burns me through the thin ceramic, but I make myself hold onto it anyway, until my fingers are burning and every muscle in my hands begs for me to just drop it.

Drop it. And I see it. See it in slow motion. The ceramic mug falling at a quicker rate than the tea inside, so the tea makes this weird column shape in the air, before tiny ceramic shards bounce back up, trying to get hold of the tea, save it maybe, before it too is on the carpet.

But then I blink and it's gone, and it's just Netty Florence in front of me. She's speaking to me in a soft voice, calming tone, but I can't make out her words. Can't really make out anything.

My hands shake. I flex my fingers, feel several knuckles crack. I make them do it again, staring at them rather than the people here. Too many eyes.

I feel my face crumpling, and I have to do something not to cry, so I stand suddenly, still holding the scalding mug, just about avoiding it dripping onto Netty Florence. It's too hot in here. Sweat's sticking my clothes to me like a second skin. And it's loud too—so much buzzing from the lights, and those mosquitoes, and everyone *talking talking talking.*

Shut up! Shut up! Shut up!

I need to get out.

We're not supposed to leave, so many people have already said that, but I weave around people, moving quickly. *Just get out, get out, get out.* Got to get away from everyone.

And then I'm… out.

The night welcomes me as I sit in the courtyard outside, a courtyard in the company's grounds, one I've not been in before, nursing the mug, feeling sicker and sicker.

You should've helped Li Hua.

You could've stopped her abduction.

You let her be taken.

Before I've even realized I'm on the move again, I'm meandering back toward the administration buildings. I'm not trying to be covert or anything, not hiding myself, nor sneaking about. But no one seems to notice me. No one at all. Like an invisible waif, I slip into the building, into the foyer that's packed with company staff.

"We need to get a handle on this right away," a man says.

Someone else agrees.

"But the journalists have already caught wind of this. I've had two voicemails from reporters at *The Daily Telegraph* already."

"Well, put a stop to it! We can't have this getting out—this will finish the school and the company. We're in enough hot water as it is with Rio and Fibonacci."

Rio and Fibonacci? I frown. That sounds like one of those companies that makes the fancy loose-leaf tea. God, I love loose-leaf tea. Had a really nice peppermint one, for the first time, when I was twelve. Bobby bought it for me after I told him that I wished we were posh. What I meant was I wanted nicer clothes, but he bought me the tea with his pocket money.

The door behind me flies open again, and Mr. Vikas enters the foyer like a whirlwind. That makes it easy enough for me to slip out. At some point, I've lost the ceramic cup of tea, because I realize it's no longer in my hands.

My hands are empty as I sneak through the back door into the dorm block.

My hands are guilty.

No.

"But I'm like Lady MacBeth," I whisper to another of those garish ballet posters with the hot-pink border. "I've got blood on my hands."

I blink and, just for a second, I see it—blood, dripping. Dripping all down me, over me, the carpet. So much blood. A sea of it.

My hands shake so much, and my head splits with a headache. I know what I need, but I haven't got any more of it. Not due to meet my dealer until tomorrow.

I could ask Mattie if he's got some left, but the chances of me getting to him, undetected by anyone else, are slim. So instead I run up the back stairs—no one uses these. It's mainly a fire exit. Voices drift toward me, through closed doors. I go to Ava's room, push the door open. Neither she nor her roommate are in here, so I go to Ava's side of the room, open her drawers. Ten leotards, neatly folded, and under them, the bottle of vodka she keeps stashed there. It's a quarter full.

I take swig after swig, until I'm numb.

We see the police outside before they make their way into the buildings. I'm not sure how much time has passed, but I'm in the diploma students' common room now. My head feels foggy.

"They're securing the area," Ty says, apparently confident that he can accurately narrate the protocol because he tells everyone he reads a lot of detective novels—I just want to scream at him. But when the officers make their way inside— so many of them, including armed officers—Ty frowns. "It's not normal to respond to an abduction that didn't even take place on this site with guns," he tells us. He's using his theatrical voice. Like this is all entertainment.

I want to hit him.

My forehead aches from how hard I'm applying my frowning muscles as I watch armed officer after armed officer go by. We've all been told to stay where we are, and there's another armed policeman outside our door. She's got a radio that she's speaking frantically into.

I look toward Madame Cachelle and Mr. Vikas. They're the two members of staff who've somehow been placed in with us. "Why are they armed?" I ask, a bad feeling making itself home in the pit of my stomach.

Neither Madame Cachelle nor Mr. Vikas reply. They just stare straight ahead, steely gazes, watching the officer at the door.

Ava's face crumples and she starts crying again. That's all she's been doing here, since I came down, the vodka warming my insides.

Ty steps closer to me. "Why?" he says, louder than my voice was.

Madame turns her head toward us. "Just precautions," she finally says.

"Must've been some kind of gun threat scare then," Felicity says.

I take my phone out and Google Roseheart—trying to find if there's anything being written online that gives us more information. But I can't find anything concrete. Just a lot of tweets about the police presence in the area and how 'something must be going down'. I change my search terms to learn more about Allegra Valenzi, but there is so little information online even on her. It's like anything meaty has been scrubbed away.

I swallow hard and try not to think about what might be happening to Li Hua right now.

The police officer stationed by the door speaks into her radio then turns to us all. Through the glass panel I see how young she looks, and then she opens the door, tells us that the whole campus has got the all clear.

"It was likely the threat was just a bluff," she says to Mr. Vikas and Madame Cachelle.

"But *what* was the threat?" I ask, and just as it seems she's about to dismiss me because I'm not management or whatever, I say, "I'm Bella—I was the one with Li Hua when she was taken."

The woman's gaze becomes a little steely. "And you're the one who's also been stalked?"

I don't know how she knows about that or who's told the police, when it seems that Mr. Vikas and Madame Cachelle don't know if their startled looks are anything to go by, but the officer tells me to come with her, that they need to get a statement from me.

My head's quieter now, and I'm not shaking, and I feel calm, so I nod. Of course I'll go with them. She leads me outside and across campus, to one of the dance admin offices on the second floor of the admin building, communicating with other officers via her radio all the way. I'd assumed I'd be taken to a station, but when I get to the office, I find it's a makeshift kind of police base, where all the officers are going to and from.

"Bella Sotheby," the woman says to a man at the door. "The witness."

The man nods. "Remi's wanting to speak to her." He looks at me and softens his voice a little. "We're just trying to get basic info at the moment—we'll ask you to come to the station tomorrow to do a formal, official statement. But right now, we need all the info we can get, as early as possible."

As early as possible.

It's been hours.

I nod and lean into the wonderful calmness spreading through my body, as another officer introduces himself to me. DC Remi Wertkin. He takes me to the room adjacent to the one they seem to be using as a base and asks me to go through the details of what happened.

I tell him about how weird it was that Li Hua invited me to go to Pilates with her when she'd just found out that I'd slept with her boyfriend. I don't tell him about her asexuality though. Even though she's missing, outing her isn't right. That, I'm sure of.

"The boyfriend," DC Wertkin says. "What's his name?"

"Trent Mason," I say, and he speaks into his radio, asking an officer to speak to Trent ASAP.

I continue, telling him how, after the class that Li Hua and I went to, we were walking to the next block, ready to be picked up. And how, when we were waiting, the van drove up, took her.

"And you were also being stalked?" DC Wertkin asks. "Have you got any notes or anything that you've been sent?"

"No, it wasn't like that. No notes. It was just… I kept hearing someone following me."

"Someone following you?" He tilts his head and leans back in his chair.

"Footsteps," I say. "And Li Hua heard them too, when we were out."

"How many times prior to this evening have you thought you were being followed?" the officer asks.

I scratch the back of my neck. My skin feels prickly, rough. "Um, once?"

DC Wertkin's eyes narrow a little as he looks at me. "Have you been drinking, Miss Sotheby?"

"I—uh, yeah. I had a bit. To calm down." Flustered, I try to continue, but he cuts me off by holding his hands up in the air.

"How much and what was it?"

"Vodka. But not much."

"And I understand you've had trouble with cocaine before?"

"I—yes." I scratch the back of my neck harder, but the skin just seems to get even rougher. Rougher and rougher. Then I feel something move there—something tiny.

I freeze.

Fleas.

No! Not again.

My heart pounds.

"Are you under the influence of any drugs right now, alongside the vodka?"

"No." I shake my head, but my head's feeling all strange. Too heavy. It's going to fall off my shoulders, roll away. "I don't think so."

"You don't think so?"

"No!" My breaths are ragged. I can't breathe properly. Why can't I breathe properly? I stand up, and the whole room sways. DC Wertkin looks a bit surprised that I'm now standing, but I've got to brush these fleas off my neck. "Look, I'm telling you about the stalking—I was being stalked too. They… they might want me as well. That could've been their plan. To take me too."

"But they didn't." His voice is lazy, yet his posture isn't… but I can't quite work out what his posture is. "And you haven't got any evidence that you were being stalked, not like the threatening notes that Miss Zhao received."

"Threatening notes?" My voice is small.

"Have you received any?"

"No," I say. "But I was being followed. I'm sure of it." *I'm not crazy. I'm not!*

"Just make sure you're sober and clean when you come down to the station tomorrow."

EIGHTEEN

Trent

"Trent, hey!" Manuel screams, his voice hoarse and grating. He's been trying to stop me for the last hour or so, from doing this—his efforts ranging from weak arguments to even grabbing my arm in the car, as if he could stop me. I've always been physically stronger than him, able to lift more in the gym and run faster.

But now we're finally here.

"I don't think you should be doing this!" he calls after me, but nothing is going to slow me or prevent me from doing exactly what I came here to do.

Anger propels me forward, and I'm running before I even realize it. Manuel's car—which he very reluctantly drove me in—is facing this way, its headlights still on, even though I'm guessing he's got out of it too now, but the lights don't stretch far enough, and now I'm sprinting through the dark gardens, ghost-gray gravel flying out from under my feet.

And there it is: the house. So grand with its stupid marble pillars and bay windows. No lights on. Of course. It's three in the morning, maybe four.

I start screaming before I'm even right up to the house. Shouting my sponsor's name. Cursing him. In the gaps in which I pause for breath, I hear Manuel shouting after me—his cries getting quieter. He's not brave enough to come right up here, not when Mr. Appleby's his sponsor too.

"You afraid to come out here?" I yell. "You're fucking afraid, are you?" My breaths come in short, sharp bursts. There's a slight pain in the right side of my chest, and I've been holding myself too tensely the whole car ride here, because there's a deep ache in my lower back. "Just tell me where she is!" I shout, and I put everything into that shout, as I bound up the white steps to the front door, my voice reverberating with my effort, my anger.

"Get down here now and talk to me like a man!" I let out another guttural scream, blinking as lights suddenly flood the area I'm in. Harsh white light that throws murky shapes over my vision as I blink. "Appleby!"

Something clunks inside the house, then lights flicker on, just visible through the heavy curtains.

I scream again, and then the door flies open. Two maids, shaking, wide-eyed. I've still got ten steps or so to take, to get up to the front door, and I bound up them. The women shrink back. "Get him down here now," I snarl.

The maids shrink back, and then a man's here, trying to close the door. It's not Mr. Appleby—I get a quick snatching glimpse of a cleanly shaven face; groundskeeper maybe—but I surge forward, get my foot in the doorway. The door slams against it, but I barely register it.

"I'm not leaving until he's told me where she is."

The maids' eyes flash, and then the groundskeeper's aggressively saying something to me, but I don't listen to his words. They fly over me, like birds. Birds freed from the house. Birds escaping. Because the monster is here.

Mr. Appleby, in a bright orange dressing gown and fluffy slippers, blinks under the light of his foyer. "You can all go," he says in a curt voice to the maids and groundskeeper, and when they falter, he barks "now!"

They scurry away, and I stare at him, feeling everything inside me ripple with revulsion.

"Where is she?" I spit the words at him. "I know you've taken her."

In one swift movement, the bastard lunges at me. His fist strikes my chest, and I'm off-balance and—

Fuck!

I fall back, stumbling. Try to grab a handrail but I'm out of reach, half-tumbling down the marble steps. I hit my shin hard, twisting around, as I land at the bottom. For a moment, I don't do anything but breathe. Breathe through my anger as I stare up at him.

"Was my word on the phone not enough?" Mr. Appleby stares down at me, and the most menacing of smiles graces his face, curling the corners of his mouth. The floodlights suddenly seem brighter, making the night look inkier around us, and the man looks so confident, so smarmy, standing up there, as if he's invincible, as if nothing can possibly hurt him.

As if he can do what he fucking wants to at any time and never have to face the consequences.

"Now isn't the fucking time to play games," I snarl. My head spins—from the tiredness, the stress, the fall maybe, and the drink I had before setting off. Because I *had* to come here. While Mr. Appleby convinced me on the phone earlier that he had nothing to do with my girlfriend's disappearance, I had to see him with my own eyes. See his face as he says the words.

"You threatened her earlier." I pull myself up, cursing as pain digs into my knee. Damn. Not that injury playing up. "You threatened Li Hua, and now this has happened." As I stare at the man who's ruined my life, I try to keep my tone as calm as possible, because I know I look a mess right now— angry, disheveled—and appearances are everything to Mr. Appleby. I need him to know he can't mess with me.

"I don't know what you're talking about," he says, his voice so... so fucking demure.

I want to strangle him. I feel it in me, this sudden force, this energy. How if I just let it control me, I'd lunge up those steps and grab him, squeeze him until he admitted the truth.

"I have of course heard about the sad circumstances surrounding Miss Zhao," Mr. Appleby says. "But regrettably, I cannot help you at all."

Sad circumstances?

Anger boils through me, and I'm climbing those steps once again, until I'm inches from the man. My chest swells with energy, with yet more anger—who even thought it was possible to feel this amount of it?—and I glare at him. "Let me through."

"I beg your pardon?"

"Let. Me. Through." I scream at him—not even words, just guttural sounds—and then he makes the mistake of touching me again.

His hand on my shoulder. "I think you'd better calm down."

I punch him, but he doesn't fall back like I expected. He grabs my arm instead.

"That was a very unwise thing to do." His voice is low, guarded.

"Just fucking tell me where she is!" I try to move past him, into the house. "Li Hua! Li Hua!"

He shoves me back a couple of steps. "If you do not leave now, I will be calling the police and having you arrested for assault."

"Assault?" A bitter, heavy laugh erupts from my gut. "You shoved me down those steps first."

"You are trespassing."

"I'm *your* dancer." I spit the words at him. I have never hated him more.

"You *were* my dancer," he says. "But I will no longer be sponsoring you, Trent Mason, so you have no right to be on my property, and I will have you charged for assault and trespassing if you do not move." He waits a moment, as if goading my reaction to be bigger. Something he can really use against me with the police.

But I won't give him that satisfaction. It's not fucking worth it. This man, this *monster*.

"And you can tell the directors and my other Roseheart danseurs yourself that *you* are the reason that they and the company will not be receiving any more funding from me." With that, he slams the door.

The slam echoes through me, and I stare at the stupid brass knocker. The fancy letter box.

The letter box.

I open it, forcing my fingers through, holding it open. "I know you're part of this," I shout into the mansion. "I know it and I will get you sent down for what you've done to her!"

Manuel isn't happy when I get back to him and the car. Not about the whole trip here, my anger, the fight—which he apparently saw enough of—and of course, his lack of sponsorship from Mr. Appleby. Manuel just stares at me, his mouth dropping open into a small 'o'. Then he shakes his head, swears twice in Spanish—words that he once taught me, so long ago—and tells me to get back in the car.

We drive in silence.

My breaths are still ragged, my heart still beating so loudly that it's all I can hear. Sweat drips down my forehead and I roll down the window next to me, only for Manuel to close the window the moment I've done so. I risk a glance at him, but he's just glaring as he drives through the night.

We get back to Roseheart in a time that seems both too quick and not long enough. He doesn't say a word as we get out, as he locks the car, as we start walking—but he speeds up, clearly not wanting to walk in-line with me.

Whatever. I shake my head at him, then raise my middle finger. It's not his girl who's been taken, is it?

I clench my trembling hands into tight fists, keep them rigid at my sides, as if I can just ball up all my energy and keep it there, ready for when it's needed. Because I'm going to need it. I'm going to need a plan. A plan to get Li Hua back.

A cool breeze ruffles over me as I step into the accommodation block. I shouldn't have got back into Manuel's car. I should've stayed there, in Mr. Appleby's grounds. Waiting. Watching the house for something. Getting ready to do something. Break in.

She's in there. He's got her.

I know he has.

"Trent?"

I blink as I step inside. There's one soft, dim light on, and I see Jaidev stepping toward me.

"You okay?"

"Do I look like I'm fucking okay?"

He holds his hands up. "Whoa. Remember who the enemy is, yeah?" He lifts his shoulders up a little, looking a bit awkward. "What the hell happened out there? Manuel's just gone storming through and—"

"Manuel?" I let out a laugh. "You're worried about him, seriously? Li Hua is missing and you're worried about him?"

"I didn't say that." He gives me a stern look. "But you need to calm down. And you need to remember who's on your side."

I ram my fist against the wall, cursing. My knuckles split open, blood oozing out—and it feels good.

"Well, that's not going to help, is it?" Jaidev shakes his head. "I'll get the medical kit. Come on. Kitchen. Now."

Everything seems to pound around me as I follow him through the hallway, into the little kitchenette. There are several in the building, and each has a small first aid kit under the sink. Jaidev retrieves the kit, makes me sit down in the only chair at the small breakfast counter.

The plastic chair creaks as I sink my whole weight into it. Jaidev takes out some wipes from the first aid kit, then offers them to me. When I don't make any movement, Jaidev starts opening the wipes himself. But I honestly don't feel like I'm here, not emotionally; I'm still back at Mr. Appleby's place… did Li Hua hear me? See me? Did seeing me get her hopes up?

Did she see me walk away from her?

Not fight for her hard enough?

My stomach roils, and then suddenly it's all pouring out of me—the frustration, the anger, the fear. I'm sobbing into Jaidev's arms, feeling pathetic and useless, and why the fuck can't I stop crying?

"It's okay," Jaidev says.

"How can it possibly be okay?"

"It's okay to cry."

Okay to cry.

I'm not one of those men who never cries. Who tries to never show emotion. Who thinks it's weak or something. That's not me. I talk about my feelings. With Li Hua. We do it—did it—all the time.

And yet there's something about the way Jaidev says the words. The effect they have on me. Like I've got permission now. Permission to just be.

Jaidev shuts the door, then stands a couple of feet or so away from me. "You know, what if your sponsor hasn't got anything to do with this? Have you thought about that? That it's not him. That it's to do with the Valenzi dancer?"

I shake my head, and my vision blurs. The wrappers of the antiseptic wipe are in tatters, next to the medical kit on the counter. "No. It has to be him."

"You want it to be him, because then you can blame him," Jaidev says. "You know who to go after. Not like with the Valenzi dancer. With no one knowing who was behind it."

Jaidev pours me a glass of water and hands me a paracetamol. He tells me he has to go up to bed now, asks if I'll be okay, sitting here. If maybe I need to get some sleep too.

I'm not sure what I say to him. But he goes. And then it's just me.

Me and my thoughts.

I don't sleep. Not really. I lie in bed, numb, detached, reading everything I can about Allegra Valenzi's disappearance, trying to ignore the scent of Li Hua on the sheets next to me. Trying to find out everything I can about the first dancer's abduction.

I've got one of Li Hua's notebooks—she made so many notes as she was reading—but I can't find any of the articles I'm sure I saw her reading. She'd printed them all out, put them in a red ring-bound folder. But that's not here—even though I'm sure it always has been. On her desk at the foot of the bed. Next to my desk. Or on the top shelf of the bookcase in the living room—only that shelf is now empty.

I made fun of her before, for how studious she was about reading up on it. Color-coding her articles. How obsessed she was.

But now I can't even find where she put her things. I never listened properly.

And now she's… gone.

And what if Jaidev is right and Mr. Appleby has nothing to do with it? What if it's Allegra's abductor, again? A low-battery warning flicks up on my phone screen, just as I'm trying alternate wording to find anything on the Valenzi girl.

But no matter how hard I look, I don't really find anything.

The only person who knows what happened is Allegra Valenzi. And she's assumed dead.

And the abductor, of course.

No one I can talk to.

No one—

My eyes widen.

There is someone.

NINETEEN

I do not want to go back to Roseheart, but Mother makes me, of course. She says everything must carry on as normal, and she tells me that Deborah will drop by to give me a lift to school and that she can also take me to the police station after my last lesson. Mother has apparently already been on the phone with officers, arranging a time for me to go in to give a formal statement.

Sitting in that police station—the same one I had to sit in so often after Allegra disappeared—was torture, and I do not want to go back there. But, like with so many things, I do not have a choice. Mother makes this very clear, and I just have not got the energy to argue with her, to fight.

I barely slept last night, and when I did, my dreams were a kaleidoscope of bright colours and gut-churning clenches of fear that had me waking up in a cold sweat, listening to the sounds of my own heart pounding as I stared around the semi-darkness of my room, looking at shapes and shadows that should be familiar—but that were not.

Everything looked wrong.

Another dancer has been taken.

And now I've got to go back to that school. The academy.

People are going to want to talk to me. I know this. I looked at my phone this morning, before heading into the kitchen to grab a bowl of cereal I knew I did not want to eat, and saw message after message after message from journalists, former friends, acquaintances. Everyone reaching out to me, wanting the latest gossip.

Now, I wait for Deborah to arrive to take me to Roseheart. Mother tells me she will not be long.

She is not.

Soon, we are in her Bently, a tense silence stretching between us as she drives. She tries to make small talk, but the woman just annoys me. Always has done, with her matching skirt suits—always a pale blue. The exact favorite color of Allegra. Deborah only adopted that color for pretty much her whole wardrobe after Allegra went missing. It annoyed Mother at first, but Deborah explained it was her way of keeping her best friend's daughter alive. And after that Mother insisted to me that it was "a very touching gesture," and that even now, we should be grateful that Deborah is still keeping this up. That ten years later, Allegra has not been forgotten.

But it just annoys me because Deborah always tries to talk about Allegra, once she's got the attempts at small talk out of the way.

"You must still miss her terribly," Deborah says. "I mean, I miss my boys—I don't believe you have met my youngest two? They do travel so much, but I miss them. And I worry about my eldest—being a policeman he's faced with so much violence, dealing with criminals. I worry so much, for all of them, yet I cannot imagine what it is like for your family. And these recent events must have really shaken up all of you."

I nod. "Yes. They have." I mean, surely she realizes she is stating the obvious?

"All we can do is take comfort in the fact that your sister is in heaven now," Deborah says.

I breathe slowly, counting to ten in my head. Deborah is religious, and I half expect her to now spout some Bible quotations to me, in her attempt to be comforting, but thankfully she does not. Just as well. I breathe out hard. Allegra isn't dead.

Deborah was one of the first to suggest to Mother and Father that Allegra might be though—back when the two dancers were freed after the ransom was paid but Allegra wasn't, Deborah came around. Offered a supporting shoulder. Said that Allegra was in a better place now.

Mother wanted to look for Allegra, there and then, I remember that. But Deborah said that the Lord wouldn't want Mother to go through the distress of finding her daughter's body. "It's best you remember Allegra as she was."

The traffic is bad—I guess it always is at this time, rush hour—but at last Deborah drops me off by Roseheart's gates and I escape from her clutches. I thank her, my voice strangely wooden, and hop out. There is an iciness to the air that seems to cut into my throat, and I wrap my jacket around me tighter, hugging it to me.

Other students are pulling into Roseheart now, but I do not recognize any. Guess they must be other day students though. They are all talking in twos or threes and several are looking across at me.

I refuse to make eye contact, just wave awkwardly to Deborah as she drives away. The tinted windows mean I cannot see if she waves back. I turn and walk and—

"Hey!"

Suddenly, a guy gets all in my face, grabs my arm. My heart pounds and for a second, I just freeze up.

But it's not the same guy as last night.

No. This guy... this guy looks terrible. Flushed skin, bloodshot eyes, greasy hair.

"I need you to tell me everything," he says, and his words are running into each other. "Everything about your sister."

I jolt, take a step back. I knew it was coming. Knew these questions would be everywhere today. And this was exactly why I did not want to come here. Exactly why—

He touches my arm and—

No.

No!

Every muscle in my body freeze. An instinctual reaction, just like it was back then, before… at the party and…

No!

My hand shakes—the first sign of it. Of *me* shaking and—

He leans closer, his mouth so close to my ear that I can feel his hot breath. His hand around my waist squeezes, squeezes so tightly, and I cannot breathe. My legs—they are not working. Not mine. They feel too soft, insubstantial. Wrong.

"I can help you," he whispers, and his words curl around me, sticking to every part of me. "Oh, darling, I can help you with everything."

My head pounds, and my eyes feel strange as he leads me away. And I do not want to go—but… but I cannot stop him. Cannot stop my feet from carrying me forward.

I try to open my mouth, try to speak, scream—something, anything.

But nothing happens. Only my eyes feeling scratchier, my head feeling heavier. Thoughts whirl through me, but I cannot quite grasp them, cannot see the contents of them.

"Here." It is his voice again. He is… back? I blink, see his keen eyes. Had he gone? Did he go? He is pressing something into my hand. A glass. "Have another drink, babe."

"Hey!" a girl shouts, jolting me, and I gasp as if I have just come up for air. The man clutching my arm looks over his shoulder, annoyance tugging at his face. "Get off her!"

As if in slow motion, I turn my head, and I see Francesca. My shoulders slacken with relief as she marches over.

"What the hell do you think you're doing?" she demands of the guy, and then she is actually grabbing him, pulling him away from me. "Did you not hear me when I said to get off her?"

The guy says something, but I cannot make out his words. Francesca just barks back at him, all fierce and lion-like. Protective.

My *friend.*

After what seems like forever, the guy backs off. He shouts something back at us, over his shoulder, but Francesca tells me to ignore him.

"He's just upset about his girlfriend—understandable. But it doesn't give him the right to be a dick."

"His girlfriend?" I ask.

"Li Hua Zhao. The Chinese dancer in the company," Francesca says. "The one who was taken yesterday."

All day, talk about Li Hua Zhao and my sister is everywhere. I cannot escape it. There are just so many gossips. So many questions. Even the staff are talking about my sister and the Chinese dancer.

I want to just run away. Scream. Cry. But I cannot seem to do anything but go through the motions of the day. A day I just want to be over.

"Come with me," Francesca says, after our lesson with Madame Jurgensen is over. A lesson in which so many of the students were whispering snidely, mentioning my sister. Mentioning me. I heard a couple of their theories—that I must know where Li Hua's been taken, because I am showing no emotion and I will not even talk about my sister to anyone that asks.

"She clearly knows," several say.

"Just come with me," Francesca says. "I'm getting coffee from the *Toast and Talk*, you know it? Just over the road. And you look like you could do with one. Don't worry—there won't be anyone from Roseheart there."

I frown. "How do you know?"

"Because pretty much every Roseheart student boycotts it. That's why I love it."

"Boycotts it? Why?"

"Something about that shop sponsoring a rival ballet school in London. Like years ago, but I guess these things stick. I've been going there for years and I've never seen a Roseheart student there. But the staff are really pretty cool. They give me half-price coffees most of the time."

"They do?"

"They do," Francesca confirms. "And why would I go somewhere else and pay full price when there's a perfectly good half-price latte with my name on it?"

Toast and Talk is a pretty artisan café. The décor is all polished wood and flowing curves, and there are artsy posters all over the walls. What space there is that has not been plastered with posters is filled with graffiti.

"Pretty cool, huh?" Francesca says. "Anyone can do it. You just ask for paints or pens at the front. They've got a whole box of them. Look—that's one I did. Not that I have a tag or anything."

I peer closer to where she points, a part of the wall near the barista's station. 'Fran' has been written in bubble writing, along with a surprisingly good drawing of a corgi.

"Cute," I say, even though that's not normally a word I use. I look around. There are a few other customers in here, but it is nothing like the atmosphere in Costa or Starbucks. Feels more intimate. Personal. And definitely not like the inside of the high-end coffee houses Mother likes. Those are too impersonal, too set on showing off how much money they have.

"Anyway, whatcha having?" Francesca props herself up against the counter, popping her hip in a way that looks kind of painful. "I'd really recommend the Lattes."

"Sure," I say.

The woman behind the counter smiles. She has got shoulder-length blond hair and so much dark makeup around her eyes that I cannot actually tell what color her eyes are. "Who's your friend, Fran?" Her accent is straight up cockney.

"This is Alessia," Francesca says, and I smile shyly. "Told you I had friends."

"Never doubted you one moment, love. I'll bring those drinks over when they're ready. You settle down."

Francesca leads me up a couple of wooden stairs into what she tells me is the balcony. It is a pretty cool space, lots of plush cushions and sofas. And it's empty.

We sit on the sofa at the back of the balcony, so we have got the view of the whole coffee shop.

"They're always saying I should bring in more Roseheart students," Francesca tells me. "Even with the boycott… Or any friends at all really." She glances through her lashes at me. "We… I don't really make friends that easily."

"That is okay. I do not either."

"Why do you always speak so formally? Like, you never use contractions."

I shrug. "It is how Mother taught me to speak." Then I laugh. "*It's* how Mother taught me to speak. She was so focused on it. We all had elocution lessons."

"I bet that set you apart from the other kids," Francesca says. "Anyway. We can be two loners together. Though I've been perfectly fine on my own, all this time," Francesca says. "It's just the staff here, thinking I need friends. Anyway, I'm sure if I brought like ten girls in here or something they'd have to stop all the discounts they give me. And the freebies. The chocolate muffins—did you see them? Most of the time if I ask if they've got any stale, or going out of date or something, they give me one for free. And those chocolate muffins are so good, believe me."

I smile, feeling a little awkward. Thankfully the barista appears, carrying our lattes on a bright orange tray. We both thank her, taking our drinks.

We sip our drinks, almost in unison.

Francesca's phone pings and when she looks at it, a smile breaks out across her face. Then her cheeks pinken considerably. She tries to hide it though, her reaction, when she looks back at me.

"Boyfriend?" I ask.

She shakes her head. "Uh, no. I, uh, I just entered a competition. That was all." But her face is red, and I am pretty sure she has just lied to me.

Well, maybe not 'lie'. That is a strong word. Just omitted to tell me the truth. Still, we are not *besties* or anything. And there are things about my life that I would not want her to know, so it is only fair she has got things she wants to keep from me. Like a boyfriend.

I have never really been into the whole dating thing. I have watched people from my year at school get together, gossip about latest crushes, sharing worries and concerns about sleeping with someone for the first time. I have never really been into it all though. Just has not appealed to me. I am much happier on my own.

I turn to look at the posters on the wall behind me, mainly for something to do because it is starting to feel a bit awkward, just drinking coffee here with Francesca. Neither of us is speaking since she lied about the boyfriend/competition thing. There are a lot of posters here, mostly advertising shows at the local theatre and some amateur dramatics groups. Most of these posters have the same logo at the bottom right corner. I lean in closer.

"Rio and Fibonacci." I frown. "What is that?"

"Ah, some big arts company," Francesca says. "They sponsor some of Roseheart's ballets, I think, but they kind of sponsor everything. Fingers in many pies, as my pa says. They do so much though. I used to play piano, when I was nine or ten, and they did this whole thing for kids from poor families, basically paying for us to have lessons in the creative arts."

Poor families? I look at Francesca and try to work out if that is still the same for her. I am not a snob or anything, but I am aware of my privileged upbringing. I know not everyone is as fortunate as me—if you can call it fortune, what with what happened to my sister. I take in Francesca's worn shirt collar and how her Converse sneakers look at least five years old as she sticks her feet out from under the table, laces fraying. And, after all, she goes to a café that gives her half-price lattes.

When Francesca heads down to the main part of the café to deposit our empty coffee cups on the counter and ask about chocolate muffins, she leaves her phone behind on the table, right next to me. It has sort of slipped under the menu that had been propped up on the table, by the unlit candle, and so I do not think she has realized her phone is even here, with me. But I am hyper-aware of it, and I am not sure why.

Then the screen lights up. Another message.

I am not being nosy or anything, but when a phone screen lights up right next to you, you cannot help but look at it. And when you notice there is text on the screen, your eyes just automatically focus on it. Read it.

Timathy: *I'll see you tonight, baby.*

I suppress a smile. She totally has a boyfriend. Timathy. Interesting spelling.

I file that name away.

TWENTY

Trent

My head pounds so much and all I want to do is sleep, not be summoned to some lousy meeting where Roseheart administration are telling us all that they're doing their best efforts to find Li Hua—even if they're really doing nothing. Even if each of them is just relieved it's not them who's been taken. Tortured.

Because Li Hua told me about that—the torture that took place. Those two dancers who were released. How their bodies were mangled with scars. How they lived after in some psychiatric home for people with unmanageable PTSD. I tried to find Li Hua's notes on it this morning, again, but came up empty handed. Still, I don't need her notes to remember. To picture it all in my mind—what is happening to my girlfriend. The woman I love.

My stomach twists violently and for a moment, I think I'm going to be sick. Right here, in the grand hall, where every single dancer in the Roseheart Romantic Dance Company is sitting on neat little fold-away chairs. The company's assistant artistic director is on stage, still speaking. Droning on and on about the actions the company and academy are taking to aid the police in their investigation. But we should be out there. All of us, looking for her. *That's* what we should be doing.

"And now we must get back down to business," Alyson Brazelton says. She looks pretty nervous up there, sweating. I don't think I've ever heard her speak before, because she never normally engages with us, and I can't help but wonder why Mr. Aleks, the company's artistic director, isn't up here. Why it's been delegated to the assistant director. "The decision has been made for the company to return to its normal schedules and endeavors. All tours will be going ahead as planned. This includes the second-division's performance of *Swan Lake*, and recasts will take place where appropriate."

There's a collective intake of breath, and then heads are turning, looking at… at me.

"This isn't right," Rosella says. She's next to me. "This is not right at all."

Replacing Li Hua. That's what they're doing.

"We will not be letting recent events derail or divert our plans," the assistant director continues. "We will not be letting those people *win*."

I try to open my mouth, try to speak—try to join in with the chorus of cries expressing outrage, because suddenly so many of the dancers around me are standing up, shouting, saying they'll go on strike, that this isn't the best thing to do at the moment—but I'm just sitting here. I can't move. My body's locked up, and it's too heavy. I haven't got the energy to move my arms, my legs.

I can't even speak.

"There is nothing that we can do but let the police do their work," Alyson Brazelton shouts. She's got a microphone now. A hand-held thing. Did she have that earlier?

"We can't pretend like nothing is happening!"

"This is a *professional* company," Alyson says, her voice sharp. "You are all *employees*. This is your work, and as I said, your tours will all be going ahead."

"She's got a point though," a danseur near me says. I look at him. First-division. Short, stocky, famous around here for his abs. "What if Li Hua is never found? We can't just not work because of her."

My left leg shakes. "She will be found," I mutter through gritted teeth, but I'm not even sure if any sound comes out bar a rasping noise that doesn't even sound human. But Li Hua has to be found.

"It is also only right that you all hear this from me," Alyson continues. "We have just had the funding from one of our main investors pulled."

I freeze. Mr. Appleby. He's done it. And I wait for Alyson to say my name. To tell everyone that I'm the reason. I feel sick as I stare at her, as I wait and wait and wait.

And she looks at me. she actually makes eye contact.

"It is therefore imperative that we secure a new investor as soon as possible," Alyson says, "and that we do not let this affect us. We will be carrying on exactly as normal. And I will be in contact with some of you regarding private performances that we can give for new potential investors."

I breathe a sigh of relief and turn. Manuel is glaring at me.

I look away.

It's strange, how quickly it happens—how within hours, the Roseheart staff are acting as if nothing has happened. It really is all back to business. Classes and rehearsals resume, and everything and everyone is just carrying on. I'd thought we'd have more of a police presence here, but I don't even see any officers. I don't see anything untoward at all.

"This is just going to be swept under the carpet again," Rosella says, then she nods more firmly. It's afternoon now, and we're the only ones in the red studio, ready for a class—a class I still can't believe we're expected to take. But I've found myself here, and early too. "And I reckon the police are in on it."

"In on Li Hua's abduction?" I raise my eyebrows. Suddenly, my water bottle seems heavier than it really is, and it takes me by surprise, like I'd forgotten that I always bring a bottle to class. I nearly drop it, so instead I carefully place it down at the side of the room. It's the only thing I've brought with me, and I suddenly realize I've got trainers on rather than my canvas flats. *Fuck.* But the police being in on the abduction? "That's highly unlikely."

Isn't it?

"No—on the cover up." Rosella pulls her phone out of her duffel bag. "Look—" She flashes the screen at me, showing messages with an unsaved number. I peer closer, trying to see what it is and why she's showing it to me. "Graziella Valenzi," she says, a triumphant look on her face that has her smiling widely, revealing the gap between her two front teeth. "She wasn't tricky to track down actually. And unlike Marco and Sofia Valenzi, Graziella was actually willing to talk to me."

"Uh, *what?*" I ask.

Outside, in the corridor, footsteps approach, and a moment later, two more dancers head inside. This barre class is for all the company dancers, regardless of division, and it normally gets pretty busy.

"Allegra's grandmother." Rosella rolls her eyes. "Come on, keep up! She lives in Camden. Got the address, which gave me the phone number too. Spoke to her last night, and she was furious it's happened again."

I take a step back. "What?"

"Is 'what' all you're going to say?" Rosella demands. "Look, it's clear the police aren't going to look too deeply—I mean, if they had, they'd have taken Bella and us all into the station for proper statements last night, rather than just asking Bella to go down at some point today. And they would've called Li Hua's parents."

My stomach drops. "Li Hua's parents haven't been told?" My eyes widen, then they smart. I think of Mr. and Mrs. Zhao—the kindest parents I can think of—and I feel sick. It didn't even occur to me to phone them last night. Why… why didn't I? "They don't know?"

"Don't think so," Rosella says. "I heard one officer say that maybe Li Hua had just got an uber to her family home—somewhere in the midlands. They were going to phone Mr. and Mrs. Zhao to check out that possibility, but—and this is the crucial part—the guy said 'Don't make them worried.'" She gives me a sharp look. "Now don't tell me that's not suspicious? Because they're going to do sods all to find her, I'm sure. And the only explanation I can come up with is that it's because the cops must know who it is. They're covering for them."

I shake my head. "Nah. Detectives and that, they're not that corrupt, are they?"

All Rosella says, as she gives me a knowing look is, "You should watch *Line of Duty*."

It's no surprise I can't concentrate on barre class—or any class or rehearsal today—and the company life all just spins around me. Everything. I try to talk to Rosella more, but she's busy with extra classes or something, and the only time I can catch her again is just before three o'clock, outside her pointe class. Her eyes are wide, and she says again about Graziella Valenzi being suspicious about the cops too.

"Then we should speak to her," I say. "Call her again—no, actually, we'll go there."

Rosella's eyebrows lift up.

"You said she lives in Camden?"

"Well, yeah," she says, twisting her hair back into a bun. The hair-tie snaps, flies across the hallway, hitting the other wall, and Rosella cusses.

"Look, Camden's not far," I say. "We can get a car over there."

"We can't just turn up there," she says. "I mean, she's an old lady. Like, really old. We don't want to scare her. It's one thing to phone her, but another to…" She looks around suddenly, behind her, her eyes wide. "Did you hear someone?"

"What? No," I say, and as soon as I've said the words, she's disappearing into her pointe class, telling me she hasn't got time.

"Okay," I say as the door shuts. "Fine."

I mean, Rosella was the one who was all for making contact with the Valenzi grandmother, right? But I don't need her to execute a plan.

I spend the next hour making calls, writing things down, thinking of all the possibilities—and I put *everything* into it.

I get out one of Li Hua's new notebooks, and I write everything down, meticulously. I use her highlighters to highlight things that seem important, like the dates that she and Allegra were taken, and the phone number and address for Graziella Valenzi which is pretty easy to find online—Rosella was right.

I even phone Graziella. A posh-sounding guy answers the phone but passes it over to Graziella in about thirty seconds. Her voice isn't what I expected it to be—what I expected, I don't know—but it's not a woman with a voice like a canary who perfectly articulates every word as if she's the queen. I'd assumed she'd have an Italian accent, but there's no trace of one to my ears.

"Thank goodness," she says. "Someone finally taking my granddaughter's abduction seriously. I'll tell Peter you are coming," she finishes the call with. "That man is a stickler for appointments. And that nice girl I spoke to last night, she is coming, too, yes?"

"Yep," I say, and the moment the call with Graziella ends, I message Rosella with the details.

I feel better now I've got a plan, like I can breathe a bit, and so I head down to the café to pick up some food. I'm not really hungry, but I can't actually remember if I've eaten today. I select the first thing I see on the counter of the café— a rice pot with a mixed bean salad—and then at the till, I pull out my credit card and tap it on the machine.

"I'm sorry but that declined," says the man.

"Declined?" I frown and try it again, but the same happens. And—*ah*. Mr. Appleby. This is the card linked to the account that he manages. The account for my expenses.

He really is cutting me off.

I let out a big sigh.

"I can get that," says a voice, and I jump and turn. Bella Sotheby stares coolly at me. Her hair is up in a perfect ballerina's bun, but she's not dressed for ballet at all. She's wearing jeans and quite a nice—albeit low-cut—top that has sequins all over it.

"No, it's fine," I say, but she's already reaching across, tapping her own card. The man looks a bit flustered but hands me my receipt and then rings up Bella's items.

"What are you even doing in here?" I ask her. "This is a café for the company. Not the academy."

There are deep bags under her eyes, bags I only notice now that I'm staring right at her, so intently.

"Netty Florence said it was okay to eat in here." She rubs the back of her right hand aggressively, then hugs her salad pot and Sprite to her chest. "It's a nightmare in the school."

"Nightmare?"

"Couldn't even get into the canteen because of the rats trying to talk to me." She looks up at me. "Don't worry though—I'll sit over there. Away from you."

And with that, she heads to the opposite corner where there's a table for one.

"Thanks for my lunch," I call after her, and I sit numbly at the nearest table. Someone else's rubbish—a half-eaten chicken salad sandwich on a tray—is still there, so I push it aside, set my rice pot down. And stare at it, feeling not hungry at all.

I can't believe that man's actually cancelled my card. My stomach twitches, and my throat feels too thick. Then again, he's cut Roseheart's funding already.

I swallow hard.

Have Manuel and Luca heard they've lost their sponsorships too?

Because of me.

More lives ruined, because of me.

I pick the plastic fork up and open the rice pot, mainly because I feel like I should be eating. Not because I'm hungry. But I've got to keep my strength up. I stir the rice and bean mixture, then pull my phone out my pocket. Rosella's replied—good.

But my heart drops as I read her message. *I really don't think we should be going to Graziella's.*

"No, no, no," I mutter. I flex my fingers, then click to call her. She answers on the second ring, and before she has a chance to say anything, I tell her, "We have to go to Graziella. She's our only lead on Li Hua."

"No, I've just been... thinking." Her voice is tinny, and there's a lot of background noise. "And it's not a lead, is it?"

I lean back and my chair creaks. "You were all for this earlier, and then outside your pointe class it was like you were doubting yourself. And now your feet are completely ice-cold. So what's changed?" My voice is blunt.

"Nothing," she says. "I'm just thinking of their family. The Valenzis have been through enough."

"Rosella." My voice is a warning. "I know you and this doesn't sound like you."

There's a grating sound, metal on metal, filling the line for a few seconds, and then a high-pitched ding. Where the hell is she? But before I can ask—or indeed that she is okay—she speaks again. Her voice is low. "Listen. There is someone out there, watching us all. And they know that I've been in contact with Graziella."

My vision glazes over, and I'm suddenly aware of how fast my heart is beating. "What are you talking about?"

"A note," she says, her voice so quiet I barely hear her. "Telling me to stay out of it. Saying…"

I wait for her to say more, but she doesn't. "Rosella?" I check my phone—still connected. "You still there?"

"Yeah," she says, but then the line disconnects.

I try to phone her back, but she doesn't answer. I try again and again.

I let out a long breath, staring across the café at the watercolor canvases on the far wall—just above Bella's head. She's hunched over, staring at her salad pot. Not eating either.

I try Rosella again, then text her. Ask her where she is. She doesn't reply. Should I go and find her? The campus is big, but it's not that big. I could search it.

Standing, I type out a message to her. *Tell the police if someone's threatening you,* I type. *It has to be someone who's involved.*

This is a clue. It has to be. And whoever is involved doesn't want us going to Graziella because Graziella must know something.

And Graziella is expecting me and Rosella to arrive. I think of what the old woman said—how warmly she spoke of Rosella. Me turning up on my own might scare her, but Rosella being there—another woman—would put Graziella at ease.

Still, Rosella's out—I feel that now, for sure. Whoever's behind the abduction has scared her off. But they don't know about me. They can't do. They've not tried to scare me off. And something tells me I need to speak to Graziella as quick as possible, before this mysterious person stops me.

I take a deep breath. Going to visit her with a woman by my side would be better. I just feel that in my gut. But it can't be done now.

In the corner of the room, Bella stands suddenly. She's still not eaten a bite, but she appears to be on her way out.

Bella.

My eyes widen. "Hey, wait!" I call, standing up. The legs of my chair squeak on the tiled floor as I push it backwards. "Bella!"

She flinches a bit, turns, looks like a deer in the headlights—the most unlike her I've ever seen her look. Because Bella's always been confident and brash, loud and enthusiastic about everything.

Still, I guess witnessing an abduction changes that.

"What do you want?" she asks me in a shaking voice, and I'm suddenly so close to her, having barely registered that I was moving.

"I've got a plan," I say, breathless. "And I need your help."

TWENTY-ONE

Bella

My head spins, and I can hardly breathe—that's what it feels like. My ribcage is too tight. Something squeaking and straining inside me with every breath I take as I stare across the table at Mr. Vikas and Madame Cachelle—and the rabbit on the desk.

It's a white rabbit with pink eyes, and I don't understand why it's here. They haven't even introduced it. Just got straight on with the meeting about my addiction problems—a meeting that I thought would've been postponed, given everything. I've already spent the morning at the police station, giving a formal statement, and then I got back and drank some vodka and did two lines while Ava tried to talk to me in the bathroom, and then we tried to get food but there were just so many eyes everywhere, watching me.

Netty Florence came to the rescue, and then I was in the company dancers' café, and then there was Trent.

Oh, Trent. Trent with his big dark eyes and the urgency in his voice, the desperation as he explained. All the while, the artificial lights were blaring down on him, making his skin look more greasy and sweaty than it realistically could be—and then I could almost see myself reflected in his sweat and it was super gross, but still he was talking of this plan.

This plan that he needs me for.

I'd asked him, of course, why he didn't just ask Alessia Valenzi to go with him. She's the obvious choice. But he admitted he'd kind of scared her earlier.

"And Rosella can't help anymore, and honestly, you're probably the best person for it because you're going to have a personal interest in finding out who it is, right? I mean, you witnessed it. You were that close"—he held up his thumb and forefinger so they were an inch apart—"to being taken too. A narrow escape, right? Plus, you owe me," was what he'd said, as he finished his pitch, and I wasn't sure what he meant by me owing him—still am not sure now, as I sit in Madame Cachelle's office, staring across at the rabbit.

Why the hell is a rabbit here? I glance up at Madame Cachelle, and then my eyes slide over to Mr. Vikas. Why aren't either of them acknowledging it?

"I know this is a really tough time," Mr. Vikas says. "But nonetheless, we have rules. And in class yesterday, you were clearly under the influence."

Madame Cachelle's eyes seem to soften, dampen a bit, like she's sad. The rabbit's nose twitches. It looks like a rabbit I saw in a pet shop once—I was, like, seven or eight, and I really wanted it. Mum said no. Bobby bought me a toy one instead for my next birthday.

But this rabbit isn't a toy.

"Do you have anything to say about this situation?" Madame Cachelle asks me, and her eyes look all disappointed now.

A moment passes. I watch the rabbit's nose twitching. It twitches in time to my heartbeat. "No," I say.

"We will have to put you on Report," Mr. Vikas says. "We cannot have students turning up to lessons under the influence of drugs nor drink." He sighs. "Miss Sotheby, I really thought you were doing well."

"This is just the stress of yesterday's events though," Madame Cachelle says, coming to my aid.

"Unfortunately, Miss Sotheby turned up to class, clearly under the influence of illegal substances, *before* Miss Zhao was abducted." Mr. Vikas folds his hands together on the desk—a sudden movement that startles the rabbit.

"Hey, careful," I say, only the moment I say the words, the rabbit disappears. I just blink and it's… gone.

Alarm pulses through me, and my skin tingles. I scratch the back of my hand, then look to the side, look all around the office for the rabbit.

"Bella, are you okay?" Madame Cachelle asks, and I'm nodding, because I will be.

I just need to find the rabbit.

My rabbit.

"We have logged that you're on Report into the system," Mr. Vikas says. "All your teachers and instructors will know, and each of them will be keeping a close eye on you. Should you turn up to any class in a less than expected state, reprimanding actions will be taken."

Reprimanding actions.

Inside my boots, my toes twitch. Twitch like the rabbit's nose. God, where is the rabbit? *God?* Wait, no. I'm not religious. Am I? My head pounds. I... I cannot remember.

Is that weird to not be able to remember that?

Madame Cachelle gives me a sympathetic smile. "We will also be carrying out daily drugs tests for the next two weeks."

Daily drugs tests. I stare at her, at the beautiful red scarf she has on. It's such a pretty color. Brings a warm glow out in her skin. "Okay."

"Okay?" Mr. Vikas says, and they both seem surprised that I've agreed. Though—I frown—what am I agreeing to? Suddenly, it's gone.

"We'll see you tomorrow morning then," Madame Cachelle says. "The tests will be conducted in the nurse's office from now on. Be there at seven o'clock sharp, please."

Seven o'clock sharp, please.

Sharp. Sharp. Sharp. "Sharp," I say.

The two of them say a few more things, and then I'm dismissed, but all the time, all I can think about is the sharpness of things. Knives and needles and lies.

And the rabbit with the twitching nose.

By the time I reach the foyer of my dorm, my phone is ringing and ringing. I'm not sure at which point it started ringing, because my head's all hazy, but I answer it. It's Trent, and he says I'm ten minutes late and where the hell am I?

Trent. The plan. Right.

He—and another dancer, a man who I briefly recognize from the other day—is waiting for me at Roseheart's gates. When I arrive—what feels like seconds later but Trent growls is fifteen minutes later—the other man smiles a bit more sympathetically at me.

"I'm Jaidev," he says in a kind voice, like he knew I'd need a reminder. "Trent told me the plan and I thought it best to come along too. In case there is anyone watching."

"Watching?" I ask.

"It's nothing," Trent says quickly. "Right, can we go now?" he snaps, his gaze zeroing in on me. "Before you bottle it."

I shake my head, even though the thought had crossed my mind, though it got stuck in all the fog in my head. It's not that I don't want to help, but I... I just don't want to go back out through the gates. Yes, that's it. The gates. I stare at them—at how big and foreboding they look now—and the thought of going back out into London, into the rest of the world, makes my stomach flip over several times.

And if someone is watching us, then I shouldn't be going out there. Li Hua was being watched and they took her.

But I've kind of agreed to help Trent. He explained it all earlier, and though my head may be hazy now, I can still kind of think about the plan. I need to be with them for this. Allegra's grandmother is probably going to feel more comfortable if a teen girl turns up. And apparently I do look really young and innocent, as Jaidev says now—earning him a dagger-filled look from Trent.

"We'll play it by ear at the door," Trent tells me and then he's stepping forward through the open gates. "It might be that all three of us can go in and speak to her. But I think we need to gauge how comfortable she is with us when we're there. It's one thing on the phone, another in person."

I nod. Jaidev nods too, doesn't say anything, but he follows Trent out of the grounds. And I? I just wobble. That's what it feels like. My legs wobble and I jab my hands in my pockets, feeling sick.

Just walk through the damn gates!

I take a deep breath and I try—but nothing happens.

"Are you coming?" Trent asks.

I let out a squeak, and somehow manage it.

You're doing well, says the white rabbit—and he's here! He's hopping along next to me. *I'll look after you.*

I glance at the guys, but neither seems to have noticed my new friend.

I smile at the rabbit. *You're mine. Just mine.*

It feels good to have something that's mine.

Trent tries to keep small talk going between the three of us as we get to the nearest Tube station and take the line toward Camden. The two guys talk the whole time. I don't, even when Jaidev asks me questions all I can do is shake my head or nod. I've just got to look after the rabbit.

He's on my lap, and he doesn't like how noisy the tube is. Poor thing, he's so scared. I can feel his little heart pounding.

"Red Deene Manor," Trent says, "should only be a ten-minute walk from the next stop."

"Manor." Jaidev nods. "Sounds posh."

"I think she's pretty rich, this Graziella. She was the chair of some big organization many years ago. I found some records online. She stepped down when Allegra went missing, wasn't really anything else on her after that. But it makes sense she'd own a nice house."

As we get nearer—just three roads away, according to Trent's maps app—I clear my throat. My pace has been slowing, because the rabbit's been slowing—he's tired, though he insisted on walking rather than me carrying him—and I know the guys have noticed it. My slowing pace, that is, not the rabbit. And the rabbit is telling me that what we're going to do is a bad idea.

"Um, I'm not really sure we actually should be doing this," I say, slowly. "I mean, we're just going to upset her. She's an old woman, right?" My words come out all quickly, jumbled up together, and I'm surprised I can get a sentence out as coherently as that. That my brain is apparently working enough for it.

"You'd rather leave Li Hua to whatever it is she's in?" Trent raises his eyebrows. "Some dingy cellar somewhere?"

Jaidev glances at me then exhales, stopping. "Or we could just let the police handle this."

"We're just visiting Graziella. That's all," Trent says, his voice firm.

Jaidev and I exchange a glance, then reluctantly follow him.

"And this should be it just up there," Trent says, tucking his phone into his pocket.

Two minutes later, I stop, staring at the house. "Oh."

It's massive. A detached building with at least thirty windows facing us. The gardens are pretty nicely done—all precise lawns and water features and several winter flowers I can't identify, lining a smooth tarmac pathway to the door. A couple of benches sit nestled in among flowers, and to the right of the house is a greenhouse where a couple of elderly women stand with a young man, potting up some cuttings or something.

Red Deene Manor Residential Home, reads the sign to the right of the garden. I turn to the guys, feel my skin goosefleshing. "This is a care home?" My breaths come in short, sharp bursts. For a second, I think I see my white rabbit, crouching under the sign, but I blink and he's disappeared. Running around maybe? Or hiding? We shouldn't be here. "We can't go in here."

"She's not going to be a resident," Trent says, but even he is frowning a bit. "A resident isn't going to have a care home listed as their address, right? She must own it or something."

I peer closer at the sign. The registered manager's name is listed in a smaller print, but it's not Graziella's.

"Where did you find this address?" Jaidev asks.

Trent shrugs. "Just online."

"*Where?*" My word is sharp.

"She's got a blog. She wrote about moving house in her last entry—only six months ago."

"Can I help you?"

Startled, I look up and see that the young man who was in the greenhouse is now walking briskly toward us.

"Uh, yeah," Trent says. "Is this where Mrs. Valenzi lives?" He looks a bit uncomfortable now.

For a moment, I think the man's going to tell us that Graziella's passed away, and I get a horrible sick feeling in my stomach. This was what my rabbit was warning us about. Oh God, why didn't I take any notice?

"Are you visitors for her?" the young man asks. He doesn't look remorseful, like he's got to be the bearer of bad news. And that's… good, right?

"Yeah, but we've not been here before." Trent shifts his weight to his other foot, glancing at me. "We didn't know if you have, like, visiting times?"

"We generally say that family and friends can visit at any time between 8am and 9pm. If it coincides with a meal time, we can have the care-user have their meal in their room, with you, so you get some privacy with them, if you wish." He glances at his watch. "Graziella has probably just finished her tea though."

"So do we just go in the house then?"

"Yeah. Jenny will be in the lounge. Just make sure you sign the visitor's book."

I feel awkward, standing here, as Trent and the man do all the talking. But apparently it's easy to feign a connection to an elderly person. Trent tells him that he's Graziella's second cousin's grandson, and that both Jaidev and I are related to him.

"We're not normally in the area," he continues. "But as we were, we wondered if we could just come and visit her."

I feel like Trent's talking too much, giving too many details and answers to unasked questions, but he manages to get us past our first potential obstacle, and what seems like seconds later, the three of us are walking up to the big front door of Red Deene Manor.

"I'm still not sure we should be doing this," Jaidev says. I meet his eyes and try to tell him that I'm feeling exactly the same way.

Trent ignores him, just knocks on the door. It takes a moment for it to be answered, and we hear a lot of clicks and beeps first, before it swings open revealing a woman in her mid-forties. She looks stressed, bags hanging under her eyes, but she frowns when she sees us. Before she can speak however, Trent says, "We're here to see Graziella Valenzi? We just spoke to your colleague over there—" He gestures behind us, toward the greenhouse, "and he said we need to find someone called Jenny and to sign in?"

I marvel at how confident he sounds. Not a waver to his voice. Nothing.

She nods and steps to the side. "Visitor's book is over there. Sign in and of course out."

We move past her, and she shuts the door behind us firmly, then presses a red button on a keypad. It bleeps once.

"You've not been here before, have you?" the woman asks.

"No. We're not normally in London—I was just telling your colleague that we're distant relations. My grandmother's Graziella's second cousin, and then Bella and Trent are my cousins, but on the other side of my family."

What? We're all cousins now? Suddenly, I want to laugh.

The woman nods. "Not often Graziella gets visitors. Not since the falling out with her son. Such a shame, that is. Anyway, she's upstairs in her room. The hairdresser's with her.

Room 43. You can wait up there with her. She'll be pleased to have the company."

And apparently, it's as easy as that.

I feel like I'm in a film or a video game or something as the three of us find our way upstairs. We pass elderly residents sitting at tables, playing board games, watching TV, reading books. In one room that we walk through there's a woman demonstrating what I think is a modified version of Pilates for a group of four women standing with Zimmer frames—and of course Pilates makes me think of Li Hua.

Trent pauses outside of Room 43. "Guess we'd better knock." A smooth white door with a sticker on it that says "G. Valenzi" with an illustration of bluebells under it. Inside the room, I can hear voices. These voices stop when Trent raises his fist to the door and knocks loudly.

I wince, glancing at Trent, but he just shrugs.

A moment later, a young woman opens the door. She's holding two pairs of thinning scissors in her hands.

"So sorry to interrupt," Trent says, a perfect smile now on his face. "You must be the hairdresser that, uh, was it Jenny who mentioned you to us?" He looks back at me and I give a small nod, but my neck creaks horribly. "We've just come to see Graziella—do you mind if we come in and see her, while you work?"

The woman turns and calls brightly, "Mrs. Valenzi! Your family's here—you were just saying they were coming!"

My eyes widen. So do Trent's.

"Bless her heart," the hairdresser says to us, then she looks directly at me. "Mrs. Valenzi is always telling me her lovely granddaughter is going to visit, and I must admit, as I'd never seen you here—and I'm here a lot—" she laughs, "I thought it was just one of her fancies. But you really are here. And don't you look like her? You've got the same eyes."

Me? Her granddaughter? My eyes? I feel them widen and—shit, they're too wide again. I'm showing too much sclera. Too much of my irises. Oh God. I narrow them. "Uh, no—I'm not—" I start to say, but the hairdresser takes me by the arm and leads me into the room. I hear Trent and Jaidev following, shutting the door, and I try not to gulp.

"Ah, so you're here after all," a strident and posh voice says, and I look to the end of the room where a very striking woman sits in an armchair. She's holding a mirror, admiring her new hair—a shock of hot pink dances through her white fringe, and when she turns her head, I see the back of her hair is a rainbow of colours. "Come, come!"

She beckons me toward her, and I find myself hurrying toward her, feeling strangely compelled. She's got a wide face, a good bone structure—I can see that clearly, even though her skin is wrinkled. She holds her head carefully. "You don't look Spanish," she says.

"Spanish?" I frown. "I'm not."

"You sounded Spanish on the phone."

"Rosella, uh, couldn't come," Trent says quickly. "But Bella, here, is just as keen to find out what happened to your granddaughter, and the latest dancer too. Bella was there when Li Hua was taken."

Graziella breathes out slowly. "Ten years. They promised they'd do it, you know?"

"Promised what?" I ask.

She turns to look at me, then focuses on Jaidev and frowns. "I know your face," she says. "Paris Ballet Company?"

He nods. "I'm in Roseheart's company now."

"Well, you'd better sit down, the three of you," Graziella says, and she gestures toward her bed at the side of the room. There are no other chairs available—and I don't think any of us want to take her armchair—so we perch on the edge of the bed, the three of us pressed together so tightly that our shoulders and arms are touching. I'm just relieved I'm on Jaidev's side, that Trent's not in the middle. That I don't have to touch him.

"How much do you know?" Graziella asks, tilting her head slightly to one side. "About Allegra?"

"Not a lot," Trent says. "There's just not that much info. Even online. And I know that Li Hua knew more—she was researching it all. Reading everything. And she had all these notebooks, but I can't find some of them now. Only found one of them, in fact. But that doesn't say a lot in it."

Graziella nods slowly. "Anyone know you're here?"

"No," Trent says, just as Jaidev shakes his head.

I'm about to say 'the rabbit does' when I think better of it.

"Well, they will do," Graziella says. "It's the investors."

"I knew it," Trent hisses suddenly. "Mr. Appleby, yeah?"

Graziella's eyes look like glass for a moment. "A group of them." Her voice is slow. "If they are the ones behind the latest abduction, they'll be watching you all."

I shudder. I knew it. I knew it. I knew it.

"I can only tell you what I know," Graziella says. "And that is my granddaughter, Allegra. She'd only just started at Roseheart, of course. But she was investigating the investors. I don't know all the details as I haven't got the case notes— and of course the police were quick to hide or destroy those, whatever it was. Either they were in on it themselves or they were worried about it all being blown open."

"Blown open?" Trent says.

"Of course, they've got to protect undercover operations," Graziella says. "I understand that. That makes sense. Even if it means not looking after their own. And Allegra, my Allegra, she had not been undercover for long either."

My head spins, and I can't take in what this woman's saying. My breaths are too noisy, and I try to distract myself from *me*, look around the room. Is my white rabbit here again?

"Are you saying Allegra was working *with* the cops?" Jaidev's voice drifts toward me, and I turn to look at him. How he's leaning forward, his elbows on his knees as he stares intently at the old woman.

"Working with them?" Graziella laughs, and her laugh grates through me—like it's got jagged little barbs, raking through my skin. "She *was* one. My granddaughter was undercover in this whole operation. They were trying to bring down the investors, but all they did was bring down Allegra."

TWENTY-TWO

"Allegra was a police officer?" A bad taste spreads across the roof of my mouth, and I glance at Jaidev. He's all wide-eyed as he turns to look at me.

Bella is still staring right at Graziella, but her gaze looks unfocused. She doesn't seem to have reacted to this revelation at all.

Graziella clears her throat, noisily. "She was the only policewoman with any ballet training, so of course they chose her." She points at the wall behind me and I turn to look. There's a noticeboard up there, one of the old-fashioned cork and pin ones, and about two-dozen photographs have been pinned up. All of them show the same person: a girl in her late teens, very pale skin and hair, light eyes. She looks happy in all the photos, smiling away.

Even in the one where she's wearing a police uniform.

"But Allegra was seventeen," I say. My head spins. "That's not old enough."

"The records at Roseheart *said* she was seventeen, yes," Graziella says. "But she was twenty-five that year."

"Twenty-five?" I blurt out.

"She had a baby face so could pass for a teenager. She told me that it made sense that she was the one chosen for that work. And I was the only one she told." She pauses. "Not even her parents."

"Why?" My word is sharp.

A look of sadness crosses Graziella's face and she pauses for a long moment, looking at her lap. When she does raise her gaze, her eyes are troubled. "The last time I saw her, she told me it was getting difficult. She thought that the person she was spying on—or whatever word she used—was onto her. The next day, she was missing, along with two other dancers. Then the dancers are found, tortured, but not my Allegra. No, they found out she was a policewoman. I'm sure. They murdered her. And I would say it is pretty obvious who was behind it."

"An investor." I think of Mr. Appleby, last night. His slippers. His orange dressing gown. That slow-spreading smile. That voice. I want to rip his head off. Behead him, like the old days.

"Why is none of this info available online?" Jaidev asks, leaning forward so his shoulder is no longer against mine.

I glance again at Bella, on the other side of him, but she's so rigid. Listening? Or—*fuck*. I clock the glazed look in her eyes. I know that look.

"The police shut it down, shut down any investigation," Graziella says. Her voice catches a bit. "I thought at first it probably was just because they had another person undercover too. That they had to keep a lid on it all to protect them. I was waiting for the big exposé to happen—I kept watching the news, trying to even keep tabs on all the investors for the school myself, though I did not know, still do not know, which investor it is that my Allegra was investigating, or why." She takes a deep breath. "But they knew that I was trying to find out info."

"*They?*" Bella asks suddenly. Her voice is shrill. "Rabbits? There's more than one of them?" She sways slightly, tilting her head from one side to another.

"The rabbits?" Graziella says, with a dark, bitter laugh. "Is that what they call themselves? Well, whichever one it is, I've had letters from them."

"Letters, where?" I jump up—can't sit still anymore—then look around, as if expecting to see these letters on the bedside table or something.

"I haven't got any of them *here*," she says. "But they'll know that I'm here."

"What did the letters say?" Jaidev asks.

"They were warnings. Threats."

Just like Li Hua received. And Rosella. My heart pounds, and I know that as soon as we leave here, I need to find her. I need to see this warning she received with my own eyes. It's got to give a clue or something.

"And that's all I know," Graziella says.

I watch her carefully for a moment. "Okay. Thank you. You've been very helpful." I wince at how formal I sound. Like I'm a cop. Not the distraught boyfriend of the investor's latest victim.

Mr. Appleby's victim.

I've got to go back to his house. Have to. He's got Li Hua in there somewhere.

We leave Graziella in her room with her coffee. My heart pounds so hard as we traipse back downstairs. I glance at Jaidev, and I know he wants to talk about this too—but we just have to wait until we get outside. Bella's just ambling along now, mumbling slightly. I can't believe she came here high.

But a cop? Allegra was an undercover *cop*? She was investigating an investor, and then she was killed. And Li Hua was investigating Allegra's disappearance. My head spins. Li Hua must have found out something. And she was already on their radar, being followed by someone. And that someone took her.

And that someone may now be onto us. I look at Bella and Jaidev, wondering if I've just put them in danger.

"Ah, I don't think we've met," a voice suddenly says, and I look up to see a woman with a blond pixie cut. She's in her late twenties and she smiles brightly—but she's talking to Bella.

Bella's stopped, a slightly panicked look frozen onto her face.

"Felicity Chambers," she says. "I'm the manager. I heard you're one of the granddaughters Graziella is always talking about? Aw, she is a lovely lady, isn't she? Such a shame she's got dementia. You can tell she used to be a writer though. Crime fiction. The things she comes out with! Honestly, you'd think we were living in a novel half the time!"

Crime fiction.

Dementia.

The things she comes up with!

Outside, I let out a massive exhale of breath, watch my breath fog white in the air. Then I look at Jaidev. He's shaking his head.

"She's got dementia," he says, his voice flat. "Can we believe any of that? Police and investors and…"

I shake my head. "Allegra *can't* have been an undercover police officer. She just can't have been." I groan. Coming here has been a waste of time. I should've just gone back to Mr. Appleby's. Broken into his house, looked for my girlfriend myself. Or I should've tried to find Rosella, check that she really is okay, and see the note she's received.

"Okay," Bella says. "But what if Graziella was right? There's a photo of Allegra in a police uniform."

"What?" I turn on her. "Anyone can buy those. She could've had it for a party or something."

Bella's eyes have lit up, and she's waving her hands excitedly—a complete change in demeanor from when we were inside the care home. "Okay, but hold on. Hold on! So, say she wasn't a cop, it doesn't mean she wasn't suspicious of the investors. She could've been. She could've told her grandmother. That part of the story could've been true. So, we need to find out which investor Allegra was looking into."

"It's got to be the Appleby Firm," I say.

"The Appleby Firm?" Jaidev frowns. "Isn't that your guy?"

"He was," I say, then I take a deep breath and I tell them how I went around to his house, before Li Hua was taken, how I told him I wanted to leave ballet, but he threatened her to make me stay. The words just all pour out of me, so quickly—like they all have to come now, or not at all. Because I can't believe I've just admitted to them that I'm not a serious dancer.

Bella's pupils are so wide now that I can barely see the blue of her irises. "We should go to his house."

"I tried—last night," I say. "Manuel went with me. All that happened was I ticked him off and he withdrew his funding from me and Manuel and Luca. Oh and the whole company and academy, I think too. Just to top it all off, you know?" I shake my head.

"Have you told the police?" Jaidev asks. "About any of this?"

"Not yet. But I've got to go down there. They want to speak to me, later today actually."

"Don't," Bella says suddenly. Her eyes spark and suddenly there's so much life in her. She throws her arms about, animatedly. "Don't tell them about this—the police are linked to at least one investor." Her words tumble out and she swipes at the back of her neck, then scratches harder. When she turns her head to look at Jaidev, exposing the back of her neck, I see four angry red marks—just made by her nails. "One of the arts groups that sponsors us, they came in last year and I found out one of them was a serving police officer."

"Well, which one?" I ask. "Which arts group?"

"I'm not sure," she says. "But, if any of this is true, that Allegra and Li Hua were both taken because they'd found out something about the investors, then the police might still just cover it up. It's all…all corrupt."

"Hold on," Jaidev says. "Bella, you just said that you found out that one of the arts group was in the police, like it wasn't information freely given?"

"It wasn't," she said. "I only knew because Mattie told me."

"Mattie?"

"Technical assistant in the company." She waves her hands at me. "I had to move some of my stash pretty quickly. But that's not the point—I mean, it is. But this means that the dodgy investor is being protected by the police. And we know that someone paid a lot to keep the police from investigating Allegra's disappearance, right? And keeping it all out of the media to stop Roseheart's reputation being ruined. So it could make sense. Maybe it wasn't just Roseheart's reputation they were protecting but themselves too—the investor's reputation, and the police were happy to comply. To help. But this also means that the dodgy investor is the same one as ten years ago. They're still active, still supporting Roseheart, which means we can look at the records, see who was sponsoring dancers then and if there are any that are the same now."

I turn over her words in my mind, knowing that if she's right, this rules out Mr. Appleby. He's only been investing in Roseheart for seven years.

"Roseheart's got investor files in the archives at the back of the library," I say. I know because when Mr. Appleby reached out to me, I made sure to research him. Everything in that file in the archives was positive. Nothing like what he's really like.

But it's a start.

It's a place to go next. And Rosella, well, I'll go to her after.

"Eight investors." I breathe out hard, looking between the lists. "Eight of them are the same as ten years ago. Stella F. Anderson, Barton and Trayner, Sheryl Courtier Ltd, Fibonacci and Rio, The Marigold Arts Company, Stars for the

Arts, Footsteps on the Moon, and Zarrow-Walker. That arts company, is that the one that's got the police officer in it?"

On the other side of the table, Bella's frowning. "I don't know. I don't recognize any of these names. I can ask Mattie? I can text him now."

I nod. "Yeah. Do that." I look at Jaidev, where he's on one of the library computers, just to my left. "And we can find addresses for all of these investors. Right?"

He's scrolling down a webpage already. "Most of them just have corporate offices," he says.

"We have to research them all," I say. "And I need to find where Li Hua's hidden her notebooks." Suddenly, it makes sense now why I couldn't find them. Li Hua was suspicious that she was going to be a target too, and so she hid them.

"Her notebooks?" Bella asks. "Where?"

"Somewhere safe," I say. "Has to be. But they'll be in our apartment, somewhere. I just need to find them."

"I can help," Jaidev says.

"Me too," says Bella.

"No." I rest my gaze briefly on her. "It's probably best that you're not in our apartment. That's mine and Li Hua's space. But somewhere, she's got to have written down the name of the investor, right? Then we'll know whose house we need to search. Right, Jaidev, if you and I go to my apartment now. Bella, you stay here and finish getting the addresses for each one. Text me when Mattie replies to you, and I'll text you if we find Li Hua's notes."

Over the next couple of hours, Jaidev and I pretty much tear apart everything in my apartment. We take every book out of the bookcases, flipping through each volume for any notes that may have been slid in. We take drawers out of the cabinets, searching through everything—contracts with Roseheart, letters to Li Hua from her grandparents in China, phone bills. I turn back the edges of the carpet in the bedroom that have always been a little loose, looking to see if there's a hiding space. We look under the cushions of the sofa, under the fridge, behind the wardrobe, but we find nothing.

"Either she's hidden this really well," Jaidev says, "or someone—the investor, if it is them—has been in here and taken them."

Someone traipsing in here, looking? The hairs on the back of my neck rise. "No, I…" But I don't know. Could that have happened?

"Where was the notebook that you have got?" Jaidev asks.

"Under her pillow," I say. "That's where she always kept her current one. The one she was writing in."

"And where were the rest of her notebooks, before she was taken?"

I point at the bookcase. The top shelf that's empty. "Up there."

"So, not hidden away." Jaidev shakes his head. "I reckon someone's been in and taken them then. Oh, look Bella's messaged." He holds my phone suddenly, which I'd left on the carpet.

I peer at the screen. *Mattie says it was the Royal Fine Arts Company, but I've just checked and they've only been sponsoring us for the last two years.*

I breathe out hard. So that rules out that one. It's got to be someone who was here ten years ago too. Right?

Unless this is a copycat? But no, that doesn't make sense. Not when Li Hua was taken because she was researching the old case.

Unless she wasn't taken because of that?

Could she have just been in the wrong place at the wrong time?

"Okay, let's go and talk to Rosella," I say. "Li Hua's notebooks clearly aren't here. And Rosella's being watched, presumably like Graziella is or was. So she's our next port of call." I look to Jaidev. "You in?"

He nods. "Of course. She'll probably be at the gym now. She and Taryn have started going together."

We head over there. The company has its own gym and leisure facilities on campus that every dancer is allowed to use as much as they want—or as little as we want, because I don't like gyms. I much prefer running outside, rather than on a treadmill. I only go there a couple of times a month for the weights. Generally, we all have our own routines, our own times that we train. It makes us predictable.

Predictable.

I turn that word over. Li Hua always went to her private Pilates class at the same time each week. Was her predictability there a factor in her abduction?

We arrive at the gym, scanning ourselves in with our passes. It's pretty busy at the moment, with figures at almost every station. I scan around the room for Rosella, but I don't see her.

"Taryn's over there," Jaidev says, pointing at the bench press machine. "Hey, Taryn!"

We walk over to her quickly, and Taryn pauses, looking up at us. She's Jaidev's dance partner, and right now she's wearing a tank top and leggings that show off her figure. She's one of the curviest of the ballerinas and when she and Jaidev joined there was a lot of talk among the straight guys about how lucky Jaidev was. Then she came out as asexual to everyone, mainly thanks to being outed, and some of the chat turned pretty disgusting. Things like 'I bet I could fix her.' I don't know if Taryn ever found out about those things that were said, but Jaidev shut them down so quickly. Half the time, I'm convinced he's in love with her, but he insists they're only very good friends. I don't think there's anything 'only' about what they've become though, in the two years since they joined the company.

"Where's Rosella?" I ask her.

"Oh, she'll be at the airport by now." Taryn sits up and reaches for her water bottle.

"The airport?" I stare at her, feel my gaze start to glass over. I blink rapidly. "What? Why?"

"She's taking a few days off," Taryn says. "Before the rehearsals ramp up ready for the next tour."

"Since when?" A slimy sensation fills my stomach and I wonder if I'm going to be sick. *She's been scared off.*

"I think it was a last-minute thing," Taryn says. "She only told me a couple of hours ago."

I pull my phone out and call her. As I count the rings, Taryn asks what's happening, but Jaidev says it's nothing. He pulls me away, calling to Taryn that he'll catch her later for training, and then he's guiding me out the gym, while I am still listening to the line ringing. At last, it clicks off. No answerphone.

"We need to see the note that she has, from the abductors." My chest rises and falls too quickly. "It's the only lead we've got." I pull a hand through my hair, feeling the buildup of grease. With my other hand, I shove my phone back into my pocket. "She has one of the single apartments, doesn't she? We just need to get a key. She might've left the note behind?"

Jaidev sighs. "Housekeeping aren't going to give us a key."

"They will if we tell them what's going on. Rosella's been scared off."

"They'll call the police," Jaidev says. "And maybe that isn't a bad thing."

But I shake my head. "If the abductors, whoever they are, are warning Rosella off like this, then I bet they know that we're onto them. They'll know that you and Bella came with me to visit Graziella. They could be watching us all. And if we go to the police about this, they're going to *know*."

Jaidev's lips set into a thin line. "Okay," he says finally. "But we need to be really careful. We don't know what they're capable of."

"Only we do," I say. "They killed Allegra Valenzi. They tortured those two other dancers. We know exactly what they're capable of."

"No ransom's been sent though, nothing's been paid. It's not like last time." Jaidev frowns.

"Not yet," I say. "Not yet."

TWENTY-THREE

"I can't believe you never told me this before," Francesca says as we head into Madame Jurgensen's room. We were both early, and we met outside in the corridor. I still do not know how she got me to talk about all this—but she has.

I drop my bag down at my desk. We are the only two in here so far—even Madame Jurgensen's not here yet. "There is not really a lot to tell."

"Um, I think there is? You're worried about a guy who used to be your friend, years ago?" Francesca's eyes sparkle. "All because some guy creeped you out in the park?"

"Yeah," I say. I am still surprised I have shared this much with her, to be honest. I look at Francesca, think about how she genuinely seems interested in me. Maybe this is what it is like to have a proper friend again. A best friend.

"I've tried to find Darius on socials," I tell her, "but there's nothing."

"But you think he'll still be at that flat?" She frowns. "I mean, it's a long shot, isn't it?"

I shrug. "Don't know really."

I have not been able to shake the nagging feeling that something is wrong. Really wrong. Maybe it's just the atmosphere here, because things at Roseheart have been unsettled and not at all calm since Li Hua's abduction. But what if that man was Darius's roommate, and maybe Darius is in trouble?

"Want me to come with you?" Francesca asks.

Do I want a friend with me on the Tube there, walking with me on roads that are going to seem dangerous and scary? Of course I do. But I also don't want to have to rely on people. "I'll be fine," I say. I mean, I still have not exactly worked out how I am going to get out there to do this anyway. Deborah is still picking me up in her Bentley, under Mother's orders. And there is no way I am asking her to drive me there.

"Okay." Francesca shrugs, and at that moment, Madame Jurgensen enters the room.

Of course, she ignores me. Since that first fateful lesson, I have kept my head down, trying to be a good student who is seen and not heard, and she has pretty much pretended I am not here. Francesca's right though—it is because I was a dancer. I have been watching Madame Jurgensen and although I am the only ex-dancer in this class, it is interesting seeing how she interacts with the other teachers. How she stays well clear of Madame Cachelle and the other ballet teachers, only sitting with non-dancers at lunch.

"Okay, turn to page twelve in your textbooks and read the two paragraphs at the top of the page," Madame Jurgensen instructs.

Page twelve is full of information I already know so I let my mind drift, wondering whether I really am being sensible with what I am planning for as soon as this class has finished. Because me going to Darius's address, it is a good idea, right?

I have got to find out what he wants me to remember.

The Tube rattles from side to side on the Northern Line, feeling even more shaky and precarious than normal. I texted Deborah and told her that there was an unexpected evening class at Roseheart and that she shall not be needed to ferry me back until nine. That should give me plenty of time.

There are not many other people in my carriage, just some college kids and two women with small toddlers.

"I am safe," I whisper, and I want to shut my eyes—only I know doing so is stupid. So, I try to distract myself. I hunch in my seat a little, knowing it is terrible for my posture—not that that matters anymore.

"The next stop is High Barnet Tube station, where this train terminates."

I stand up, grabbing my tote bag. Everyone else begins to stir too, getting ready. And now I realize what I am doing—how silly it might even be, walking around a part of London I am not even that familiar with, trying to find the flat that I do not even know whether Darius still lives at.

The last time I saw him was at this flat in Chipping Barnet. I was twelve or thirteen. He had run away from home—or been kicked out, I am not sure—but he was rooming with two other guys and a woman, all of whom I suspected had addiction problems. They were all so jittery, so angry. And thin—the woman was gaunt, her bones protruding through paper-thin skin. I remember staring at her, how the nodules of her spine stuck through her tight cami top when she bent forward to grab the mangy cat from the floor. Her spine was like a series of water droplets.

Darius asked me for more money then. Of course he did.

The roommates asked for it too.

"I am so sorry," I said. "I have not got any."

It was the truth, but they did not believe it. For a moment, I had thought I would not get out of there. All four of them blocking my exit. But I whispered I was sorry, and then Darius nodded.

I slipped out, and I remember thinking then that I would not ever be coming back. That my friendship with Darius was over. It had to stop. He just... he was not the same person any more.

I wonder if the flat will still smell of sadness.

That is what I think it smelled like, before, in my memory.

I walk slowly, under weak amber lights of the streetlamps, two of them flickering. Two have already gone off.

I pass a group of teenagers standing in tracksuits, smoking. One of them shouts something at me, but I force myself not to react. To remain calm. My hands are clenched into fists in my pockets, and in my right hand, my keys protrude from the gaps between my fingers.

The teens do not come after me, and I walk quickly. My phone vibrates, and I check it quickly. A message from Tiger, on WhatsApp, asking if I am okay. I have not been as active on the WhatsApp group recently. Or at all really.

I leave her message on read, will reply later. Maybe when I am back on the Tube.

I turn left, then right. My memory is usually good, but now that I am here, faced with finding a flat I was last in over two years ago, I am unsure. Is it that way? I pause.

"All right, love?" a woman with curly gray hair and missing front teeth asks me.

"Uh, looking for Old Court Terrace?" That was the name of his block, right?

The woman eyes me up and down, and for a moment I think she is going to ask for money in exchange for helping me, but she does not. "Down there," she says. "Two rights, then a left. Go under the bridge, and turn right after, by the chippy."

I thank her and her gaze lingers on me, but she nods, then shuffles on, pulling a holdall behind her. My heart pounds as I follow her directions, wondering if maybe I should not even be here.

But that man in the park. I try to recall whether he could've been one of the roommates I met before, but I did not really see enough of him. I do not really remember the roommates either. All I recall is how skinny they were.

But he told me Darius needs me.

I get to the chippy, and turn right. Blue lights are flashing down the road. Two cop cars. It makes me pause for a moment, linger, but then I press on. Cannot see anything anyway. But I do recognize the roads now. And… and the whole of Darius's block of flats has been taped off with blue-and-white police tape.

I flex my fingers, my key dropping into my hoodie's pocket. My movements are small, a little wooden, but I am still walking. Closer and closer.

Darius?

An officer sees me coming, and for a moment, I do not know whether to make eye contact or not. But I am still moving, toward him, toward the block—and I feel it. Feel it deep in my bones now. Something has happened to Darius.

"Miss, this is a crime scene." A white policeman reaches out to physically stop me, and I recoil back.

"But I'm just here to see my friend." My voice wobbles. "Darius. Is he… is he okay?"

"Darius Longbourne?" the copper asks. He has got a bristly, red moustache and a couple of his hairs turn inward, scratch against his front teeth as he speaks.

I nod, then a bad taste starts to spread across the back of my mouth.

But before I can say or do anything else, the policeman is pressing a button on his radio. "Ma'am, we've got a friend of Darius Longbourne out here. Miss…" He looks toward me.

"Valenzi" I say. "Alessia Valenzi."

I wait for his eyes to widen in recognition at my name, but if he knows of me, he doesn't let on. "Miss Valenzi. If you leave your details with my partner, then we can contact you in the morning once we know more." He points toward the nearest police car. Its engine is off but its lights are still flashing. I can just about make out a figure sitting inside.

"Is Darius okay?" My voice trembles, and suddenly I am picturing it all: Darius, dead, in the flat. An overdose. Or, I do not know, a gunshot wound. He has got in serious trouble, pissed off the wrong people, stolen money—I don't know.

But all I know is it is too late.

I am too late.

Darius needs you to remember.

"There's just been a very serious incident," is all the policeman says as he leads me to the car.

TWENTY-FOUR

Bella

Numb, head ringing, I find myself in the studio the next morning, after doing the mandatory drug test—which I failed—trying to run through combinations, practice choreography, do anything to distract myself. Reporters are now swarming Roseheart's gates, TikTok investigators are ramping up the public's interest in Li Hua's abduction, and everywhere I look, she's there. Her name, her photos: *her*. There was a heartbreaking broadcast on TV this morning from her parents, expressing shock and anger over her abduction and how the police hadn't told them right away.

As I watched her father say this, I felt like he was looking directly at me. Why didn't I tell him?

I only have to close my eyes, and I'm back there. On that street, watching her be taken.

Letting her be taken.

I didn't do a fucking thing.

My mum always says that guilt is the most powerful emotion. It's the one that can change the way you think and feel about everything. It can make you do things you wouldn't normally, and it can make you so sleep-deprived that you can't think because it's just hanging over you.

I feel guilty about Li Hua. I know that.

But I couldn't have stopped her abduction. Ava said that to me this morning. She saw the news report too. She begged me to agree with her. To believe that there was nothing I could've done. But it doesn't change how I feel.

When it becomes obvious I can't lose myself in ballet the way I normally do, I ring my mum, putting my phone on speaker as I untie my pointe shoes, the need to talk to her so strong, but it just goes to her voicemail. Of course, it's early. Still 7am. And a Saturday. She'll have only got in from her shift at the hospital in the early hours.

I don't leave a message. I don't want to worry her. But I know I have got to tell her that I witnessed this whole thing. At some point, my name's going to be out there too, as the witness. I don't want her to think I'm keeping secrets from her. Not any more secrets than usual, anyway.

I stare at the barre, running through the order of things in Miss Potts's class, and then persuade myself to try again with the ballet. I retie my shoes.

I work on my stability and strength, trying to improve my core. A muscle in the corner of my right eye twitches a little every time I look in the mirror, but I think I'm making good progress.

Have to be, right?

"Right." I repeat the word several times, over and over, in time with my pliés. But then I feel a bit unsymmetrical, so I start saying, "Left," instead.

Left. Left. Left. Right. Right. Right. Not that it has any bearing on the movements I'm doing. Oh damn. Maybe it should have. A proper dancer would make it have bearance. Bearance—is that a word?

"Hey."

I turn at Ava's voice. She's standing in the doorway, and I wonder how long she's been there. I hadn't heard her. Then again, I was just concentrating on my movements and saying *right* and *left*.

"Okay if I come in?" She's already making her way toward me though, so it's not really a question, is it? She stops in front of me and tilts her head slightly to one side. Classic worried Ava look. "Bells, I'm worried about you."

"I'm fine."

"Are you? Because this has shaken me up, so I hate to think what it's done to you. And, well…" She looks down at her hands. Which are fidgeting a lot.

"What?" I ask. "What is it?"

"I'm wondering if you've got PTSD." She keeps her voice so calm, so level. "And I think you might need help."

"Help?" I sit down abruptly—on the hard floor. Pain snakes up my spine. My butt feels numb.

"I've thought it for a while. You just…."

Ava's still talking but now I crawl along the floor—crawling suddenly seems like the most efficient way of moving—and I grab my bag. Pull my phone out. Ring Trent. I need to talk to him. This is what I should've done earlier—and I don't know why I didn't. We need to work out what we're going to do next.

The line rings and rings and rings.

He doesn't answer.

"Bella, uh, why don't you come to the cinema with me and Stacia later?"

I shake my head, my mind so busy all of a sudden with all the things that Trent and Jaidev and I are going to need to do. The guys didn't find Li Hua's notebooks, so they have been taken. I'm sure of that. And the person who has taken them might know about the three of us investigating this.

We need to stick together. We have to.

"I've got plans," I say, and I keep saying the words over and over until Ava finally leaves.

Trent doesn't answer his phone during the next hour that I ring it. I haven't got Jaidev's number, but I find him on socials, add him. I wander around the company's part of campus, hoping to bump into either of them, but I don't. So,

I do two lines of coke in my bathroom, then realize I'm nearly out of it.

Damn. Damn. Damn.

So, I find myself walking that familiar route, down to Mac's place. A route I've never taken in the light before—and it kind of looks different. The same, but different. "Uncanny valley," I mutter, only it's not really uncanny valley, so I'm not sure why I say that.

I get to Mac's doorway, but it's shut. His door's always been open when I've gone before. Maybe he only opens it when he's got customers coming. And now, even though I have this urge to speak to him, to go inside there and buy more gear, just because it's my normality, I know I can't intrude. His door's shut. I haven't got an appointment.

So I just keep walking. Not back to Roseheart, but farther on. My feet seem to know where they're going, and so I walk for a while, until my heels are aching and the bunion on my right foot seems to be bleeding again.

I pause, sitting on a bench, and look up at the sky—and would you believe it but those clouds kind of look like Mac's silhouette. I've never really gotten a good look at him, but he has pretty springy, curly hair. Pretty like Mattie's hair actually. Huh. Fancy that. Two boys with perfect curls.

Two men whose lives couldn't be farther apart, even if they were brothers. Brothers—could they be?

Nah. I let out a laugh. "The same hair does not a family make." And I don't even know why I say that, why I say it out loud so that the people around me are suddenly looking at me. But it makes me laugh. Makes me laugh a lot.

And I'm laughing and laughing, until I'm crying and crying, completely lost.

TWENTY-FIVE

It is later than I intended to arrive at the police station, but Mother and Father know my timetable. Father dropped me off at Roseheart this time, and Madame Jurgensen then saw me arriving, so of course I had to do her lesson. Francesca was absent—ill, apparently—but at last the lesson was over and I was able to get out and walk to the nearest police station, following directions on my phone.

I tell them that I am here to find out if Darius Longbourne is okay, and the officer on the desk looks vague. I tell him there was an incident in Chipping Barnet last night, and I do not know if he is okay. I ask if he can phone the station over that way. For a moment, I do not think that this officer will, but he shrugs, nods.

I take a seat and wait. A minute later, the policeman comes up to me and says that the investigating officer of that case is wanting to speak with me.

Oh goodness. No. He's dead.

I feel it.

Darius is dead.

The policeman shows me to an interview room, on the second floor of the police station. It's so cold, clinical. Just a table and two chairs. The walls are an eggshell blue, but the texture looks rough, like if I was to drag the back of my hand across it, it would come away bleeding.

My shoulders tighten, and the roof of my mouth is suddenly too dry.

"Detective Matthews shouldn't be long," the man who showed me here says. "Just wait here."

He smiles but it is a professional smile that does not reach his eyes, then asks if I would like any water. I shake my head, and he leaves.

And I try not to think. Try not to remember.

"It's not going to be like before," I whisper to myself, as I look around the interview room again.

Before. Allegra. The tortured girls.

It's not long before the door opens, and a man steps inside. He looks a bit scruffy, his shirt untucked on one side, and his tie at an angle. His face is beet-red and his forehead has collected an astonishing amount of sweat.

"Is Darius okay?" I ask.

"We have arrested Mr. Darius Longbourne on charges of producing, supplying, and possessing with intent to supply Class A substances to minors."

I stare at the officer, unable to actually contemplate what he is saying. Darius—a drug dealer? I almost want to laugh. That is not him. Except I… I do not know him anymore.

"Can I ask why you were visiting Mr. Longbourne's flat yesterday evening?" the officer asks me. "You are of course here voluntarily and not under caution, but I'm just trying to understand what Mr. Longbourne's social group looks like."

"He… he's just a friend," I say.

"A friend who gets you gear?"

"No," I say. "I… I do not do drugs or anything."

He folds his arms. "Look, Miss Valenzi, I know you're at Roseheart, and I know the kinds of things that go on in that place. So when I'm asking why you went to Mr. Longbourne's flat, I want the truth."

The hairs on the back of my neck rise, but I look him right in the eye. "I do not do drugs. I have never touched them. Ever. I would not!"

"Too high and mighty for all that, are you?" He leans back in his seat. The chair creaks. "Let's just say I've got a lot of experience, dealing with druggies." He spits the last word like it's contagious, like he needs to get it out of his mouth as quickly as possible. "And I know what druggies look like. Their body type."

I hold my head high and grit my teeth. "I do not do drugs."

"You wouldn't be the first dancer to need a little…help."

"I am *not* a dancer." I keep my breathing even, low. "And like I said, I do not do drugs."

"Then why were you visiting Mr. Longbourne's flat?"

"He's a friend. Was a friend. We went to school together, but I have not seen him in a couple of years." I fidget a little.

"So why go and visit now?"

"I… I bumped into someone who knew him," I say. "At the park. A couple of nights ago." Immediately, I wince, wondering if this is going to get back to the officers I spoke with at our apartment—officers who I failed to mention the man to.

"What park?"

I describe the location, and then of course he asks me about the man I saw. I take a deep breath. "I don't really know who he was, but he knew me—knew my name. And he said Darius needed me to remember." As I speak, I wonder if I am saying too much, sending Darius in deeper. Because whatever happened last night with Darius, then the man with the scars who spoke to me, he must have been aware of it. He came to find me—knowing I would be in that park?

"What did he need you to remember?" the detective asks.

"I do not know—that is why I was going there, to see him."

He frowns. "So, let me get this right? A man who you've never met before surprises you in the park and says that Darius—a man you've not seen in a couple of years—needs you to remember something. You don't know what this thing is, or what it means, so you get the Tube over to Barnet to go and see him?"

I nod.

"You see, Miss Valenzi, I don't buy it. Do you want to know why? Because why would you drop everything and go there at that time to see a man you've not seen in a long time? It just doesn't make sense."

"But we were best friends!" I cry.

"But not for the last couple of years."

"I thought he might be in trouble." And that is the truth. But I don't know how I can get this policeman to believe me because when he says it like that, it does sound unlikely. Like I'm hiding something. Even though I'm not.

"Do you want to know what I'm thinking, Miss Valenzi?" He doesn't give me a chance to answer, but just leans forward, meeting my gaze with his steely-gray eyes. "I think this mysterious sentence of 'Darius wants you to remember'—if that even *was* the sentence that was said—was a code. A phrase that has an entirely different meaning for someone in the drug ring." He looks at me expectantly. "Care to translate it for us?"

"I'm not in their drug ring!" I cry. "I'm not in any drug ring."

He makes a considering sound deep at the back of his throat. "Let's hope you're not hiding anything or trying to protect Mr. Longbourne," the detective says. "Because two of the children he supplied Class A drugs to are currently in hospital, fighting for their lives. One has had a heart attack, the other a stroke. And let me tell you, it's not looking good at all."

Children? Children are involved in this?

Oh, God. Darius, what have you been doing?

"And we're going to crack the whole drugs ring—and if that includes you, Miss Valenzi, well, let's just say I won't be as lenient with you if I have to interview you a second time."

TWENTY-SIX

Bella

It's dark when I get back to Roseheart. My feet are bleeding. I lost one of my shoes. I'm not sure how.

In my room, Stacia watches me with troubled eyes. "Have you let Ava know you're back? She's been worried, you know. She's not gone to her D&D club. That's how worried she is."

Stacia's eyes turn accusing, and they're suddenly too bright in the semi-dark of our room. The main light is off and only her bedside lamp emits a soft glow, so there are shadows everywhere. And her eyes.

I just need to get into bed. I pull my remaining shoe off, slide my body into my sheets, and stare straight up.

"Uh, Bella?" Stacia's worried eyes hover over me. "You're bleeding. You're bleeding a lot." She grabs my arm suddenly, and I wince at the pain. "What's happened to you?"

What has happened to me?

There's nothing in my brain. Nothing at all. Just this numbness. The faint recognition of pain.

"I don't know."

"We should go to the nurse. Have… have you been in a fight?"

A *fight*. A fight over what?

The *cocaine*.

Damn. I jump up, nearly slamming my skull into hers. I'm still dressed, but my jacket—where's my jacket? There. In a crumpled pile by the door. I throw myself over there, somehow curling my toes so the carpet burns against the bleeding cuts, and grab my jacket. I breathe a sigh of relief as I pull out the baggies of cocaine. They're still there. Safe.

I want to be safe.

"Uh, Bella? You shouldn't have that."

I turn to find Stacia looking shocked and so, so judgmental. Like she's never done anything illegal in her life. Then again, looking at her—all goody-two-shoes and no fun—she probably hasn't. Her love for gossip is probably her biggest vice, and that's hardly a vice, is it?

"I'm going to get Ava," she says, more to herself than me, then pads out the room in her slippers.

I can't bear the thought of Ava coming in here and looking at me, all concerned and disappointed and worried, so I grab the coke, slip on my Crocs—I normally only wear them in the shower as I hate standing bare-foot in any showers—and head out. Stacia's just disappearing down the other end of the corridor, but she doesn't look back. Doesn't see me.

I go the other way. Turn right. Two lefts. Fire escape. And I'm outside.

I clutch the coke in my hand, squeezing it so hard I almost expect it to burst. He won't be long. Yes, I need to be giving this to Mattie. Half of it is his.

Normally I message him when I've got more gear, but I think my phone must be in my room. Oh well. I know which block his room is in. And it's late, so he'll be there. I'll deliver it. Door-to-door service. Proper little courier, me.

Smiling, and feeling very proud of myself, I walk to the company's side of campus and find the building where Mattie lives. I go to the fire escape again, just in case he's there, but of course he isn't. So I push the door, but it doesn't open.

Of course. It opens from inside. Or you need a company ID card.

Tears come to my eyes suddenly and I try to blink them away, but it's pretty futile. Why won't anything ever go to plan?

I let out a frustrated growl, then force myself to think. The front of the building. I've just got to wait until someone else goes in or out, and then I can slip in too. Yes. That's what I'll do.

I step in something wet and sticky and my left Croc nearly falls off my foot. I curse, but I keep going. As I walk around to the front of the building, I become more aware of the pain in my arms. The streetlights illuminate jagged cuts, and a faint memory of falling into a bramble bush fills my head for a second. Then I blink and it's gone.

"Bella? Hi!"

I jump at the voice. It's Netty Florence. She's sitting on the steps outside the building, a vape pen in hand.

"You okay?" she asks. She's clearly looking at my arms, and I wish I'd put my jacket back on. Wish I could cover them. Cover all the hurt.

"I'm looking for Mattie?" I say. "Mattie Levenson."

Netty Florence stands up—all elegance and beauty—and then she gets her ID card out. Swipes it on the front entrance of the door. "Room 38B," she says. "It's the third floor. End of the corridor."

"Thanks." My word feels thick, smoky.

"Are you okay though, Bella?" she calls after me, but I don't stop. The door to Mattie's block is open now.

I glide in, my head feeling a little heavier than it should. I realize I'm still holding the baggie of cocaine in a very visible way—that Netty Florence would have definitely seen it. Then again, she was vaping, so maybe we'll both keep each other's secrets.

I see no one as I climb the flights of stairs, as I wander down the corridors until I find Room 38B. I knock on the door, and I want to laugh when the door opens a moment later—I don't know why. But Mattie stares at me.

"Shit, Bella, you look awful."

I walk past him, holding up the coke. "Where shall I put this then? Do you want to do some now, together? That would be a great idea, right! Yes, we totally need to do that."

His flat's pretty nice. I mean, it's small. It's poky. It's—

"Bella, no—what the hell are you doing?"

I spin around to find Mattie right behind me. "Look, you've really got to go. Now isn't a good time," he says—and that's when I hear it. A murmur—a voice calling his name in a strong Scottish accent.

Oh.

"You have to go," Mattie tells me.

"You've got a girlfriend?" I don't know why I sound surprised—why this feels like such a shock.

And she's Scottish.

"You can't tell anyone," Mattie says, his voice low and urgent.

"What?"

"She's a student—so you can't tell anyone."

A *student*? My mind is bleary. Which dancer?

And I'm not the only student who's got with someone in the company… an adult.

Mattie presses the coke back into my hand—I hadn't realized I'd put it down on his coffee table. "Just take all this. Give me mine, tomorrow. Okay?"

I nod, numb, and he pushes me gently out of his flat. The door slams shut and I lean against the wall, feel my body sliding down it, until I'm slumped on the grimy carpet, staring at my Crocs.

And I just want to disappear. Melt right into this carpet. Disappear forever.

I open the baggie of cocaine. *Okay, then.*

TWENTY-SEVEN

Bella

I am staring at three coffins. Three coffins on the woodland floor. The air is damp, woody, and the moss has a pungent smell. The coffins are closed, and every time I try and take a step back from them, the coffins shuffle toward me, together.

I swallow hard, a pounding in my head.

"Hello?" I call out, and I'm not sure why I call out. Because there's only me and the coffins here in the woods— but the moment I speak, the lids of the three coffins creak open.

They move so slowly, and then the ground underneath my feet is tilting, prompting me to look inside each one. I don't want to look—I try to turn, try to run.

But I can't.

I can't move my body.

All I can do is stare at the coffins and the bodies inside them. Dancers.

Each with a pink leotard and tutu. Creamy skin, slightly blue. Cold.

I don't want to look at them.

Don't want to see their faces.

But the ground's tilting again, forcing me to look.

Allegra is in the middle coffin. Her face is peaceful. Her hair is no longer in the ballerina's bun but lies perfectly around her shoulders.

Her lips are blue.

A strangled sound escapes me. I try to look away from her, but all I succeed in doing is staring at the coffin on the left. The ballerina inside it. I cannot see her face—no matter how hard I try to look at her face—I can't. I just... can't.

But I see her arms. So thin, skinny. And the welts on them. The bruises. Purple and black. The red marks around the wrists. Ligature marks.

The third ballerina is the same. Bruised, broken. Faceless.

I am screaming but my screams are soundless.

I turn, suddenly able to move. Damp twigs crackle under my feet and—

There's a person.

A person walking toward me.

A woman.

There's a light behind her in this dim darkness, like she's got a halo.

"Li Hua?" I breathe as she gets closer.

Her lips are blue, bruised. Blood sits neatly around her neck. She, too, is wearing a pink leotard and tutu, but her tutu is bigger than the others'. It's so big, and sharp—it has knives in it, knives that slash me when she gets close enough.

I cry out, clutching my thigh and the gashes across it, but I can't look away from Li Hua, even as wetness bathes my hands, as blood pools around my feet.

My blood.

Li Hua's eyes are sad. "Why did you let them take me?" she asks. A baby voice. So small, soft, innocent. "Why didn't you help me, Bella? Why?"

I wake, coughing, spluttering. Strings of vomit fly from my mouth, and my head pounds as I roll over. Pain lassoes my neck and I stare up at a flashing red light above me. A very small light.

I blink, frown. There's no one here.

And carpet—I'm lying on carpet.

My head spins, makes me woozy as I sit up. I cough— more vomit. A bitter taste in my mouth. My chest heaves. Eyes watering, I try to see—there's a door next to me. Room 38B, it says.

"Help," I whisper, dizzy. Can't move much. The huge tide of dark fatigue hovers over me. "Please help."

"No one's coming, Bella," says Li Hua—and suddenly she's here. In this corridor, kneeling in front of me. She's just so suddenly here. "No one's coming to help you, just like no one is coming to help me."

She says the words so simply. So matter of fact.

"And when they take you, there'll be no one to help you, either."

I try to reach out to her, my hand stretching to hers—I just need to touch her, I just need to know that she's real—but then Li Hua shimmers, and she's gone.

And it's just me here with my vomit.

Crying.

Alone.

TWENTY-EIGHT

Francesca is beginning to get on my nerves. She finally told me about her boyfriend—pronouncing *Timathy* in the most exaggerated way, drawing out the '*maaa*'—but now all she wants to talk about is him.

"We actually met in *Toast and Talk*," she tells me the next morning. "Linsey actually introduced us."

"Linsey?"

"The barista there. She, like, knows *everyone*. And she thought that I'd already know him, given he works at Roseheart. But of course he's in the company and we're not."

Great. She is with a dancer. I want to scream. I just want to get away from ballet.

"Plus, he's older," Francesca continues. "That's why Linsey said she was a bit worried at first, about introducing us, but she just thought we'd click. And we really have."

I am starting to understand why Francesca does not seem to socialize with the other choreography students. There is a big group of them that I have noticed tend to hang out together, after class. Of course, I am not in that group, but I'm also noticing that Francesca is never with anyone outside of me. At least I also see the girls in the support group, messaging them on WhatsApp. I have other people.

Even though Francesca's now got a boyfriend, she still seems to be hanging around me just as much. If not *more*. She even tells me that Timathy has said he does not want to be one of those boyfriends who completely monopolizes all of his girl's spare time, and he has even suggested that the three of us get together some time.

"Maybe," I say to Francesca, but the thought of third-wheeling them is not appealing, to say the least. And I just hope that she does not bring it up again.

But of course, she does—because she is everywhere I am.

I finish a private review with Madame Jurgensen—which goes terribly—and Francesca is there afterward, leaning against the corridor wall, ready to pepper me with questions of how it went.

I step out of the girls' bathroom and there she is, waiting outside, a huge smile on her face as she loops her arm in mine—totally unsolicited—talking nineteen to the dozen about *EastEnders,* which I do not even watch.

I pop into the canteen at Roseheart to buy a coffee, and low and behold, Francesca happens to pop in there too, about five minutes after me. Each time this happens, she always giggles loudly, claims it is a coincidence—"Great minds think alike!" is becoming quite a popular and prevalent saying with her—and then sits with me at my table.

I just want space.

When Darius and I were friends, best friends, it was natural. It was easy. But with her… well, my heart just is not in it now—it is too full on too soon—even though I am trying to be friendly. And she has never once asked me about my sister either—which should make it easier to feel friendly, kindly, toward her.

But all this… it is just too much—too quickly. I like my own space. I need my own space. Just the other afternoon, I was heading into the academy's library—mainly to see if the administration had kept anything on Allegra's disappearance—when Francesca popped up.

"I was just having a look," she told me. "Dancers' biographies. I love them."

There is a part of me that cannot help but wonder if she is following me now. Not that there is really anything sinister going on. I know that. But it makes me think about her, makes me think she is always hovering nearby, and so now, as I sit in the common room for the day students, in one of those rare times when she is not here for she told me she has got a meeting with her tutor, I search for Francesca on socials. I do not know what makes me do it, but I do. I try Facebook and IG, then Twitter, Snapchat. I cannot find her.

But I also do not know her last name. I thought it was Jones—but now I am not so sure. I do not think I have ever asked her. This makes me feel pretty silly, especially when I get the feeling she knows a lot about me. I take a deep breath. Maybe I will just ask if she wants to add me on Snapchat or something? She would probably jump at the chance. Track my location, my every move.

Not that I want her seeing everything I post, but it cannot be a bad thing to know more about her and maybe even learn *why* she is so keen to be friends with me. Either she is lonely and she is worried about mentioning my sister, or she is trying to get close to me because of who my sister is. And if it is the latter, then I am not sure what her end plan is.

I take a deep breath, look at the time. Oh, no. I gather my things, nearly dropping my water bottle in the process. I'm going to be late for the next community center meeting—another 'evening lesson' in the eyes of my parents—if I do not get a move on.

"There is just too much going on," I say to that stupid poster that haunts me at the support group, later that day. *We are all Survivors.* It is our second session and it seems like a lifetime has passed since the first one. And now I am early—twenty minutes early because I managed to make an earlier Tube connection that I had not thought was possible—and the only one here, and I am talking to a poster. "A dancer at Roseheart's been abducted, exactly like what happened with my sister. And my former friend has been arrested for supplying drugs. And… and…"

But I do not even know how to get the huge vat of sadness out from inside me. Or what exactly it is. It is just always there. This feeling of gloom. This heaviness.

I clam up as soon as the door opens though, about five minutes later. Two girls enter, cautiously. I recognize them from last time, but I cannot remember their names. I have had way too many new names to learn recently. It is only really Tiger and Annmarie that I want to see, I realize, thinking of them as my friends in this group.

But neither turns up.

In fact, there are only about a quarter of us here this time. I message Tiger and Annmarie. Both give explanations and I cannot tell if they are excuses or genuine—library books needed returning and having to babysit younger siblings—but this meeting feels very much different to the last one.

None of us really talk. Or at least we do not talk about what has happened. We talk about our hobbies. It is more like a group of young women meeting up and trying to be friends with each than a support group. And it feels forced.

I watch the clock, relieved when finally the hour is over, and I can head out. I mean, I do not know why I felt the need to stay the whole hour—maybe because none of the other girls were leaving—but now I cannot get out of the community center quickly enough.

My phone rings, just as I am opening the door to the main corridor. It is a withheld number, and I do not normally answer these calls, but something in me makes me click 'accept'.

"I'm so sorry," a man's voice says, but I do not recognize it.

"Sorry, who is this?"

"It's me, Darius."

Darius. I stop and two of the girls behind me crash into me. "Sorry," I say to them as I move to the side of the corridor. "Darius?"

He's sobbing now. "You don't understand—they're watching you, Alessia. They're watching so many of you at that school. You can't trust anyone."

"What are you talking about?"

There's a hissing down the line, and then he asks if I am on my own.

"Uh, hold on." I head outside, waving bye to the other girls, and then I lean against the wall. It is one of the warmest days in January so far and for once, the sun has warmed the evening air. "Okay, I am on my own now."

A notification pops up—Darius wants to turn it into a video call. I frown. *Okay.*

The video is grainy at first, but then it gets clearer, and I see him. See him properly. His lined face—*God, he looks old.* He holds his hand up suddenly, so I can see the inside of his wrist. There's a tattoo there. A crescent moon.

"Anyone with this—you don't trust them, okay?" His voice is gruff.

"The tattoo?" I say, frowning. I have seen one like that before. Like…

My eyes widen. *Allegra.* She wanted one. Of course as a dancer, she could not get any tattoos, but I remember the design she wanted. She talked about it to no end.

"The BGG Group. Don't trust them," Darius says.

"The BGG Group? What's that?"

He holds his phone closer, so mainly just the top part of his face is visible. There's a scar next to his right eye that looks fairly new. The skin's all jagged, raw, inflamed. "I can't tell you over the phone—it's too dangerous. They could even be listening in now. Just don't trust anyone okay, not until we've met."

"Met?"

"We have to meet. Tomorrow, 6pm. I'll come to you. To the park where Juan met you before."

"Juan? Is that that man, the one who said you needed me to remember?" I grip my phone tighter.

He nods. "Juan's trustworthy," he says. "About the only person in the BGG I can trust now. Look, Lessie, I can explain everything tomorrow, okay?"

Lessie. My heart does a jolty movement. It's been years since anyone called me that.

"I can get away—when they're not watching," Darius says. "But be careful, please. You're on their watch list. You're *all* on their list. And they'll stop at nothing—I mean nothing—to get what they want."

TWENTY-NINE

Bella

I don't know how I got back to my room. Whether I walked there. Whether Mattie came out and found me, helped me back, but I woke up in my bed, the crustiness of dried vomit around my mouth.

Stacia was already up, so I was able to wash my face with a damp flannel without any questions. Change into clean clothes. Try and breathe and not cry, with no audience.

And I've stayed in my room the whole day.

Because someone is watching me. That feeling again. Everywhere I walk, my skin is burning. It's not fleas, it can't be—I haven't got fleas. So the only explanation is that I'm being watched. Stalked. Of course I am. Just like Li Hua was. And Rosella too. Just like Graziella warned us.

I gulp. There's been nothing on Li Hua's case. No developments, nothing more released in the media, though the girls in the dorm are watching it relentlessly, putting updates on their socials like they're their own personal blogs.

I pace back and forward now, in my room. Stacia is out, but Ava's here. Watching me. Shaking her head, softly as I try to peer through half-an-inch's gap in the curtains—curtains that I've got drawn across, even in the daytime—to see if anyone's down there, standing outside the dorms. Waiting for me.

I pull the curtains together firmly, holding the two pieces of fabric together so hard that my knuckles whiten. "I'm not sure what to do." I look back at Ava. "Because every time I'm outside of this room, they're watching me again. They're going to take me, I'm sure."

"Bella, listen, please," Ava begins, but I cut her off.

"I think they're going to hurt me. And I can't tell who it is, but they're on campus. These people are watching me, everywhere I go." I flick my head back around, checking on the white rabbit. He's sitting on my pillow, sort of lying down with his back legs at an angle. He's a pretty good pet— I've not even found any of his droppings anywhere, so he's clearly litter trained and a dream to own—but I'm worried that these bad people are going to be after him too. That's what always happens. In films. Books. You name it. They go after your pet first.

Ava opens her mouth, as if to speak, but then shuts it again. Her brows furrow and a small vertical groove appears between them. Then she looks at me more certainly. "Bella, we're all worried about you. Ty said you've not even gone to your extra practices the last couple of days?"

Ty. The extra practices. The studio.

I look back out the window, pushing the curtains ever so slightly apart, suddenly sure that someone is down there. The person. I just need to know who it is.

"You've been doing more lines, haven't you?" Ava doesn't even need to ask because I haven't cleaned up the things from earlier—it's all spread out on my desk, right next to my bed, where she is currently sitting so prim and proper, on the edge.

I'm not sure when I started cutting the cocaine in my room, rather than the bathroom. My head feels all floaty and heavy when I try to think about it. Not that it matters. It doesn't matter, right?

But, shit, I've got a pet now. My rabbit. I glance at him, still lying lazily across my pillow. He won't lick any of that, will he?

Of course I won't, he says, and that's good—that's reassuring—so I look back out the window. Can focus just on this.

"Bella, there isn't anyone out there after you," Ava says, a note of irritation in her voice now.

"Li Hua might've thought that and she's been taken." I shake my head so hard my neck cricks. I carefully arrange the curtains again, then turn back to her. "I can feel it, Ava. They wanted to take me too then. That was their plan. It didn't work, did it? But it doesn't mean they're giving up. They're not going to. They're going to get me."

Ava sighs, all dramatically, but then she kind of stiffens, her face pinching inward a little.

"What?" I look at her.

"Your brother's messaged me," she says after a long moment.

"Bobby? Why?"

"Because you've not been replying to his messages. Or your mum's. They're worried about you."

"What have you said?" My eyes widen.

"Nothing about the drugs," she says. "But they've heard about Li Hua, obviously. They don't know you're the witness yet. But they're going to find out."

Of course they will. I grit my teeth. I even realized this before, tried to phone Mum on Saturday. But then I… forgot. It just slipped my mind completely.

"Isn't it Bobby's birthday soon?" Ava says.

I raise one eyebrow at her, trying to work out her intention, because she knows perfectly well it's my brother's birthday next week—because it's the day before her own. We discovered this in our first few days of the diploma, when general talk got around to birthdays. For some reason when Ava told me hers, I had the need to blurt out that Bobby's was the day before. As if that would be important to her.

"You haven't got him anything yet have you?" Ava asks. "We could go out shopping again? Like last year?"

Last year, we made a whole day of it. Traipsing around Primark and Next and H&M, trying on clothes and then getting food at Pho, before deciding what I'd actually buy Bobby. And of course I was able to get Ava her present too— a scarf that she really liked in H&M.

I feel the muscles in my eyes tighten and my vision blurs for half a second before it rights itself. "I can't really go out," I say. "they're going to find me. I don't want them to find me."

Ava tilts her head farther to the side. "But you said they're on campus—this would be us going away from campus. You'd be safe there."

"I… I don't know." I sit down heavily on the bed suddenly, only a foot or so away from her, but I may as well be miles away. That's how lonely it feels. Because it is lonely, being watched, stalked, when no one believes you.

And I do want to go out and be normal and forget all this, because who wouldn't want to do that?

"I think you just need to get out a bit," Ava says. "You've stopped doing all the things you love."

"I haven't stopped dancing," I say. "I love dancing." I'm still going to classes, aren't I? Even if I've missed one or two… but that's to be expected, in the circumstances.

"When was the last time you drew?" Ava stands and reaches for the sketchpad on my desk. My baggie of cocaine is propped against it and it falls, makes a soft plopping sound on the wooden surface, as she pulls the sketchpad toward her.

"You used to love drawing roses. You were always drawing them. But you're not now. Stacia has noticed it. And you're not going on walks—the rose gardens here. You were always out there. But you're not now." She says the words triumphantly, like she's made a really good point.

But she just doesn't get it, does she?

How can she? She's not the one being stalked.

"I can't leave my room except for when absolutely required," I say. "For class and that."

Ava purses her lips then breaths out hard, puffing her cheeks up for a long moment, before she releases the air. "Bella, you know there's a thing called drug-induced paranoia, right?"

"I'm not paranoid!"

"I'm not saying you are. I'm saying there's this condition that exists." She gives me a long look. "I'm trying to help you. Look, I'm just suggesting shopping."

"I don't want to go shopping."

She shakes her head. "Maybe I should get the nurse?" She says it like it's a test. Like she's trying to get a reaction from me. But I don't react, because that's what she wants.

I blink and for a moment, superimposed on the wall behind her, I see three coffins. Three coffins with alabaster-white figures in. Naked, this time.

My stomach roils.

"Fine, I'll go and get her. I'll get Madame Cachelle and Mr. Vikas too, while I'm at it," Ava says. And then she's flouncing out of the room. "We'll see what they have to say about this."

She's trying to get a reaction from me. I know that. Trying to shock me into doing something. But I just watch her leave. The three girls in the coffin are watching me. Just like the white rabbit used to—

Wait.

Where *is* my rabbit?

I look around for him, and I think I hear him laughing. But I can't see him.

My body jolts a bit, and it's like my brain catches up, finally understands Ava's threat. Mr. Vikas and Madame Cachelle *cannot* see me like this.

Fine. I'll prove it. "I'll prove it!" I yell, as if Ava can hear. "I'll go for a walk!"

And before I can talk myself out of it, I head straight out of my room. "Be good until I'm back," I whisper to the rabbit, wherever he is, but I'm already out in the corridor now, and I'm not sure he can hear.

I walk, forcing one foot in front of the other, realizing only when I get to the stairwell that I'm barefoot. I stare at the red nail polish on my toenails. When did that get on there? I… I don't paint my nails. Do I?

I rub my forehead, but as I descend the stairs and look at my feet again, I realize I was mistaken. There's no nail polish.

A strange laugh rises up inside me.

I continue on.

The rose gardens. I realize pretty quickly that that's where I'm heading. Of course it is. Damn. I should've brought my sketchbook with me. I curse loudly, startling two blackbirds, and then sit down on the bench—the one that Trent punched.

"Poor bench," I say, patting its arm. It's wobbly and for some reason that makes me giggle. Makes me call my rabbit—summoning it toward me. And here he is, bounding over.

He jumps up onto the bench, next to me, stretching his head up so he can use the wobbly arm as a chin-rub and—

Something flashes in the corner of my vision—a sharp, light flash, like a camera. A photo being taken.

I whirl around, looking in that direction and—

And there is a person.

There is!

A person holding a phone up, toward me. As if they are taking a photo.

Taking a photo—because they're watching me. Watching me.

Stalking me.

My mouth dries.

It's Mattie.

"Mattie?" I call his name, starting to move toward him. But instead of smiling and waving or saying my name or anything, he just moves—moves quickly. Away from me.

He's running. Running as fast as he can, away from me, until he's out of sight.

I breathe deeply.

Why the hell was Mattie Levenson taking a photo of me?

THIRTY

Bella

For several minutes, I don't know what to do. What it means. But suddenly I'm back to the day when Li Hua went missing. To the hours before, when she was asking me about him.

Li Hua was investigating Allegra's disappearance.

And she was asking about *him*.

Mattie Levenson.

I feel sick. I can't breathe. *It's him. It's him. It's him.* The voice in my head won't shut up, because I know it's right. I'm onto something.

And he's onto me. He's the one who's been following me.

He… he knows that I know. Even though I don't know much—like where she is or what's happened to her or why he's taken her.

But I know it's him.

And he's… he's with a student. Someone on the diploma, someone I know.

But—no. I heard her voice. Scottish.

There aren't any Scottish dancers in the diploma. Not in my year, and I don't think there are any in the year below either.

I frown.

Did I… did I imagine all that?

I move slowly out of the gardens, half expecting to see Mattie crouching in the bushes, hiding behind the water fountain. Watching me. My head feels numb and with every step part of me expects to fall over, so I'm walking with my arms spread wide, like I'm a tightrope walker or something. Fogginess spins around inside my mind, and I try to keep thinking as clearly as I can.

Just got to concentrate.

One step at a time.

There are some students up ahead, on the picnic tables. Day students I think—non-ballet courses, because they're not dressed like dancers and they've all got their hair down. I focus on them, and… and isn't that Alessia Valenzi?

She's sitting a little way off from the bulk of the girls, all alone at a table. She's reading a novel, and I might've thought she was engrossed in it, if it wasn't for the way she keeps looking up, around her, checking her surroundings. The other students don't do this. They're completely focused on their conversations, their gossip.

"Hey!" I call to Alessia, and then I'm suddenly much closer to her—time doing one of its weird jumps—and I slide onto the bench opposite her, lean across the table and look right at her. "Is there a Scottish student here who's seeing Mattie Levenson?"

She frowns, looking up at me with distrustful eyes. Carefully, she puts a bookmark in her novel and then levels a cool gaze at me. "I don't know."

"What? Are there a lot of Scottish girls on the course?" I look around, trying to listen to the accents of the other students talking—but they're all jumbling up together.

"Uh, just Francesca," Alessia says. "But her guy's called Timathy."

I stop. "Then who is it who's seeing Mattie?"

Alessia shrugs. "It is not Francesca."

"Come on, this is important!" I almost want to grab hold of her shoulders, shake her, make her really understand.

"I don't know!"

"Look, whoever it is, you need to tell them that Mattie Levenson is dangerous, okay? Tell her to stay away from him."

But Alessia just shakes her head. "Look, I have heard about you. Always so high you can never see things properly. So paranoid you think stuff is going on when it is not. But unlike you, some people actually have things to do. Important things. So can you just leave me to read in peace please?"

I let out a shaky breath, but I move. No point wasting time on her. Not when there's one more person I can go to.

"Seriously?" Trent stares at me. "You think you're in danger? That you're being stalked by Mattie Levenson? That guy is a drip."

"I *am*!" I'm breathing hard, can hardly think straight. I look around—but there's no one else in here, in the studio. One of the company studios. I just waltzed in, checked room after room until I found him. Was going to check every room of every company building, until I found him. "I'm being followed too, just like Li Hua was!"

"No! You're not!" he yells. "You're just paranoid because you're off your face on drugs all the time, and now you want to be a victim! You're making this all about you, when *my* girlfriend is missing."

"Li Hua was asking me about him!" I cry. "The day she went missing, she asked me about him."

Trent looks at me slowly. "What did she ask?"

"I—I can't remember. I thought she was wanting drugs but it can't have been that, and I… I can't remember."

"You can't remember?" He stares at me, then shakes his head. "Just get lost, Bella. You're just making things worse, throwing accusations around."

"I'm not, no! But I think it's him, Trent. I really do. He took Allegra and the other two girls—tortured them. And now he's got Li Hua."

"Mattie Levenson, the tech guy?" He stares at me, then shakes his head. "You're really fucked up, you know."

"Why don't you believe me?"

"Why would I believe you?" he snarls. "Ever since we slept together, my life has fallen apart. And guess who's suddenly in every single part of my life now? *You*, Bella. You're doing this. You're ruining everything. I wish it was you who was taken."

THIRTY-ONE

Trent

I ditch the rest of my training session, skip company class. I can't face it. Not with the way my head's pounding. I've really let Bella get to me, get under my skin.

As if Mattie Levenson is capable of pulling off an abduction, let alone four. I mean, it's just preposterous! That guy is such a drip. It's—

My eyes widen.

Four.

Allegra's assumed dead, but the other two who were taken aren't. They came out alive. I… I can speak to them. I *have* to speak to them. My head pounds. What are their names? I can't remember their names. Did I ever know their names?

But they'll be able to tell me, these women, who's involved. Won't they?

"Don't you think they would've told the police?" Jaidev says. We're in the library, looking through the archives, trying to find a name for either of the two dancers that were taken alongside Allegra Valenzi. We've got a box file and two large folders out, but so far we've found nothing.

"They might have been scared to," I say. "But they'll tell me."

They have to tell me.

Only there's no mention of either of their names.

"Every article either refers to them as the other two abduction victims of Roseheart Academy," Jaidev says with a frown. "Or there's this one where the names have been redacted." He holds up a piece of paper from the box file. A small amount of text has been blotted out with a black marker.

I take the paper from him, holding it up to the window, trying to see if there's any way to see the info underneath. But it's futile. "Are there any others like this?"

Jaidev shakes his head. "Do you think Li Hua found out who they are?"

"I don't know." But I'm sure wishing I actually had listened to her more. All those evenings when she was bright-eyed with adrenaline, telling me about this case and what she'd discovered, and I just didn't really listen. "Their names have got to be here though. Someone has to know them." I drum my fingers on the desk. "Think the police might tell us?"

"We can try," he says. "But what about Alessia Valenzi? Wouldn't she know? Or even the grandmother? Wouldn't they have been Allegra's friends."

I bite down on my bottom lip for a moment, so hard that it hurts. A sweet kind of pain though. The kind of pain that makes this real. "Someone has to." I swallow hard. "Okay. Here's what we'll do. If you can reach out to Alessia—you're probably going to be better received than me, think I scared her the other day—and I'll phone Graziella. And… and we need a list of all the Roseheart Academy students for the ballet course, ten years ago too. That's going to give us a starting point with names. We then just have to narrow it down. Staff too—there's going to be some who are the same. We just have to talk to everyone."

"Everyone." Jaidev gives a glum kind of smile. "Not many then."

Jaidev's messages to Alessia go unanswered. Unread. He reached out to her on Messenger, but of course she's not a friend of his on Facebook, so it's probably in her message requests. Unseen.

My phone call to Graziella proved no help. All she could say was that she once knew, but her memory is a bit watery now.

"Do you think it's worth talking to Allegra's parents?" Jaidev asks.

"Might have to," I say. "If we don't get anywhere here."

He taps his pen on the notebook where we've made a list of current staff members who were here ten years ago; there are only three of them. One's a caretaker, one's a canteen worker, and one teaches literature in the lower school. It's doubtful whether Allegra would've had any contact with any of them, though they still might remember the names of the other girls who were abducted. They'd have to, right?

But the most interesting discovery though is Madame Jurgensen, the current head of the choreography courses. She was originally on the ballet diploma, training during the same year as Allegra.

"Right," I say. "I'll pay Jurgensen a visit. You all right to see the caretaker? He's probably still around. We can sort out contacting one of the Valenzis if we don't get anywhere with any of this."

The door to Madame Jurgensen's office is wide open, and upon approaching, I can hear the clack-clack-clack of keys being hit. Almost sounds like a typewriter. Upon entering her office, I see the sound is a result of her very long, very pointy-looking nails. She's perched on a bar stool at her desk, and her computer's monitor has been raised up with several thick books. She's wearing a long, dark-purple dress that almost looks like a Halloween costume. If she had the witch's hat on, it would just complete the look.

Madame Jurgensen remains staring at her screen, her side profile to me, apparently oblivious to my presence, so I clear my throat. I expect her to react, to half acknowledge me at least. But she does not. She just stares at the computer screen.

She looks older than late twenties. At least ten years older. But on the way over here I worked out how old she'd have to be. The same as Allegra.

"Hello," I say, and my word gets stuck in my throat.

Without looking away from her screen, she asks, "Do you have an appointment with me?"

"No," I say, "but—"

"Do you have an office hour booked?"

"No." I try again. "But—"

"Then you can make an appointment for next week." Clack-clack-clack go her nails on the keyboard.

I don't move, just shift my weight a little, so it's distributed more evenly across my legs. "I need to talk to you."

Finally, she looks at me. There are deep bags under her eyes, and her nose looks a little too large yet also too thin for her face. It gives the impression of her forehead being too small and her mouth and chin all squashed up in comparison.

"Are you a student of mine?"

"No."

"Then we do not need to talk."

I stare at her. "Are you always this rude?"

"You may think you've got it all, as a company dancer—I assume—but I assure you, young man, that respecting other people's time and commitments will get you much farther than this entitled attitude you have."

"This is important. I need the names of the other two dancers who were abducted ten years ago, alongside Allegra."

For a moment, Madame Jurgensen doesn't react. She doesn't blink, doesn't even seem to breathe. But then her posture straightens a little, and her shoulders hunch together. Her voice wavers when she speaks. "Why would you need those?"

"I need to speak to them."

"You cannot," she says. "You must not."

"I have to. It's my girlfriend who's been taken this time." I take a small step toward her. "I just need their names. Need to find them."

Madame Jurgensen stands up. "Do you know why their names were never in the public record? Why everyone here worked so hard to keep them anonymous?"

"No. And that's the problem—I don't know everything. And I need to know."

She takes a deep breath. "The two other girls. They weren't diploma students. They were in the lower school."

"What? I thought they were like Allegra."

"No. These girls were seven and nine years old. Their identity had to be protected."

"So they're like seventeen, nineteen now?" The age of the dancers on the diploma. Could it be one of them? My mind spins, and I know it's unlikely.

"They would've been," Madame Jurgensen says. "One of them never recovered from her injuries. She died four months later. And the other?" Her breath shakes and she reaches out for the edge of her desk, steadies herself with it. "My sister would've been just turning seventeen."

"Your *sister*?" My eyes widen.

"She took her own life, because of what those people did to her."

An icy chill fills the room.

"I am so sorry," I say. "I… I just need to know who those people are."

"You think I don't?" she asks, her voice cracking. "You think I haven't been out looking, since Li Hua was taken?"

"You have?" I ask. I can't hide my surprise.

"Of course I have. I owe it to my sister. But they are watching me, and I cannot be too obvious. None of us can."

"*They*?" I ask. "Who are they? Who's taken her?"

"If I tell you, I'm putting you in danger," she says.

"I don't care about that."

"They're likely already watching you. You and your friends. Everyone here."

"Who are they?" My words shake.

"They call themselves the BGG Group," she says. "There's at least one investor of Roseheart involved in a big way, but I have not been able to identify who it is, despite my best efforts. The same with the other parties."

I let out a long breath. An investor. I knew it. "What does BGG stand for?"

She shrugs. "Anyone's guess. But you must promise me that you do not breathe another word of this to anyone. If they find out I've blabbed—"

"They won't," I say.

"Do not say things you cannot guarantee," she says. "Now, excuse me, but I have a class to teach. And you—well, you'd do well to know that this conversation never happened." And without another word, Madame Jurgensen sweeps past me, her long purple dress trailing behind her.

THIRTY-TWO

Alessia

Six o'clock this evening cannot come soon enough. Just two more hours.

I have been restless all day, constantly looking out for people who are watching me—and I have not been able to find a thing really. Nothing to say that I am being watched. Which of course means that these people are good. This BGG Group. And I have not got a clue who they are.

"You okay?" Francesca asks me during the break of Madame Jurgensen's class. "You know, you're proper quiet all of a sudden."

I take my time before replying, trying to read her. She has been overkeen to be friends, and she has appeared in so many places where I am. Could she be part of this group, whatever the BGG Group is? I Googled them on the Tube on the way back yesterday evening, of course I did, but I did not find anything. I searched socials for any trace of their group too, but there was nothing.

No traces at all online of the BGG Group.

Because these people are good at what they do.

Because they are an organized crime group?

I swallow hard. What has Darius got himself involved in?

What are we all involved in?

I glance at the clock. Just another couple of hours and I will find out.

"I'm fine," I tell Francesca.

She nods and pushes her red hair back from her face. She has got a half-up, half-down style today, and I am not too sure it suits her, but she told me that Timathy really likes it.

"I just really can't wait for tonight," Francesca tells me. "Timathy's taking me out tonight, again. He knows this person who runs a private cinema and he found out that *Marley & Me* is my favorite film, so he's arranged a completely private viewing of it."

I may not watch a lot of films, but I have seen this one. And I can't believe she's having it as a date choice. "Really? You ready for him to see you crying at the end?"

"I won't cry," she says with a look of mild alarm. "But if I do get upset, then I've got my man to comfort me. And Timathy is just so caring. Very gentle. You know, I always thought men smell—like bad. But he actually doesn't. It's like he actually showers twice a day and uses deodorant."

"Okay, everyone. Break's over," Madame Jurgensen says, striding back into the room.

She has been very snappy today, even more short-tempered than usual, and she has already had a big go at me about my homework. Apparently, I should not have used ballet as the example dance in more than two of the exercises.

"I do not even know why she's teaching at Roseheart—which is primarily a ballet school—when she seems to hate it so much," I say in a low voice to Francesca, who just shrugs.

The rest of the class has fallen silent, and we all watch as Madame Jurgensen writes on her blackboard. No sooner has she written a couple of words on it—words that are still hidden from us by her body—when the door to the classroom creaks open.

Three people stand there. I recognize one as a receptionist at Roseheart, but the other two are unfamiliar. A white man and a Black woman, both dressed in neat suits.

"Can Alessia come with us please?" the receptionist says.

Madame Jurgensen turns slowly and her eyes fall on me before she looks back at the trio. "Is this necessary to interrupt my class for?"

The man and woman in suits look particularly grave, and that's what makes my stomach suddenly drop. I'm standing up before I realize, moving forward, almost gliding out of the room.

"If you just come to the office with us, Alessia," the receptionist says. She is trying to smile, but her smile is not right. It is not proper, not true, not organic.

Something has happened.

Something has really happened.

I start shaking. First at my knees, then my whole legs. It is a challenge to place one foot in front of the other.

"Is it my parents?" I ask. "Allegra?"

Has she… has she been found? My sister… Her… her body.

No! She's not dead! She's never been dead! She's Greece or Turkey or somewhere!

"Let's get to the office," the woman says, and it is then that I realize she is police. The man too.

It seems to take an eternity to get to the office—a pale-yellow painted room with two sofas in it. I sit on one. The receptionist and the police sit on the other.

"We are sorry to tell you this," the policewoman begins, "but earlier today we recovered the body of Darius Longbourne."

THIRTY-THREE

Alessia

Suicide. That's what they're saying.

Darius couldn't cope with the guilt. The guilt of harming children.

I feel numb as things happen around me. People offering me tissues.

"We know you were friends," the policewoman says. "And he did leave a note—addressed to you."

"Me?" I sit up a little straighter. "Where is it?"

"Our team are taking it to forensics," the policeman says. "Standard procedure, but it will be returned to you after, should you wish to have it."

"What does it say?"

The two police officers glance at each other for a moment, then the woman nods. The man gets his phone out and reads. "'Alessia, I am sorry I can't keep you safe. But know this, please, you're the best friend anyone could wish for, and I am so sorry for what's happened. Please, stay safe and don't look into things.'"

It takes me a moment to realize the policeman has got a photo of it there, this note from Darius.

I gulp.

"Do you know what Mr. Longbourne meant by 'keep you safe,' Alessia?" the woman asks me.

The receptionist, opposite me at the end of their sofa, gives me an encouraging look, then adjusts how she is sitting. She crosses one leg over the other, and in doing so the bottom of her trouser leg rides up a little, revealing skin. And a tattoo. My eyes widen.

I cannot tell what the tattoo is, but that does not seem to matter because… *I can't keep you safe from the BGG Group.* That's what Darius meant. And he said they are watching me. What if they are part of the school?

"No," I say. "I do not." And I am trying not to look at the receptionist. Trying not to make eye contact. But is she part of this group? Or is that just a coincidence, her tattoo innocent?

I look back at her leg, but her trousers are lying differently now and I cannot see the tattoo. My chest rises and falls too quickly and I feel like I am going to choke. Is she onto me? Part of this drugs operation that Darius got caught up in?

"I am sorry," I say. "I do not know anything."

I do not go back to Madame Jurgensen's lesson. Several staff offer to book me a taxi to take me home, but I tell them I want to study in the library. Which I do. Numb, gaze glazed over, heart pounding, trying to ignore the stares of other students, not taking a word in from the textbook page I must have read a hundred times, until six o'clock. The time I was supposed to meet Darius.

Now, I am out here, at the place that Darius and I had arranged. Because maybe someone else is going to show instead. Someone who can explain what all of this is. I need answers.

A light rain fills the air. My coat has not got a hood. It is handmade, from alpaca wool—waterproof, warm, but I can feel the iciness getting into my ears, my head. As I wait, the rain gets worse. There were a few parents with children here, but as the weather worsens, they pack up, go home.

I look for the man with the scars—*Juan*, if that is his name—rehearsing in my head my side of the whole conversation that we'll have. But no one shows at the park. No one.

The air turns a thick gray, and I shuffle about, trying to shelter under the bandstand. Turning around every so often to look a full three-sixty.

Wait—there *is* someone.

My heart pounds, and my mouth suddenly feels too dry. I swallow hard, trying to wipe the water—rain and my tears, I realize—from my eyes. The person is not coming over.

They're on the other side of the park, a dark figure in the grayness of winter.

Are they watching me?

I cannot tell, but they are not sheltering from the rain. No dog is with them.

Maybe it is him.

I force my feet to move. One step in front of the other. Heading for him.

It is Francesca's boyfriend, Timathy. I recognize him from the photos Francesca has showed me. His curly blond hair may be hidden under a hood, but I am sure it is him.

I wonder if I should call out to him as I get closer. He sees me, makes eye contact, and then quickly looks away. A second passes, and he shoves his hands deep into his pockets and turns, walks away as fast as possible.

He *was* watching me, I know he was. And that—that doesn't make sense. If he was worried about me, if Francesca has somehow found out what has happened and told him, why would he not come over? Unless he is going to get her?

Though she will probably be at home now.

They're watching you. That is what Darius told me. The last words he said to me.

I take a deep breath. Is it Timathy? Is Francesca in danger?

Look, whoever it is, you need to tell them that Mattie Levenson is dangerous, okay? Tell her to stay away from him.

Bella's words suddenly float back to me, wrap around me, and I do not know why. Why I am thinking about her warning now? Because Timathy is not—

"Oh my goodness." My words are raspy.

Timathy. Mattie.

Is it the same person?

My eyes widen.

Mattie is short for Timathy.

THIRTY-FOUR

Trent

My phone rings and I grab it from my desk. *Jaidev.*

"Yep? We need to meet." I slam my laptop shut, not giving him any time to speak. I've been trying to find out more about this BGG Group all afternoon and because of his timetable, I've not yet been able to update him. This information seems too important to send via text.

"No, listen," he says. "Alessia Valenzi is sobbing in the common room. She's desperate to speak to you."

"Me?"

"Mate, just get down here. She's distraught."

I inhale sharply. "I'll be there in a second."

Alessia Valenzi—the sister. Going to tell me something. I practically fly out of my apartment. My heart pounds all the way down to the common room, and there, I'm greeted with quite the commotion.

Several dancers are trying to console Alessia, who's got tears running down her face. She looks up as I enter, and then she's breaking free of the comforting arms, lurching toward me.

"I cannot find her!" Alessia sobs into my arms—actually sobs—and I don't know what to do.

"None of us can," I say, glancing at Jaidev. Netty Florence and Sonia hover anxiously. Netty Florence mouths something at me, but I can't make it out.

"No, not Li Hua!" Alessia cries, hiccupping. "Bella!"

"Bella?"

"She was right," Alessia says. She looks around suddenly, then she's tugging at my arm. "Outside. Now."

I follow her back out into the corridor. Jaidev follows and she looks at him suspiciously.

"He's cool," I say.

She wipes her nose on her sleeve. "It's Timathy Levenson, Mattie—Bella was right. He's involved in something bad, and I think it's called the BGG Group."

My eyes widen. "You know about that?"

"The what?" Jaidev asks.

"It's a drugs ring," Alessia says, "and Darius was in it, I think. He is my friend… was my friend. Uh, he is dead now though. The police told me today. They are saying it is suicide, but I… I think they have murdered him. He told me he wanted out of it. And he has got a friend called Juan who wanted out of it as well. And I thought Juan was going to come and meet me, but then I saw Timathy—uh, Mattie—and he was just watching me. And Darius told me that the BGG are watching me, that they are watching loads of people. People at Roseheart. It must be."

"Do they know that you know about them?" I ask her.

Alessia gulps. "I… I don't know. Darius was trying to protect me so maybe not."

"Okay. Do you know where these people meet? Any addresses?"

"I know Darius's."

I look back at Jaidev. "And have you still got the addresses we came up with, of the investors ten years ago who are still investing now?"

Jaidev frowns. "Yes. They're in my room. I can get them, but I don't understand—you think this drugs ring took Li Hua?"

I nod. "Madame Jurgensen told me that the BGG Group is behind the abductions, and that they can influence the police, the media."

"The *abductions*?" Alessia's voice is small, and she looks confused.

I lean back against the wall. "Okay, so we think that Mattie Levenson is part of this group, but we don't know who else is. That right? And Jurgensen says there is an investor involved. They've got money. Of course they have if they're a drugs ring." I let out a shaky breath. "But these people have got Li Hua."

"And Bella," Alessia whispers.

"What?" I stare at her.

"I told you. I can't find her! She came to warn me about Timathy—Mattie—and I didn't listen. But she was onto him and now she's missing."

"Are you sure?" I ask. I pull out my phone and dial her number.

"Her friend checked her room, said she was not there." Alessia dissolves into fresh tears, making it harder for me to hear the ringing line.

But Bella doesn't answer.

"Okay. We're going to find her. Just like we're going to find Li Hua. We've got an address—this Darius person, right? We'll go there."

"We need to tell the police," Jaidev says.

"The police are involved in the BGG Group," I say. "We cannot trust them. But we've got an address—a small chance of getting Li Hua back. We're taking it."

Jaidev looks doubtful.

"You in?" My tone is sharp.

He nods.

"Yes," Alessia says.

THIRTY-FIVE

Bella

I search Mattie Levenson's flat, pulling drawers out of his cabinets, looking under cushions. Everything.

I've just got to find the name of his girlfriend. Or a picture. Anything.

I need to warn her.

I couldn't save Li Hua, but I can save her.

I can—

But Mattie didn't take Li Hua.

But I don't know that he didn't.

All I know is that Li Hua was being stalked before she was taken. And I'm being stalked by Mattie. I still can't believe it.

I take a shaky breath, moving onto the next room. His bedroom.

It was easy to break into his flat. I kicked the door in. No one else was about. No one heard anything, or if they have, they haven't come to stop me.

Mattie's bedroom is all dark colours. Navy walls. Black sheets. A dark-gray duvet. There's a table in one corner with a computer, and a pretty rancid, gone-off smell fills the whole room. I wrinkle my nose for a moment, then continue my search.

But there are no signs of her. No photos, no love letters—if people even write those anymore—no bras, not even a second toothbrush in the bathroom I checked earlier. There's just nothing.

My gaze falls on his laptop. It's on the table, closed.

I open it—the lid's quite stiff and my fingers ache a moment. There's a bit of pink paper enclosed inside. A Post-it note. Small, square writing.

"What the hell?" I whisper as I stare at the words.

Possible recruits:

Francesca Jones-Marshall – for drop-offs. Will do as I say.

Bella Sotheby – already engaging with Mac. Easy. But if refuses, sort out.

And then at the bottom of the Post-it note:

Trent Mason and Jaidev Ngo may be onto us. Sort them out.

Everything whirls around me, faster and faster. Francesca. Is that his girlfriend? And… and Trent and Jaidev being sorted out?

Damn. Damn. Damn.

My head spins even more frantically as I look at the Post-it note and I almost can't take this all in. It's all just…

I sit down heavily in the desk chair. It creaks, shakes a little. I go to pull my phone from the pocket of my gym leggings, only my hand slaps against my leg. Shit. Left it in my room. Must've.

Get out of here, the voice in my head says.

I grab the Post-it, crumple it in my fist, and run.

"You've not been kidnapped?" Trent stares at me. He was right outside Mattie's block when I sprinted out the front entrance, and I practically ran straight into him.

"What?" I stare at him, heart pounding. Jaidev's with him and… "Alessia?"

The girl looks awful. Her face is all puffy, her eyes red with crying.

"What's happened?"

"We've got an address," is all Trent says, his voice firm. "We need to go there now. We might be able to get Li Hua back."

"An address?" My heart pounds.

"You're coming with us," Trent says. "We need to stick together."

"We're being watched," Alessia says. "All of us."

"By Mattie," I say, glaring at Trent. "Like I told you."

"It's not just Mattie," Jaidev says. "It's a whole organized crime group."

My eyes widen, and I try to show them the Post-it note, trying to work out what it means. *Possible recruits?*

"We'll all share everything we know on the way there," Trent says. "Car should be at the main gates now. Come on."

I feel sick as I climb into the taxi. My legs won't stop shaking, even when I'm trying to physically hold them still. Trent's sitting up front with the driver—a different driver, a completely different company to the taxi that Li Hua got—and I'm in the middle of Jaidev and Alessia.

In the passenger seat, Trent turns around and looks back at us. "Okay. Who wants to go first?"

"I don't know if we should be talking about all this," Alessia says. She flicks her eyes toward the driver and keeps her voice low. "We don't even know who he is."

If the driver hears, he doesn't react.

"Write it down," I say. "Oh, damn. I've not got my phone."

"It's okay," Jaidev says, pulling his out. "We'll put it all on my phone. Pass it around. Read it all."

It seems like an awfully convoluted process, and it's time-consuming, waiting for each of us to write out what we know, but by the time we get to the drop-off point, some corner in Chipping Barnet, we've all read the notes we've made on Jaidev's phone:

The BGG Group is a drugs ring and behind the abductions. The two girls taken along with Allegra were 7 and 9 years old. One was Madame Jurgensen's sister.

Unknown why they took Allegra and the two girls. Because they found out or something more sinister? Trafficking? The two girls were tortured and released. Both now dead.

Allegra never found.

Li Hua taken because she possibly found out identity of some of the BGG—was asking questions about Mattie. He is in the BGG. So is Mac, Bella's dealer.

They want to recruit Bella and Francesca. They also know that Trent and Jaidev are onto them and want to 'sort them out'.

The BGG have people everywhere. At least one investor (maybe Rio and Fibonacci), likely people at the school are involved. Maybe the receptionist with the dark bob? Police are definitely helping to cover it up.

BGG have tattoos.

Darius was involved. He wanted out, and they murdered him. His friend Juan also wants out.

Seeing it all written down makes it real. Makes it very real. My teeth chatter and my whole body trembles. Alessia puts her arm around me in what has to be the most awkward way.

"How do we know it's Rio and Fibonacci?" Trent asks. We're standing at the side of the road, the taxi having just driven away. "Who wrote that part?"

"Me," Jaidev says. "I had a look at their website the other day, and I only remembered when writing that. I can't believe I didn't make the connection—his photo's right there."

"Whose photo?"

"Mattie's. Deborah and Kyle Levenson own Rio and Fibonacci. And they've got three sons. Hold on, let me show you," he says, and then he's typing on his phone. A moment later he shows us the webpage.

There's a family photo on the About page. A middle-aged woman, a man who looks a bit older, and three grown-up sons. One's unfamiliar to me, wearing a police uniform—huh—and one's definitely Mattie, no doubt about it. My eyes widen. And the other—

My eyes widen, and then next to me, Alessia stiffens.

"Timathy and Maxwell Levenson," Jaidev says.

"That—that's *Mac*." My chest tightens. "The dealer." I shake my head. "Mattie never even *needed* me to get him the coke. It's his own brother."

I glance toward Alessia but she's completely frozen, still staring at Jaidev's phone. "What is it?" I ask.

"That… woman is Mother's best friend," Alessia says, her voice small. "She was visiting our apartment only the other day. When… when Li Hua went missing. She was there, supporting my parents—they thought I was missing too. She… she's been driving me to Roseheart. She… she cannot be involved. She would not be. She knows how Allegra's disappearance has affected Mother. She would not be behind that. This just… cannot be right. If you are saying… but Allegra is not…she was not…"

"We have to assume that Rio and Fibonacci are most definitely involved," Trent says firmly. "We assume the parents are dangerous too. And—fuck." His eyes widen. "They approached Li Hua, a few months ago. Wanting to sponsor her."

"Was that when she started investigating Allegra?" I ask.

"Yeah." Trent lets out a long shaky breath. "Okay. No, this is good. We've got information now. We've got leads." He looks at Alessia. "Show us the way to Darius's flat. If this Juan guy is still there, and still wants to get out of this gang or whatever it is, he's likely to help us."

"And if he won't help us?" I ask.

Trent glances at Alessia. "Then we go to Deborah."

Alessia gulps. She's ashen-faced, shaking. "She… she was the one that really stopped Mother from wanting to look for Allegra, after those two girls were released and she wasn't. She made Mother think Allegra was dead, that she was in heaven now." She runs a hand through her hair, then blinks several times. "It cannot be her. It cannot be Deborah. I mean, just because her sons appear to be involved, it does not mean she is."

"Well," I say. "If it's not her, then we wait for whoever it is to recruit me, if Mattie's Post-it was correct. We'll get in some way. We'll get Li Hua back." I try to say the words as confidently as possible.

"That's too dangerous," Jaidev says. "That's akin to getting yourself kidnapped too, just to see if you end up in the same place as Li Hua."

Trent nods. "Right. Alessia, lead the way to this flat."

THIRTY-SIX

Alessia

I hover outside the entrance of Darius's block, my head spinning. *Deborah.* She's involved? Or at the very least her son is. Timathy. Mattie. Whatever name he goes by. He hasn't been away traveling, like Deborah told me both her sons were. She lied to me, even when driving me to Roseheart, the very place one of her sons was. Why? To hide the connection.

I feel sick.

"Is this it?" Trent asks, gesturing at the building.

Police tape is still there, but it has been torn down. There is a man lying in the doorway, moaning a little. I cannot tell if he is unconscious, but I do not want to step too close to him. "Yes," I say.

"Righto," Bella says, "off we go." And with an astonishing amount of vigor, she surges inside, jumping neatly over the slumped man.

Trent heads in after her, and Jaidev glances at me, asks if I'm okay to do this. I just nod, and I force myself to go next. *This is for Allegra. To find out what has happened.* Because now, well, now I cannot shake the feeling that I have been wrong all the time about my sister. Was it just hope that really made me believe she'd escaped ballet, escaped this life for a better one where she was away from us but very much alive.

She's in a better place now, with our Lord.

I cannot get Deborah's voice out of my head. She knew something. She *knows* something. I pause. "I think we should just go straight to Deborah now," I call after Trent and Bella. "And I need to warn Mother."

"You can't," Bella says. "If your mum's friends with them, she might be in on it too—"

"What, killing her own daughter?" I stare at her. "She is not in on anything. Mother is—"

"She might inadvertently warn the Levensons," Trent says. "And we're sticking to our plan. Okay? We've come all the way over here. We may as well check the flat in case this Juan guy is here and will help us. Give us some knowledge anyway, so we know more about what we're dealing with."

"And anyway," Jaidev says, "we can't just go to the Levensons. Not without a plan. They're powerful people, right?"

I nod and I try not to breathe as we walk through urine-smelling corridors. The carpet is sticky and damp. Brown marks cover most of the walls. Some of the doors we pass have been damaged, others kicked in entirely so we can see into flats. Dark rooms. Someone moaning, like they are in pain.

Bella and Trent disappear around the corner ahead, and I have this sudden moment of panic. This deep foreboding sensation in my gut. We should not be here.

"All right?" Jaidev asks me, his voice low. He is right behind me, and I turn and—

The tears just start. So many of them. I cannot breathe. I cannot see. I cannot—I cannot be here.

"Hey," Jaidev says, and he's reaching out for me.

I freeze.

No.

Jaidev stops, holding his hands up. "It's—it's okay."

"Okay?" I say. "How can it ever be okay? My… my sister is *dead.* And Mother's best friend is…" Suddenly, it is too hot in here. I am sweating buckets, and it is all collecting under my arms and down my spine, sticking my clothes to me.

"You are being so strong," Jaidev says. "So, so strong. And we just need you to be strong for a little longer, just in case we can find where Li Hua is. Okay? Can you do that?"

His words float over me, but then they come back, wrap around me, this invisible hug. Support. And I am staring at him, still crying. But I nod.

For Allegra.

For Allegra.

I take a deep breath, and we continue on. We walk through more corridors, catch up with Bella and Trent, and the four of us pull ourselves up two flights of stairs with their graffitied walls and urine pools. The air is thick, rancid in my throat. Bella stretches her sleeve over her hand, uses it to open the door onto the third floor. And—

And that's when a lot of things happen at once.

People race past us, shoving us back. I cry out, bang my head on a wall or something solid, losing my balance, and then Trent's falling onto me. I twist, rolling out from under him, taste blood at the back of my mouth, and—

A knife flashes into my vision, and then someone grabs my arm, roughly. I yelp, twisting around, but the person—a man, I think—steps behind me.

"Hey," Bella screams just as another man appears. His hood's up, but I catch a glimpse of white skin as he turns on Bella. "You scum!" she hisses.

And—

"Fuck," Trent says.

I stare at the men. Not just knives, but guns.

One points at each of us.

"There's an easy way to do this, and a hard way," the man nearest me says.

"Just let us go," Jaidev says. "We haven't got any money."

"Money? You think *we* need money?" The man laughs, and then all of them are laughing. "This has never been about the money."

"Then what is it about?" Trent asks. His voice trembles a little, but I can tell he's trying to put on a brave front. He glances back at the rest of us, and then Trent's moving his body ever so slightly. Like he's trying to stand more in front of Bella and Jaidev and me—even though there are men on each of us.

"This is about people poking their noses into business that don't concern them," the man spits.

I gulp. The gun nearest to me keeps going in and out of focus. But they would not actually shoot us, would they?

"Look, we're not," Jaidev says. His voice shakes. "We're… we were just going to go."

"Do you think we're fucking stupid?" the man in front of him snarls. "We've been watching you. All of you. And you clearly know too much. Now, there's an easy way to do this. Or a hard way. But either way, the four of you are coming with us and—"

Bella makes a run for it. I see it all in slow motion. The way she turns her head first toward me, makes eye contact, widening her eyes, and then yanks her arm from the man holding her. There's a shout—from the men, from her, I do not know—but then she is free. She is running, running down the corridor and—

A gunshot blasts through the air, swiftly followed by a second.

THIRTY-SEVEN

Alessia

I run and run, nausea hurtling through me. I'm outside. Fresh air, cold. Rain. Streetlights.

Jaidev is right behind me, keeps shouting stuff at me, but I cannot stop. Cannot answer him. Just have to keep running. Keep running because then it will all go away. It will all go away and—

The gunshot.

Bella—falling.

A second shot.

Trent.

The gurgling sound he made before…

The men shouting at each other, angry. "That wasn't the plan!"

And me… running.

I do not know how I even got out of the block of flats, alive, unharmed. How I managed to get free. Or how Jaidev did.

But we both ran.

We ran and ran and ran. And kept running. And I cannot stop running. Nowhere is safe.

Nowhere at all.

"Alessia," Jaidev pants, and I slow just enough for him to reach me, run next to me. His eyes are frantic. "Where do we go?"

I risk a glance behind. We're on another road I don't recognize—it's all been roads I don't know. No traffic at all. "Are they coming?"

"Don't… don't think so." He pulls his phone out, and I see him type '999.'

"No!" I cry. "The police are in on it."

"Trent and Bella need ambulances," he says, and I hear a car engine, somewhere.

I look around, panicked, but I can't see anyone. No men coming after us.

"Are they both…" I swallow hard. I cannot say the word. *Dead.* Because saying it will make it true.

Jaidev's breathing hard. "I don't know," is all he says. "But we can't not call one… We…."

There's a car—a car coming toward us. My heart pounds and I step back, nearly trip on a lump of concrete. The vehicle slows as it approaches us, and my stomach flips.

No… no… no!

Jaidev grabs my hand, pushes me to the other side of him, so he's nearest the car and—and there's someone getting out.

"Madame Jurgensen?" I stare at her, feel… I do not know. *Deflated.* Numb. Like all of this is wrong… because she is with them? Of course. They've got people in the school.

"Get in the car *now*," she says.

Ice fills my body.

"No," Jaidev says, and then he's trying to pull me along.

"I'm not with the BGG Group," she says. She hovers right by her open door. "I've been following you—followed you to their flats. I called an ambulance for Bella and Trent, but I think they've likely already moved them and—"

I stare at her, feel my knees weaken.

"Get in the car now," she says. "We haven't got long until they're out here. The police are already en route, but we—"

"What?" I say. "They're on this! They all are."

"Some of them," she says. Her brow furrows for a moment. "And there are corrupt officers, yes. But just get in the car. We've got to get to safety."

Jaidev looks at me. "I think it's okay," he says.

"We do not know that though!"

"Her sister was taken too," he reminds me, his voice low. "If we can trust anyone, I think it's her."

Numb, I watch as he gets into Madame Jurgensen's car. As the door shuts. She's still standing by the open driver's door.

"Alessia?" Her voice wobbles.

I take a deep breath and nod.

The moment I get into her car, I burst into tears, leaning back against the padded leather. *I am safe. I am safe. I am safe.*

But Bella… Trent… Allegra… Li Hua….

Nausea twists my gut into knots.

"We're going to the hospital," Madame Jurgensen says. "That'll be the safest place."

"And Bella and Trent will be there?" Jaidev asks. He's in the front, next to her. I stare at the backs of both their heads.

"I've been…observing them for years," Madame Jurgensen says. "Subtly. Nothing like what the four of you have been doing." She tuts under her breath. "I've got names. I've got people I think are in the BGG. And Roseheart is…" She shakes her head. "The more I've watched, the longer the list is. These people are dangerous, and I cannot believe you went after them like that."

"We had to do something for Li Hua," Jaidev says.

"The police *were* doing something—the non-corrupt ones."

They continue talking, but I cannot take any more in. I just lean back, stare out the window. Watch as building after building zooms past.

In my pocket, my phone buzzes. Just one buzz. A text. I pull it out. Maybe it's Bella? Or Trent…

But it's not.

I stare at my screen. An unknown number, texting me another number that begins +30. An international number. Then another message comes through from the same person. *Phone this if you want answers.*

THIRTY-EIGHT

Bella

"Hey… uh, can you hear me?"

"She's bleeding a lot—have they shot her too?"

"What's her name? Does anyone know who she is?"

I open my eyes… slowly… everything's… wrong… different…

Shapes blur above me… a face blurs above me… a woman… no, a girl… and…

A strange high-pitched sound fills my ears. Someone shrieking and shrieking. The girl's face gets nearer, and she's saying something to me, I think—but I can't tell what because the person shrieking isn't stopping, and all I can see are these girl's lips moving as she speaks.

I try to tell her I don't know what she's saying, but I move my head a little, just a fraction and I realize I'm the one shrieking. The sound is coming from me.

Me.

Me.

Pain surges through my body, and I twist, as if my spine's contorting, being folded up. My whole body, in two and—

"Hey! Hey! Don't panic! Stay calm!"

The words filter through to me, and then the light in here gets a bit brighter. Too bright. I squint, blinking, feel more pain, this time in my eyeballs. Something's buzzing near me.

Calm box. Calm box. Calm box.

"Stella, she's bleeding too much. I don't know what to do," the girl is saying. She's pretty. Very pretty. And young.

But then I realize there are others in here. More faces. Their faces just kind of hover, like they're all bodiless.

Like we're all bodiless and—

I was shot.

I jolt, and I feel it. The pain, so rich, so forceful, a river gushing from me. I let out a cry as I try to sit up, try to see and—

My hip. The girl has her red-dyed hand on it, pressing down, but I see flesh and tissue. My flesh and tissue. And white bits, and something sinewy and the bone and—

My stomach twists violently, and I throw up. Hands pat me, and I lean back, dizzy. My fucking hip—I've been shot. I've been shot. I've been shot. Actually shot.

I stare around at the other… other girls. I blink, my vision blurry. They're… they're so young. Like, barely teenagers.

"What's happening? Where…" I wince as white-hot pain flashes through me.

"They shot you," one of the girls says. "But don't look."

"But who… What… Where are my friends? A girl and…" More pain lassoes my head, and I feel like there's something vibrating inside my skull. My teeth chatter.

I look around the room—a small room. One naked lightbulb hangs from a wire on the ceiling. There's a fly buzzing around it. There are two doors, both next to each other. Both are shut, and I assume they're locked.

"What do we do with her though?" one of the girls asks. She's dark-skinned and dark-haired and has big, worried eyes as she looks at the girl next to her. "We can't take her with us—she can't walk. We can't carry her."

"We'll work something out." The girl nearest me nods firmly and then looks back at me. "What's your name?"

"Bella." My voice is weak, breaks after the first syllable. Dizziness wraps around me and I lean back, my head clunking against the wall.

"Right. I'm Dominicia," she says. "These are Terri, Daria, Lawana, and May. The others are next door, but we've got a plan."

"The others? Alessia and Trent and—" A wracking cough cuts me off and I throw up again, slimy stringy stuff. And— and blood.

I lean back, even dizzier. They shot me. Those men. They actually shot me.

"They're going to get us out," the first girl—Dominicia—says firmly. "We're all going to get out." She squeezes my shoulder, then she's sort of sitting next to me, her arm around me. "You've got here just in time, you know," she says. "If it had been tomorrow, we'd have all been gone."

"Gone?" I mumble, tasting copper and vomit. My tongue feels too big, and my eyes—something's wrong with my eyes. *Just breathe. Concentrate on breathing.*

"She's so clever, you know," one of the other girls says. "We're all going to get out and be safe."

"If it works," one of the other girls mutters.

"It will," several of them snap.

Dominicia hugs me tighter, and I lean against her, my head pounding, and I shut my eyes, stare at the redness that fills the insides of my eyelids.

"Why?" I whisper. "What is this…"

"They want to sell us," Dominicia says. "They've advertised us already. Probably not you. Not yet…" She trails off, and I open one eye, see her looking at my hip. The gunshot wound.

Selling us… advertising us…

But not me—it hits me. They've shot me. They've put me in here, left me to bleed out. Oh fuck. I'm dying.

I'm actually going to die.

Dominicia rubs my upper back. "Would you like me to sing to you?"

"What?"

"My mother always sang to me when I was scared."

I don't know if I answer her, if I ask her to sing, but a few moments later, a soft melody fills the room. I close my eyes.

I think of my mother. Of Bobby.

I'm not going to see them again.

The BGG Group, they've won. They've…

It'll be okay.

This will all be over soon.

My breaths hitch, like something in my chest is catching them. A raspy sound. A whimpering noise fills the room and it takes me a moment to realize it's me, once again.

The girls start talking, but their words are hazy, a mess that just spirals round and round and round and round and….

Something squeaks and clicks—*a key in a lock.*

My eyes flutter. The girls are all standing and the door on the left is opening and—

"Are you ready? Come on," says a voice. A voice I recognize. "We've not got a lot of time, and we've all got to get out."

I try to lift my head, try to see better, but fresh pain weighs me down, and I'm falling, sliding down the wall.

"We can't leave her though." Dominicia's voice. I can't see her. All I can see is darkness. My eyes are shut. I can't open them. "They've just brought her in. An hour ago."

"Who?" says the voice, and my heart surges.

It's… it can't be… But it's…

I fight to open my eyes. Really fight. Put everything into it, and I manage it. They crack open, the smallest amount. I inhale sharply, a breath that makes something in my chest squeak loudly, but I see her.

My mouth opens and the words are inside me and I'm staring at her.

"Bella?" Li Hua rushes toward me, and then her face is wobbling, blurring, and I… my eyes… "Bella, stay awake! Come on, stay with us!"

THIRTY-NINE

Trent

"Hi," Li Hua smiles shyly at me, then offers me her hand. To shake. Like we're… I don't know, being really formal or something.

But I take her hand—soft skin, warm. There's a tenderness in her eyes. "It's nice to meet you," I say. And I don't know why I've even said that, because I haven't just met her. We've danced together several times during the last couple of weeks, ever since we began the Roseheart diploma.

Madame Cachelle had everyone partner with everyone, pretty much. She watched us, making notes, observations. "My dears, you must put everything into this. You must imagine that each new partner is your partner. I want to feel the romance, the love, the energy."

The romance, the love, the energy—those are the words I think of now, as I look into Li Hua's eyes. So dark, so much swirling within. Energy and vibrancy and excitement. Partners.

The two of us will be dancing together for the rest of the diploma. If we graduate top of our year, we'll get places in the company. Dancing together.

"Me and you," I whisper, and she smiles that shy smile of hers again.

This is the start. The start of everything that could be.

The start of forever.

I am… silent.

My head's floating, and I'm aware that I'm silent… as I lie here. *Bleeding.*

I can feel it. Everything inside me, gushing out.

But I can't feel the pain. I thought I would. I thought it would be unbearable, all that I could concentrate on.

If I think really hard, I can hear the sound of the gunshot. I can feel it ripping into me—feel tearing sensations and something pulling, and ripping—but I can't feel pain.

There's…

There's no pain.

It's so… Easy…

I bring my face close to Li Hua's, my lips brushing hers, softly. She murmurs something against my mouth, then her hands are reaching for me—her fingers are in my hair, and she's pulling me close.

I kiss her.

I kiss her with everything I have.

Our bodies melt together, and it's in a totally different way to when we dance. And I mean, when we dance, that's just...amazing. We fit together. We're dance soulmates, as Madame Cachelle once said.

But now...

Now we are so much more.

I ...can't.... can't breathe... My head... it's not.... It's...

It's so dark in here, now.

I blink... darkness and... I can't feel my legs... Can't...

Above me, the ceiling glistens. It's moving, again. Wobbling.

My head's...

Everything's wet. I can feel my shirt, and it's soaked. My jeans... everything and... the urine-stench in this place is worse. Stronger than ever... it's all I can smell.

My stomach roils.

I don't know... Can't think....

There's a humming. A buzzing. A light maybe—only there's no light now.

Or flies… I don't know… but there's… there's a raspy sound, too. And it's high-pitched as well. Every breath I take. Every…

It's okay, says a voice.

A deeper sense of darkness shifts over me. A swirling spiral, spinning round and round. I try to reach for it, because there's glitter in it, too, and I don't understand but there's something in me telling me to just touch it. Embrace it.

And I see her.

Her face.

Li Hua's soft eyes blink. She's smiling, smiling at me, and just seeing her again, it does something. It reaches inside me—she reaches inside me. My soul, in her hands. Safe.

It's okay, she whispers, and her voice wraps around me. The warmest hug. *It's okay. I forgive you. I love you. It's okay.*

She's wearing her Odette costume, only it's different now. It's adorned with so many white feathers and each feather glistens, sparkles, and her dress looks softer than anything I can imagine.

Li Hua's closer to me now, her face inches above mine. There's a light layer of powder on her skin, and when she blinks—those beautiful dark lashes—a dusting of powder floats down toward me.

I feel it land on my face. Lightness and hope.

It's okay.

"I love you." My voice croaks. "I'm sorry."

But I don't hear my words. I don't hear anything. The humming has gone… and Li Hua's gone.

And everything's… gone.

FORTY

Alessia

The hard plastic chair digs into the backs of my thighs. Its seat is too short, the edge too sharp. I shift my weight. There's a clinical smell in the air. Disinfectant. Cleaning products.

Jaidev's next to me, staring down at his phone. He's typing away.

I can't even look at my phone. That text I got. There's something about it that makes me feel sick. I swallow hard.

Madame Jurgensen has just popped to the toilet. She's been with us the whole time, and I'm not even sure how much time has passed, since we arrived here. We're in A&E. Madame Jurgensen said we both needed to get checked out. Her police contacts—officers that she insisted, *promised* are safe—arrived pretty soon after we got here. They had me and Jaidev and Madame Jurgensen moved to a private room in the A&E wing.

One of the officers has stayed with us the entire time, and I cannot help but watch her. Is she really safe? Or is she one of them?

But as I look at her, she looks back at me. Makes eye contact.

I look away, but she is approaching us now. She's got a radio in her hand. She was speaking into it a lot earlier. Hushed voice, too quiet for me to hear.

Now, she stops in front of me and Jaidev.

"We've got Bella Sotheby," she says. "She's unconscious, but I'm told she's stable, though she's lost a lot of blood."

I breathe out a shaky breath that leaves me more lightheaded than anything.

The officer smiles. "And we've got Li Hua."

"Li Hua?" My eyes widen.

Jaidev claps a hand to his mouth and when I look at him, I see tears glistening in his eyes. "Is she okay?"

"She had actually escaped, herself. And got thirteen young girls out too—as well as Bella. It really was a whole trafficking operation being run by this group. But Li Hua got herself, Bella, and these thirteen girls out. They flagged down a car outside and called emergency services."

I let out a small, warbled cry. "Was there… was there anything about my sister?" I ask. And I know the answer even before the officer shakes her head, because Allegra went missing ten years ago.

Ten bloody years.

"I'm sorry," the officer says.

I nod. Numb.

"What about Trent?" Jaidev asks. "Trent Mason?"

The officer shakes her head. "Nothing yet." She looks at me. "What time are your parents getting here?"

"I do not know." My head pounds. Did I call them? I cannot think.

"We will need to speak with them, of course."

"Of course," I echo, then feel my face crumble. Yet more tears. And I'm just so tired. Tired of crying, of sitting here, waiting. And not knowing. Not knowing if my sister really is dead.

Phone this if you want answers.

I think of that text. The text I have not told anyone about, but the police are going to look through my phone, aren't they? As part of this investigation. They are going to find out. And what if I want to find out first?

"Can I just go and get some air?" I ask.

The officer nods, and then Jaidev is asking her more questions. I slip out.

I look a mess—I know—because people in the hospital, nurses and doctors and visitors in the corridor, they are all looking at me with concern. I realize I am still crying, tears sliding down my face. But I get to an outside door. It leads to a little courtyard. With a bench.

I sit on it. My left leg trembles violently as I navigate to the text with the number. *Phone this if you want answers.*

There is a child's teddy bear on the end of the bench. Left behind. Lost.

I pick it up. "I want answers," I tell it, squeezing its padded belly.

I *need* answers.

But I still feel sick as I press 'connect.'

The line rings and rings, and then just as I think it's going to disconnect, it clicks. There's a brief moment of static interference, and then I hear background noise. Someplace noisy. Like a pub or something. Voices and chatter and laughter and the clinking of cutlery and plates. Then there's an intake of breath and a woman says, "Γειά σου."

Her voice is soft, tranquil tones. Even speaking a different language.

I freeze. All the hairs on the back of my neck stand on edge. I open my mouth to speak, but only a raspy sound comes out. I clap a hand to my chest, feeling sick, feeling so many things at once.

"A-Allegra? Is that you?" A whisper is all I manage, but a whisper is all I need.

I hear her intake of breath, so loud, so suddenly. I reach out and grab my teddy bear, squeeze it tightly. And I wait for the woman to speak again, for her to say I've got the wrong number, even though I know it's her.

I know this is my sister.

She's alive.

Allegra is alive.

Relief floods through me.

"Alessia? Oh my God. You called—you finally called!" Something clatters in the background where Allegra is, and then she says, "Hold on, give me a minute—I just need to get out of here. Somewhere quiet."

My heart pounds as I wait for her to move. Hear her speaking a different language. Greek, maybe? She always did want to go to Greece. My heart races as the line gets quieter, so quiet until I think it's disconnected again. And then she says, "It's really you, isn't it?"

"It's me." My voice is raspy, and I lick my lips, as if that will help. "Why did you…" I can't finish the sentence. Why did you leave me? Why did you stage your own abduction? Why did you let two innocent dancers get hurt?

"Why didn't you call me sooner?" she asks.

Me? Me call her? My head spins. "I… I thought you were dead."

"Harrison was supposed to reach out to you, let you know. I didn't want Mother to know—she'd be right out here and—wait. You haven't told her, have you?"

"Allegra, no, I haven't—but… have you any idea what our lives have been like?"

She's quiet for a moment, so quiet that again I think she's gone, the call has ended. "I had to get out," she whispers. "This was the only way. But I planned it all. And Harrison was supposed to tell you."

"Harrison didn't," I say. *Whoever the fuck Harrison is.*

"But he must've now—we're speaking." She laughs, but it sounds so different to my sister's laugh.

"He did not. I…" I shake my head. "It is too complicated to explain."

"You can't tell Mother and Father that I'm out here," she says.

I swing my legs under the bench, back and forth, mainly to stop them shaking. "I do not even know where out here is."

"Alessia, I mean it!" She sounds panicked now. "Promise me?"

I squeeze the teddy bear tighter. "Allegra, this BGG group, these people are criminals."

"They helped me," she whispers. "When I had no one else, they helped me."

"They are traffickers and drug dealers," I counter. "But of course you know that."

"I did what I had to do."

FORTY-ONE

Bella

THREE WEEKS LATER

Alessia and I huddle together at the side of the graveyard. She's sort of supporting me, because I'm still not great at the crutches. But at least I've had my last surgery now.

Ava's on my other side, and Madame Cachelle too. There are lots of people here for the funeral. All dressed in black. Somber-faced, crying, hysterical, deadpan. We've got the whole gamut of expressions here.

The coffin's being delivered into the ground. Delivered. I don't know why I think of that word, as I watch.

That could've been me.

Li Hua's next to the coffin, closest to it, being supported by her mother and Trent's mother—though all three women are crying, all hugging each other, holding each other up.

"You okay?" Madame Cachelle asks me.

I nod.

Things have been so different, since it all… happened. The police took down everyone—everyone they thought was involved in the BGG Group. Their own officers, the whole Rio and Fibonacci organization, the Levenson family, and four members of staff at Roseheart. Three of them I didn't know. But one of them I did.

I still can't believe that Mr. Vikas was one of them.

It makes me feel sick just thinking about it. About him. Doing my drug tests, meeting with me about my addiction, knowing that his organization had encouraged it. Mattie got me into drugs, purely for the BGG's benefit. He got me addicted, so they could control me, recruit me. Ruin my life.

But most of all what makes me feel sickest is knowing that Trent's…dead. That we didn't win. That Li Hua was already rescuing herself, and the others. If we had just waited, everyone would be alive.

Everyone.

There's a reporter outside Roseheart when we get back; the woman's being filmed, cameras set up on her.

It's a whole group of us which walks past her—Madame Cachelle and Madame Jurgensen, me and Ava and pretty much all of the company dancers. I didn't really want to come back here. It was bad enough getting out of the grounds earlier, all the journalists about. I wanted to just leave with Alessia after the funeral. She did offer, said that I could go to her apartment. Her father was picking her up.

But I have to come back here. To pack.

And so our whole group goes right past the reporter, and the reporter doesn't even stop her spiel. We all hear her words.

"With the recent revelations of Roseheart staff involvement in the abduction of Li Hua Zhao, the historical abductions of Allegra Valenzi, Marta Davenport, and Freja Jurgensen, and the murder of company dancer Trent Mason, some of the biggest funders of the school and company have lobbied for the immediate closure of this institution. Currently, I am told, the academy and company have lost the majority of their funding, and unless no new investors can be secured, we are looking at the imminent closure of both the school and the company. Given that this institution seems unable to keep its students and dancers safe, this closure does not appear to be a bad thing."

I taste dankness on the roof of my mouth. Of course we've already been told this. We've also been told not to listen to the news or the journalists, not to read all the posts on social media, not to engage with any of it. But people are. Felicity gave an interview the other day, before she left. She managed to get a transfer to a different school.

That's what a lot of dancers are doing. Transferring. Going for auditions. No one wants to be associated with the institution where members of staff were involved in the BGG Group, an organized crime gang that has been trafficking girls out to other countries and dealing drugs. Lots of drugs.

I've even heard that some of the staff involved had specific jobs: to look for vulnerable dancers. Girls and boys, men and women, who they could push drugs on, people they thought would become addicted easily. Or individuals that they thought could be recruited into the BGG Group. It appears they never wanted to abduct the dancers though—they wanted us to help with the drugs side of things—and the girls they mainly took were from impoverished areas of London or were runaways. People they didn't think would be missed.

But Roseheart's name is associated with it all now. Just because of four members of staff.

Madame Cachelle cried the other day, when she visited me in hospital. She doesn't know if Roseheart can ever recover. None of the administration or faculty do.

And me? Well, I don't know what to do now. I look down at my crutches, my hip, my leg.

I don't know if I'll ever dance again.

"You okay?" Ava asks me.

I nod. "Let's just get back inside. I need to pack my things, before Mum and Bobby get here."

They've been staying in a hotel nearby, pretty much ever since it all happened. They visited me every day in hospital.

They offered to come to the funeral, but I felt it was better if they didn't.

But we're going to go home tonight, the three of us. Family. I taste the word—salty—and I want to cry. For everything. Everything we've lost. Everything we've learnt.

For my love of dance and my broken body.

For my desperation for more coke and my brain that just won't stop.

But most of all for Trent.

Acknowledgments

Swans in the Dark was one of those books that I thought was going to take me a long time to write; I'd spent a couple of years thinking about it, ever since the publication of my first Roseheart book, *The Rhythm of My Soul,* but I felt intimidated every time I tried to start it. Writing a sequel— even though I've written sequels for other books—seemed so daunting, but when I finally sat down to write it, I was able to get a first draft out within five months. And pretty soon after that, I got this book into shape. There are of course many people that I need to thank.

To my critique partners—S.E. Anderson and Attiya Khan— thank you for reading early drafts, providing edits, workshopping problems with me, and generally letting me talk about these characters for as long as I needed to. You are both awesome!

Sophie Doolan and Kayleigh Talbot, thank you also for your wonderful feedback. Your insightful comments have really helped develop this story.

When selecting beta-readers for this novel, I was lucky enough to be able to connect with a number of Sixth Formers at Exmouth Community College; working with such enthusiastic readers has been a delight, and each of you has helped shape this book. So, a big thank-you goes to Luke James, Rosa Smith, Lyra Berndt, Isla Burley, Olivia Price, Amber Milne, Sophie Hardiman, Sophie Pallister, Jackson Loman, Echo Niedzialko, Chelsea Williams, Emma Rose, Daisy Jones, and Hope Eaton-Terry. (And a huge thank you must also go to Sam Prior for facilitating this!)

Sarah Anderson, your phenomenal design work has made this book so special. I still can't believe how gorgeous this cover is!

And thank you to Madelaine Couch for your meticulous proofreading.

To my parents, my brother, my aunt, my in-laws, and my husband Michael: thank you always for all your support.

And finally, to my guinea pigs Louisa, Ariadne, and Genevieve who live in my office and provided just the right amount of distraction when I should have been writing: so, thank you!

About the Author

Madeline Dyer (she/her) is a novelist, anthologist, poet, and literary academic, drawn to dark and monstrous stories. Her debut anthology *Being Ace* (Page Street YA, 2023) received a starred review from *School Library Journal* and was named a 2024 Lammy Award Finalist at the Lambda Literary Awards, commemorating "outstanding LGBTQ+ literature from 2023." Her debut novel *Untamed* (Prizm Books, 2015) also won the 2015 SIBA award for Best Dystopian Novel. She is currently a postgraduate researcher in Creative Writing at the University of Bristol.

Madeline also writes romance and light-hearted contemporary fiction as Elin Annalise.

Swans in the Dark is her nineteenth book.